THE ADVENTURES OF
PIPPI
LONGSTOCKING

THE ADVENTURES OF
·········· PIPPI ··········
LONGSTOCKING

by Astrid Lindgren

illustrated by Michael Chesworth

Viking

VIKING
Published by the Penguin Group
Penguin Putnam Inc., 345 Hudson Street, New York, New York 10014, U.S.A.
Penguin Books Ltd, 27 Wrights Lane, London W8 5TZ, England
Penguin Books Australia Ltd, Ringwood, Victoria, Australia
Penguin Books Canada Ltd, 10 Alcorn Avenue, Toronto, Ontario, Canada M4V 3B2
Penguin Books (N.Z.) Ltd, 182–190 Wairau Road, Auckland 10, New Zealand

Penguin Books Ltd, Registered Offices: Harmondsworth, Middlesex, England

First published in 1997 by Viking, a member of Penguin Putnam Inc.

24

Pippi Longstocking
Copyright The Viking Press, Inc., 1950
Copyright renewed Viking Penguin Inc., 1978

Pippi Goes on Board
Copyright © Astrid Lindgren, 1957
Copyright renewed Astrid Lindgren, 1985

Pippi in the South Seas
Copyright © Astrid Lindgren, 1959
Copyright renewed Astrid Lindgren, 1987

Illustrations copyright © Michael Chesworth, 1997
Afterword copyright © Penguin Putnam Inc., 1997
All rights reserved

LIBRARY OF CONGRESS CATALOGING-IN-PUBLICATION DATA
Lindgren, Astrid, date
The adventures of Pippi Longstocking / by Astrid Lindgren ;
illustrated by Michael Chesworth.
p. cm.
Summary : A collection of three previously published books: Pippi
Longstocking, Pippi Goes on Board, and Pippi in the South Seas.
ISBN 978-0-670-87612-9
[1. Humorous stories.] I. Chesworth, Michael, ill. II. Title.
PZ7.L6585An 1997 [Fic]—dc21 97-20035 CIP AC

Manufactured in China
Set in Aldine 721

Contents

• •

PIPPI
LONGSTOCKING

translated by Florence Lamborn

CONTENTS

Pippi Moves in to Villa Villekulla

● ●

Way out at the end of a tiny little town was an old overgrown garden, and in the garden was an old house, and in the house lived Pippi Longstocking. She was nine years old, and she lived there all alone. She had no mother and no father, and that was of course very nice because there was no one to tell her to go to bed just when she was having the most fun, and no one who could make her take cod liver oil when she much preferred caramel candy.

Once upon a time Pippi had had a father of whom she was extremely fond. Naturally she had had a mother too, but that was so long ago that Pippi didn't remember her at all. Her mother had died when Pippi was just a tiny baby and lay in a cradle and howled so that nobody could go anywhere near her. Pippi was sure that her mother was now up in Heaven, watching her little girl through a peephole in the sky, and Pippi often waved up at her and called, "Don't you worry about me. I'll always come out on top."

Pippi had not forgotten her father. He was a sea captain who sailed on the great ocean, and Pippi had sailed with him in his ship until one day her father was blown overboard in a storm and disappeared. But Pippi was

3

absolutely certain that he would come back. She would never believe that he had drowned; she was sure he had floated until he landed on an island inhabited by cannibals. And she thought he had become the king of all the cannibals and went around with a golden crown on his head all day long.

"My papa is a cannibal king; it certainly isn't every child who has such a stylish papa," Pippi used to say with satisfaction. "And as soon as my papa has built himself a boat he will come and get me, and I'll be a cannibal princess. Heigh-ho, won't that be exciting?"

Her father had bought the old house in the garden many years ago. He thought he would live there with Pippi when he grew old and couldn't sail the seas any longer. And then this annoying thing had to happen, that he was blown into the ocean, and while Pippi was waiting for him to come back she went straight home to Villa Villekulla. That was the name of the house. It stood there ready and waiting for her. One lovely summer evening she had said good-by to all the sailors on her father's boat. They were all fond of Pippi, and she of them.

"So long, boys," she said and kissed each one on the forehead. "Don't you worry about me. I'll always come out on top."

Two things she took with her from the ship: a little monkey whose name was Mr. Nilsson—he was a present from her father—and a big suitcase full of gold pieces. The sailors stood upon the deck and watched as long as they could see her. She walked straight ahead without looking back at all, with Mr. Nilsson on her shoulder and her suitcase in her hand.

"A remarkable child," said one of the sailors as Pippi disappeared in the distance.

He was right. Pippi was indeed a remarkable child. The most remarkable thing about her was that she was so strong. She was so very strong that in the whole wide world there was not a single police officer as strong as she. Why, she could lift a whole horse if she wanted to! And she wanted to. She had a horse of her own that she had bought with one of her many gold

pieces the day she came home to Villa Villekulla. She had always longed
for a horse, and now here he was, living on the porch. When Pippi wanted
to drink her afternoon coffee there, she simply lifted him down into the
garden.

Beside Villa Villekulla was another garden and another house. In that
house lived a father and mother and two charming children, a boy and a
girl. The boy's name was Tommy and the girl's Annika. They were good,

well brought up, and obedient children. Tommy would never think of biting his nails, and he always did exactly what his mother told him to do. Annika never fussed when she didn't get her own way, and she always looked pretty in her little well-ironed cotton dresses; she took the greatest care not to get them dirty. Tommy and Annika played nicely with each other in their garden, but they had often wished for a playmate. While Pippi was still sailing on the ocean with her father, they often used to hang over the fence and say to each other, "Isn't it silly that nobody ever moves into that house. Somebody ought to live there—somebody with children."

On that lovely summer evening when Pippi for the first time stepped over the threshold of Villa Villekulla, Tommy and Annika were not at home. They had gone to visit their grandmother for a week; and so they had no idea that anybody had moved into the house next door. On the first day after they came home again they stood by the gate, looking out onto the street, and even then they didn't know that there actually was a playmate so near. Just as they were standing there considering what they should do and wondering whether anything exciting was likely to happen or whether it was going to be one of those dull days when they couldn't think of anything to play—just then the gate of Villa Villekulla opened and a little girl stepped out. She was the most remarkable girl Tommy and Annika had ever seen. She was Miss Pippi Longstocking out for her morning promenade. This is the way she looked:

Her hair, the color of a carrot, was braided in two tight braids that stuck straight out. Her nose was the shape of a very small potato and was dotted all over with freckles. It must be admitted that the mouth under this nose was a very wide one, with strong white teeth. Her dress was rather unusual. Pippi herself had made it. She had meant it to be blue, but there wasn't quite enough blue cloth, so Pippi had sewed little red pieces on it here and there. On her long thin legs she wore a pair of long stockings, one brown

and the other black, and she had on a pair of black shoes that were exactly twice as long as her feet. These shoes her father had bought for her in South America so that Pippi would have something to grow into, and she never wanted to wear any others.

But the thing that made Tommy and Annika open their eyes widest of all was the monkey sitting on the strange girl's shoulder. It was a little monkey, dressed in blue pants, yellow jacket, and a white straw hat.

Pippi walked along the street with one foot on the sidewalk and the other in the gutter. Tommy and Annika watched as long as they could see her. In a little while she came back, and now she was walking backward. That was because she didn't want to turn around to get home. When she reached Tommy's and Annika's gate she stopped.

The children looked at each other in silence. At last Tommy spoke. "Why did you walk backward?"

"Why did I walk backward?" said Pippi. "Isn't this a free country? Can't a person walk any way she wants to? For that matter, let me tell you that in Egypt everybody walks that way, and nobody thinks it's the least bit strange."

"How do you know?" asked Tommy. "You've never been in Egypt, have you?"

"I've never been in Egypt? Indeed I have. That's one thing you can be sure of. I have been all over the world and seen many things stranger than people walking backward. I wonder what you would have said if I had come along walking on my hands the way they do in Farthest India."

"Now you must be lying," said Tommy.

Pippi thought a moment. "You're right," she said sadly, "I am lying."

"It's wicked to lie," said Annika, who had at last gathered up enough courage to speak.

"Yes, it's very wicked to lie," said Pippi even more sadly. "But I forget it

8

now and then. And how can you expect a little child whose mother is an angel and whose father is king of a cannibal island and who herself has sailed on the ocean all her life—how can you expect her to tell the truth always? And for that matter," she continued, her whole freckled face lighting up, "let me tell you that in the Congo there is not a single person who tells the truth. They lie all day long. Begin at seven in the morning and keep on until sundown. So if I should happen to lie now and then, you must try to excuse me and to remember that it is only because I stayed in the Congo a little too long. We can be friends anyway, can't we?"

"Oh, sure," said Tommy and realized suddenly that this was not going to be one of those dull days.

"By the way, why couldn't you come and have breakfast with me?" asked Pippi.

"Why not?" said Tommy. "Come on, let's go."

"Oh, yes, let's," said Annika.

"But first I must introduce you to Mr. Nilsson," said Pippi, and the little monkey took off his cap and bowed politely.

Then they all went in through Villa Villekulla's tumbledown garden gate, along the gravel path, bordered with old moss-covered trees—really good climbing trees they seemed to be—up to the house, and onto the porch. There stood the horse, munching oats out of a soup bowl.

"Why do you have a horse on the porch?" asked Tommy. All horses he knew lived in stables.

"Well," said Pippi thoughtfully, "he'd be in the way in the kitchen, and he doesn't like the parlor."

Tommy and Annika patted the horse and then went on into the house. It had a kitchen, a parlor, and a bedroom. But it certainly looked as if Pippi had forgotten to do her Friday cleaning that week. Tommy and Annika looked around cautiously just in case the king of the Cannibal Isles might be sitting in a corner somewhere. They had never seen a cannibal king in all their lives. But there was no father to be seen, nor any mother either.

Annika said anxiously, "Do you live here all alone?"

"Of course not!" said Pippi. "Mr. Nilsson and the horse live here too."

"Yes, but I mean don't you have any mother or father here?"

"No, not the least little tiny bit of a one," said Pippi happily.

"But who tells you when to go to bed at night and things like that?" asked Annika.

"I tell myself," said Pippi. "First I tell myself in a nice friendly way; and then, if I don't mind, I tell myself again more sharply; and if I still don't mind, then I'm in for a spanking—see?"

Tommy and Annika didn't see at all, but they thought maybe it was a good way. Meanwhile they had come out into the kitchen, and Pippi cried,

Now we're going to make a pancake,
Now there's going to be a pankee,
Now we're going to fry a pankye.

Then she took three eggs and threw them up in the air. One fell down on her head and broke so that the yolk ran into her eyes, but the others she caught skillfully in a bowl, where they smashed to pieces.

"I always did hear that egg yolk was good for the hair," said Pippi, wiping her eyes. "You wait and see—mine will soon begin to grow so fast it will crackle. As a matter of fact, in Brazil all the people go about with eggs in their hair. And there are no bald-headed people. Only once was there a man who was so foolish that he ate his eggs instead of rubbing them on his hair. He became completely bald, and when he showed himself on the street there was such a riot that the police were called out."

While she was speaking Pippi had neatly picked the eggshells out of the bowl with her fingers. Now she took a bath brush that hung on the wall and began to beat the pancake batter so hard that it splashed all over the walls. At last she poured what was left onto a griddle that stood on the stove.

When the pancake was brown on one side she tossed it halfway up to the ceiling, so that it turned right around in the air, and then she caught it on the griddle again. And when it was ready she threw it straight across the kitchen right onto a plate that stood on the table.

"Eat!" she cried. "Eat before it gets cold!"

And Tommy and Annika ate and thought it a very good pancake.

Afterward Pippi invited them to step into the parlor. There was only one piece of furniture in there. It was a huge chest with many tiny drawers. Pippi opened the drawers and showed Tommy and Annika all the treasures she kept there. There were wonderful birds' eggs, strange shells and stones, pretty little boxes, lovely silver mirrors, pearl necklaces, and many other things that Pippi and her father had bought on their journeys around the world. Pippi gave each of her new playmates a little gift to remember her by. Tommy got a dagger with a shimmering mother-of-pearl handle and

Annika, a little box with a cover decorated with pink shells. In the box there was a ring with a green stone.

"Suppose you go home now," said Pippi, "so that you can come back tomorrow. Because if you don't go home you can't come back, and that would be a shame."

Tommy and Annika agreed that it would indeed. So they went home—past the horse, who had now eaten up all the oats, and out through the gate of Villa Villekulla. Mr. Nilsson waved his hat at them as they left.

Pippi Is a Thing-Finder and Gets into a Fight

● ●

Annika woke up early the next morning. She jumped out of bed and ran over to Tommy.

"Wake up, Tommy," she cried, pulling him by the arm. "Wake up and let's go and see that funny girl with the big shoes."

Tommy was wide awake in an instant.

"I knew, even while I was sleeping, that something exciting was going to happen today, but I didn't remember what it was," he said as he yanked off his pajama jacket. Off they went to the bathroom, washed themselves and brushed their teeth much faster than usual, had their clothes on in a twinkling, and a whole hour before their mother expected them came sliding down the bannister and landed at the breakfast table. Down they sat and announced that they wanted their hot chocolate right at that very moment.

"What's going to happen today that you're in such a hurry?" asked their mother.

"We're going to see the new girl next door," said Tommy.

"We may stay all day," said Annika.

That morning Pippi was busy making *pepparkakor*—a kind of Swedish

13

cookie. She had made an enormous amount of dough and rolled it out on the kitchen floor.

"Because," said Pippi to her little monkey, "what earthly use is a baking board when one plans to make at least five hundred cookies?"

And there she lay on the floor, cutting out cookie hearts for dear life.

"Stop climbing around in the dough, Mr. Nilsson," she said crossly just as the doorbell rang.

Pippi ran and opened the door. She was white as a miller from top to toe, and when she shook hands heartily with Tommy and Annika a whole cloud of flour blew over them.

"So nice you called," she said and shook her apron—so there came another cloud of flour. Tommy and Annika got so much in their throats that they could not help coughing.

"What are you doing?" asked Tommy.

"Well, if I say that I'm sweeping the chimney, you won't believe me, you're so clever," said Pippi. "Fact is, I'm baking. But I'll soon be done. You can sit on the woodbox for a while."

Pippi could work fast, she could. Tommy and Annika sat and watched how she went through the dough, how she threw the cookies onto the cookie pans, and swung the pans into the oven. They thought it was as good as a circus.

"Done!" said Pippi at last and shut the oven door on the last pans with a bang.

"What are we going to do now?" asked Tommy.

"I don't know what you are going to do," said Pippi, "but I know I can't lie around and be lazy. I am a Thing-Finder, and when you're a Thing-Finder you don't have a minute to spare."

"What did you say you are?" asked Annika.

"A Thing-Finder."

"What's that?" asked Tommy.

"Somebody who hunts for things, naturally. What else could it be?" said Pippi as she swept all the flour left on the floor into a little pile.

"The whole world is full of things, and somebody has to look for them. And that's just what a Thing-Finder does," she finished.

"What kind of things?" asked Annika.

"Oh, all kinds," said Pippi. "Lumps of gold, ostrich feathers, dead rats, candy snapcrackers, little tiny screws, and things like that."

Tommy and Annika thought it sounded as if it would be fun and wanted very much to be Thing-Finders too, although Tommy did say he hoped he'd find a lump of gold and not a little tiny screw.

"We shall see what we shall see," said Pippi. "One always finds something. But we've got to hurry up and get going so that other Thing-Finders don't pick up all the lumps of gold around here before we get them."

All three Thing-Finders now set out. They decided that it would be best to begin hunting around the houses in the neighborhood, because Pippi said that although it could perfectly well happen that one might find a little screw deep in the woods, still the very best things were usually found where people were living.

"Though, for that matter," she said, "I've seen it the other way around too. I remember once when I was out hunting for things in the jungles of Borneo. Right in the heart of the forest, where no human being had ever before set foot, what do you suppose I found? Why, a very fine wooden leg! I gave it away later to a one-legged old man, and he said that a wooden leg like that wasn't to be had for love or money."

Tommy and Annika looked at Pippi to see just how a Thing-Finder acted. Pippi ran from one side of the road to the other, shaded her eyes with her hand, and hunted and hunted. Sometimes she crawled about on her hands and knees, stuck her hands in between the pickets of a fence, and then said in a disappointed tone, "Oh, dear! I was sure I saw a lump of gold."

"May we really take everything we find?" asked Annika.

"Yes, everything that is lying on the ground," said Pippi.

Presently they came to an old man lying asleep on the lawn outside his cottage.

"There," said Pippi, "that man is lying on the ground and we have found him. We'll take him!"

Tommy and Annika were utterly horrified.

"No, no, Pippi, we can't take an old gentleman! We couldn't possibly," said Tommy. "Anyway, whatever would we do with him?"

"What would we do with him? Oh, there are plenty of things we could do with him. We could keep him in a little rabbit hutch instead of a rabbit and feed him on dandelions. But if you don't want to, I don't care. Though it does bother me to think that some other Thing-Finder may come along and grab him."

They went on. Suddenly Pippi gave a terrific yell. "Well, I never saw the like," she cried, as she picked up a large, rusty old tin can from the grass. "What a find! What a find! Cans—that's something you can never have too many of."

Tommy looked at the can doubtfully. "What can you use it for?"

"Oh, you can use it in all sorts of ways," said Pippi. "One way is to put cookies in it. Then it becomes a delightful Jar with Cookies. Another way is not to put cookies in it. Then it becomes a Jar without Cookies. That certainly isn't quite so delightful, but still that's good too."

She examined the can, which was indeed rusty and had a hole in the bottom.

"It looks almost as if this were a Jar without Cookies," she said thoughtfully. "But you can put it over your head and pretend that it is midnight."

And that is just what she did. With the can on her head she wandered around the block like a little metal tower and never stopped until she stumbled over a low wire fence and fell flat on her stomach. There was a big crash when the tin can hit the ground.

"Now, see that!" said Pippi and took off the can. "If I hadn't had this thing on me, I'd have fallen flat on my face and hurt myself terribly."

"Yes," said Annika, "but if you hadn't had the can on your head, then you wouldn't have tripped on the wire fence in the first place."

Before she had finished speaking there was another triumphant cry from Pippi, who was holding up an empty spool of thread.

"This seems to be my lucky day," she said. "Such a sweet, sweet little spool to blow soap bubbles with or to hang around my neck for a necklace. I'll go home and make one this very minute."

However, just at that moment the gate of one of the cottages nearby opened and a boy came rushing out. He looked scared, and that was no wonder, because head over heels after him came five other boys. They soon caught him and pushed him against the fence, and all five began to punch and hit him. He cried and held his arms in front of his face to protect himself.

"Give it to him! Give it to him!" cried the oldest and strongest of the boys, "so that he'll never dare to show himself on this street again."

"Oh," said Annika, "it's Willie they're hurting. Oh, how can they be so mean?"

"It's that awful Bengt. He's always in a fight," said Tommy. "And five against one—what cowards!"

Pippi went up to the boys and tapped Bengt on the back with her forefinger. "Hello, there," she said. "What's the idea? Are you trying to make hash out of little Willie with all five of you jumping on him at once?"

Bengt turned around and saw a little girl he had never seen before: a wild-looking little stranger who dared to touch him. For a while he stood and gaped at her in astonishment; then a broad grin spread over his face. "Boys," he said, "boys, let Willie alone and take a look at this girl. What a babe!"

He slapped his knees and laughed, and in an instant they had all flocked around Pippi, all except Willie, who wiped away his tears and walked cautiously over to stand beside Tommy.

"Have you ever seen hair like hers? Red as fire! And such shoes," Bengt continued. "Can't I borrow one? I'd like to go out rowing and I haven't any boat." He took hold of one of Pippi's braids but dropped it instantly and cried, "Ouch, I burned myself."

Then all five boys joined hands around Pippi, jumping up and down and screaming, "Redhead! Redhead!"

Pippi stood in the middle of the ring and smiled in the friendliest way. Bengt had hoped she would get mad and begin to cry. At least she ought to

have looked scared. When nothing happened he gave her a push.

"I don't think you have a very nice way with ladies," said Pippi. And she lifted him in her strong arms—high in the air—and carried him to a birch tree and hung him over a branch. Then she took the next boy and hung him over another branch. The next one she set on a gatepost outside a cottage, and the next she threw right over a fence so that he landed in a flower bed. The last of the fighters she put in a tiny toy cart that stood by the road. Then Pippi, Tommy, Annika, and Willie stood and looked at the boys for a while. The boys were absolutely speechless with fright.

And Pippi said, "You are cowards. Five of you attacking one boy! That's cowardly. Then you begin to push a helpless little girl around. Oh, how mean!

"Come now, we'll go home," she said to Tommy and Annika. And to Willie, "If they try to hurt you again, you come and tell me." And to Bengt, who sat up in the tree and didn't dare to stir, she said, "Is there anything else you have to say about my hair or my shoes? If so, you'd better say it now before I go home."

But Bengt had nothing more to say about Pippi's shoes or about her hair either. So Pippi took her can in one hand and her spool in the other and went away, followed by Tommy and Annika.

When they were back home in Pippi's garden, Pippi said, "Dear me, how awful! Here I found two beautiful things and you didn't get anything. You must hunt a little more. Tommy, why don't you look in that old hollow tree? Old trees are usually about the best places of all for Thing-Finders."

Tommy said that he didn't believe he and Annika would ever find anything, but to please Pippi he put his hand slowly down into the hollow tree trunk.

"Goodness!" he cried, utterly amazed, and pulled out his hand. In it he held a little notebook with a leather cover. In a special loop there was a little silver pencil.

"Well, that's queer," said Tommy.

"Now, see that!" said Pippi. "There's nothing so nice as being a Thing-Finder. It's a wonder there aren't more people that take it up. They'll be tailors and shoemakers and chimney sweeps, and such like—but Thing-Finders, no indeed, that isn't good enough for them!"

And then she said to Annika, "Why don't you feel in that old tree stump? One practically always finds things in old tree stumps."

Annika stuck her hand down in the stump and almost immediately got hold of a red coral necklace. She and Tommy stood open-mouthed for a long time, they were so astonished. They thought that hereafter they would be Thing-Finders every single day.

Pippi had been up half the night before, playing ball, and now she suddenly felt sleepy. "I think I'll have to go and take a nap," she said. "Can't you come with me and tuck me in?"

When Pippi was sitting on the edge of the bed, taking off her shoes, she looked at them thoughtfully and said, "He was going out rowing, he said, that old Bengt." She snorted disdainfully. "I'll teach him to row, indeed I will. Another time."

"Say, Pippi," said Tommy respectfully, "why do you wear such big shoes?"

"So I can wiggle my toes, of course," she answered.

Then she crept into bed. She always slept with her feet on the pillow and her head way down under the quilt. "That's the way they sleep in Guatemala," she announced. "And it's the only real way to sleep. See, like this, I can wiggle my toes when I'm sleeping too.

"Can you go to sleep without a lullaby?" she went on. "I always have to sing to myself for a while; otherwise I can't sleep a wink."

Tommy and Annika heard a humming sound under the quilt; it was Pippi singing herself to sleep. Quietly and cautiously they tiptoed out so that they would not disturb her. In the doorway they turned to take a last look toward the bed. They could see nothing of Pippi except her feet resting on the pillow. There she lay, wiggling her toes emphatically.

Tommy and Annika ran home. Annika held her coral necklace tightly in her hand.

"That certainly was strange," she said. "Tommy, you don't suppose—*do* you suppose that Pippi had put these things in place beforehand?"

"You never can tell," said Tommy. "You just never can tell about anything when it comes to Pippi."

Pippi Plays Tag with Some Policemen

●●

It soon became known throughout the little town that a nine-year-old girl was living all by herself in Villa Villekulla, and all the ladies and gentlemen in the town thought this would never do. All children must have someone to advise them, and all children must go to school to learn the multiplication tables. So the ladies and gentlemen decided that the little girl in Villa Villekulla must immediately be placed in a children's home.

One lovely afternoon Pippi had invited Tommy and Annika over for afternoon coffee and *pepparkakor*. She had spread the party out on the front steps. It was so sunny and beautiful there, and the air was filled with the fragrance of the flowers in Pippi's garden. Mr. Nilsson climbed around on the porch railing, and every now and then the horse stuck out his head so that he'd be invited to have a cookie.

"Oh, isn't it glorious to be alive?" said Pippi, stretching out her legs as far as she could reach.

Just at that moment two police officers in full uniform came in through the gate.

"Hurray!" said Pippi. "This must be my lucky day too! Policemen are the very best things I know. Next to rhubarb pudding." And with her face beaming she went to meet them.

"Is this the girl who has moved into Villa Villekulla?" asked one of the policemen.

"Quite the contrary," said Pippi. "This is a tiny little auntie who lives on the third floor at the other end of the town."

She said that only because she wanted to have a little fun with the policemen, but they didn't think it was funny at all.

They said she shouldn't be such a smarty. And then they went on to tell her that some nice people in the town were arranging for her to get into a children's home.

"I already have a place in a children's home," said Pippi.

"What?" asked one of the policemen. "Has it been arranged already then? What children's home?"

"This one," said Pippi haughtily. "I am a child and this is my home: therefore it is a children's home, and I have room enough here, plenty of room."

"Dear child," said the policeman, smiling, "you don't understand. You must get into a real children's home and have someone look after you."

"Is one allowed to bring horses to your children's home?" asked Pippi.

"No, of course not," said the policeman.

"That's what I thought," said Pippi sadly. "Well, what about monkeys?"

"Of course not. You ought to realize that."

"Well then," said Pippi, "you'll have to get kids for your children's home somewhere else. I certainly don't intend to move there."

"But don't you understand that you must go to school?"

"Why?"

"To learn things, of course."

"What sort of things?" asked Pippi.

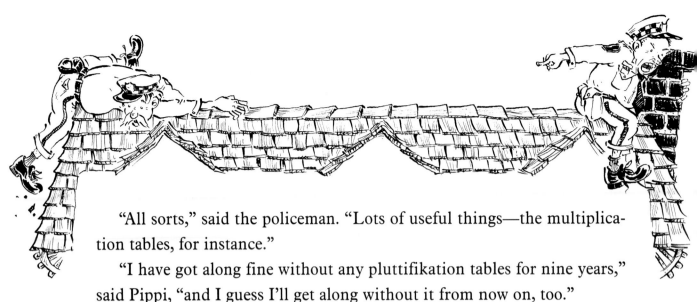

"All sorts," said the policeman. "Lots of useful things—the multiplication tables, for instance."

"I have got along fine without any pluttifikation tables for nine years," said Pippi, "and I guess I'll get along without it from now on, too."

"Yes, but just think how embarrassing it will be for you to be so ignorant. Imagine when you grow up and somebody asks you what the capital of Portugal is and you can't answer!"

"Oh, I can answer all right," said Pippi. "I'll answer like this: 'If you are so bound and determined to find out what the capital of Portugal is, then, for goodness' sakes, write directly to Portugal and ask.'"

"Yes, but don't you think that you would be sorry not to know it yourself?"

"Oh, probably," said Pippi. "No doubt I should lie awake nights and wonder and wonder, 'What in the world is the capital of Portugal?' But one can't be having fun all the time," she continued, bending over and standing on her hands for a change. "For that matter, I've been in Lisbon with my papa," she added, still standing upside down, for she could talk that way too.

But then one of the policemen said that Pippi certainly didn't need to think she could do just as she pleased. She must come to the children's home, and immediately. He went up to her and took hold of her arm, but Pippi freed herself quickly, touched him lightly, and said, "Tag!" Before he could wink an eye she had climbed up on the porch railing and from there onto the balcony above the porch. The policemen couldn't quite see themselves getting up the same way, and so they rushed into the house and up the stairs, but by the time they had reached the balcony Pippi was halfway up the roof. She climbed up the shingles almost as if she were a little monkey herself. In a moment she was up on the ridge-pole and from there jumped easily to the chimney. Down on the bal-cony stood the two policemen, scratching their heads, and on the lawn stood Tommy and Annika, staring at Pippi.

"Isn't it fun to play tag?" cried Pippi. "And weren't you nice to come over. It certainly *is* my lucky day today too."

After the policemen had stood there a while wondering what to do, they went and got a ladder, leaned it against one of the gables of the house and then climbed up, first one policeman and then the other, to get Pippi down. They looked a little scared when they climbed out on the ridgepole and, carefully balancing themselves, went step by step, toward Pippi.

"Don't be scared," cried Pippi. "There's nothing to be afraid of. It's just fun."

When the policemen were a few steps away from Pippi, down she jumped from the chimney and, screeching and laughing, ran along the ridgepole to the opposite gable. A few feet from the house stood a tree.

"Now I'm going to dive," she cried and jumped right down into the green crown of the tree, caught hold of a branch, swung back and forth a while, and then let herself fall to the ground. Quick as a wink she dashed around to the other side of the house and took away the ladder.

The policemen had looked a little foolish when Pippi jumped, but they looked even more so when they had balanced themselves backward along the ridgepole and were about to climb down the ladder. At first they were very angry

25

at Pippi, who stood on the ground looking up at them, and they told her in no uncertain terms to get the ladder and be quick about it, or she would soon get something she wasn't looking for.

"Why are you so cross at me?" asked Pippi reproachfully. "We're just playing tag, aren't we?"

The policemen thought a while, and at last one of them said, "Oh, come on, won't you be a good girl and put the ladder back so that we can get down?"

"Of course I will," said Pippi and put the ladder back instantly. "And when you get down we can all drink coffee and have a happy time."

But the policemen were certainly tricky, because the minute they were down on the ground again they pounced on Pippi and cried, "Now you'll get it, you little brat!"

"Oh, no, I'm sorry. I haven't time to play any longer," said Pippi. "But it was fun."

Then she took hold of the policemen by their belts and carried them down the garden path, out through the gate, and onto the street. There she set them down, and it was quite some time before they were ready to get up again.

"Wait a minute," she cried and ran into the kitchen and came back with two cookie hearts. "Would you like a taste?" she asked. "It doesn't matter that they are a little burned, does it?"

Then she went back to Tommy and Annika, who stood there wide-eyed and just couldn't get over what they had seen. And the policemen hurried back to the town and told all the ladies and gentlemen that Pippi wasn't quite fit for a children's home. (They didn't tell that they had been up on the roof.) And the ladies and gentlemen decided that it would be best after all to let Pippi remain in Villa Villekulla, and if she wanted to go to school she could make the arrangements herself.

But Pippi and Tommy and Annika had a very pleasant afternoon. They went back to their interrupted coffee party. Pippi stuffed herself with fourteen cookies, and then she said, "They weren't what I mean by real policemen. No sirree! Altogether too much talk about children's homes and pluttifikation and Lisbon."

Afterward she lifted the horse down on the ground and they rode on him, all three. At first Annika was afraid and didn't want to, but when she saw what fun Tommy and Pippi were having, she let Pippi lift her up on the horse's back. The horse trotted round and round in the garden, and Tommy sang, "Here come the Swedes with a clang and a bang."

When Tommy and Annika had gone to bed that night Tommy said, "Annika, don't you think it's good that Pippi moved here?"

"Oh, *yes*," said Annika.

"I don't even remember what we used to play before she came, do you?"

"Oh, sure, we played croquet and things like that," said Annika. "But it's lots more fun with Pippi around, I think. And with horses and things."

Pippi Goes to School

Of course Tommy and Annika went to school. Each morning at eight o'clock they trotted off, hand in hand, swinging their schoolbags.

At that time Pippi was usually grooming her horse or dressing Mr. Nilsson in his little suit. Or else she was taking her morning exercises, which meant turning forty-three somersaults in a row. Then she would sit down on the kitchen table and, utterly happy, drink a large cup of coffee and eat a piece of bread and cheese.

Tommy and Annika always looked longingly toward Villa Villekulla as they started off to school. They would much rather have gone to play with Pippi. If only Pippi had been going to school too; that would have been something else again.

"Just think what fun we could have on the way home from school," said Tommy.

"Yes, and on the way to school too," said Annika.

The more they thought about it the worse they felt to think that Pippi did not go to school, and at last they determined to try to persuade her to begin.

"You can't imagine what a nice teacher we have," said Tommy artfully to Pippi one afternoon when he and Annika had come for a visit at Villa Villekulla after they had finished their homework.

"If you only knew what fun it is in school!" Annika added. "I'd die if I couldn't go to school."

Pippi sat on a hassock, bathing her feet in a tub. She said nothing but just wiggled her toes for a while so that the water splashed around everywhere.

"You don't have to stay so very long," continued Tommy. "Just until two o'clock."

"Yes, and besides, we get Christmas vacation and Easter vacation and summer vacation," said Annika.

Pippi bit her big toe thoughtfully but still said nothing. Suddenly, as if she had made some decision, she poured all the water out on the kitchen floor, so that Mr. Nilsson, who sat near her playing with a mirror, got his pants absolutely soaked.

"It's not fair!" said Pippi sternly without paying any attention to Mr. Nilsson's puzzled air about his wet pants. "It is absolutely unfair! I don't intend to stand it!"

"What's the matter now?" asked Tommy.

"In four months it will be Christmas, and then you'll have Christmas vacation. But I, what'll I get?" Pippi's voice sounded sad. "No Christmas vacation, not even the tiniest bit of a Christmas vacation," she complained. "Something will have to be done about that. Tomorrow morning I'll begin school."

Tommy and Annika clapped their hands with delight. "Hurrah! We'll wait for you outside our gate at eight o'clock."

"Oh, no," said Pippi. "I can't begin as early as that. And besides, I'm going to ride to school."

And ride she did. Exactly at ten o'clock the next day she lifted her horse off the porch, and a little later all the people in the town ran to their win-

dows to see what horse it was that was running away. That is to say, they thought he was running away, but it was only Pippi in a bit of a hurry to get to school.

She galloped wildly into the schoolyard, jumped off the horse, tied him to a tree, and burst into the schoolroom with such a noise and a clatter that Tommy and Annika and all their classmates jumped in their seats.

"Hi, there," cried Pippi, waving her big hat. "Did I get here in time for pluttifikation?"

Tommy and Annika had told their teacher that a new girl named Pippi Longstocking was coming, and the teacher had already heard about Pippi in the little town. As she was a very pleasant teacher, she had decided to do all she could to make Pippi happy in school.

Pippi threw herself down on a vacant bench without having been invited to do so, but the teacher paid no attention to her heedless way. She simply said in a very friendly voice, "Welcome to school, little Pippi. I hope that you will enjoy yourself here and learn a great deal."

"Yes, and I hope I'll get some Christmas vacation," said Pippi. "That is the reason I've come. It's only fair, you know."

"If you would first tell me your whole name," said the teacher, "then I'll register you in school."

"My name is Pippilotta Delicatessa Windowshade Mackrelmint Efraim's Daughter Longstocking, daughter of Captain Efraim Longstocking, formerly the Terror of the Sea, now a cannibal king. Pippi is really only a nickname, because Papa thought that Pippilotta was too long to say."

"Indeed?" said the teacher. "Well, then we shall call you Pippi too. But now," she continued, "suppose we test you a little and see what you know. You are a big girl and no doubt know a great deal already. Let us begin with arithmetic. Pippi, can you tell me what seven and five are?"

Pippi, astonished and dismayed, looked at her and said, "Well, if you don't know that yourself, you needn't think I'm going to tell you."

All the children stared in horror at Pippi, and the teacher explained that one couldn't answer that way in school.

"I beg your pardon," said Pippi contritely. "I didn't know that. I won't do it again."

"No, let us hope not," said the teacher. "And now I will tell you that seven and five are twelve."

"See that!" said Pippi. "You knew it yourself. Why are you asking then?"

The teacher decided to act as if nothing unusual were happening and went on with her examination.

"Well now, Pippi, how much do you think eight and four are?"

"Oh, about sixty-seven," hazarded Pippi.

"Of course not," said the teacher. "Eight and four are twelve."

"Well now, really, my dear little woman," said Pippi, "that is carrying things too far. You just said that seven and five are twelve. There should be some rhyme and reason to things even in school. Furthermore, if you are so childishly interested in that foolishness, why don't you sit down in a corner by yourself and do arithmetic and leave us alone so we can play tag?"

The teacher decided there was no point in trying to teach Pippi any more arithmetic. She began to ask the other children the arithmetic questions.

"Can Tommy answer this one?" she asked. "If Lisa has seven apples and Axel has nine apples, how many apples do they have together?"

"Yes, you tell, Tommy," Pippi interrupted, "and tell me too, if Lisa gets a stomach-ache and Axel gets more stomach-ache, whose fault is it and where did they get hold of the apples in the first place?"

The teacher tried to pretend that she hadn't heard and turned to Annika. "Now, Annika, here's an example for you: Gustav was with his schoolmates on a picnic. He had a quarter when he started out and seven cents when he got home. How much did he spend?"

"Yes, indeed," said Pippi, "and I also want to know why he was so extravagant, and if it was pop he bought, and if he washed his ears properly before he left home."

The teacher decided to give up arithmetic altogether. She thought maybe Pippi would prefer to learn to read. So she took out a pretty little card with a picture of an ibex on it. In front of the ibex's nose was the letter "i."

"Now, Pippi," she said briskly, "you'll see something jolly. You see here an ibex. And the letter in front of this ibex is called *i*."

"That I'll never believe," said Pippi. "I think it looks exactly like a straight line with a little fly speck over it. But what I'd really like to know is, what has the ibex to do with the fly speck?"

The teacher took out another card with a picture of a snake on it and told Pippi that the letter on that was an *s*.

"Speaking of snakes," said Pippi, "I'll never, ever forget the time I had a fight with a huge snake in India. You can't imagine what a dreadful snake it was, fourteen yards long and mad as a hornet, and every day he ate up five Indians and then two little children for dessert, and one time he came and wanted me for dessert, and he wound himself around me—uhhh!—but I've been around a bit, I said, and hit him in the head, bang, and then he hissed uiuiuiuiuiuiuiuitch, and then I hit him again, and bingo! he was dead, and, indeed, so that is the letter *s*—most remarkable!"

Pippi had to stop to get her breath. And the teacher, who had now begun to think that Pippi was an unruly and troublesome child, decided that the class should have drawing for a while. Surely Pippi could sit still and be quiet and draw, thought the teacher. She took out paper and pencils and passed them out to the children.

"Now you may draw whatever you wish," she said and sat down at her desk and began to correct homework. In a little while she looked up to see how the drawing was going. All the children sat looking at Pippi, who lay flat on the floor, drawing to her heart's content.

"But, Pippi," said the teacher impatiently, "why in the world aren't you drawing on your paper?"

"I filled that long ago. There isn't room enough for my whole horse on that little snip of a paper," said Pippi. "Just now I'm working on his front legs, but when I get to his tail I guess I'll have to go out in the hall."

The teacher thought hard for a while. "Suppose instead we all sing a little song," she suggested.

All the children stood up by their seats except Pippi; she stayed where she was on the floor. "You go ahead and sing," she said. "I'll rest myself a while. Too much learning breaks even the healthiest."

But now the teacher's patience came to an end. She told all the children to go out into the yard so she could talk to Pippi alone.

When the teacher and Pippi were alone, Pippi got up and walked to the desk. "Do you know what?" she said. "It was awfully jolly to come to school to find out what it was like. But I don't think I care about going to school any more, Christmas vacation or no Christmas vacation. There's altogether too many apples and ibexes and snakes and things like that. It makes me dizzy in the head. I hope that you, Teacher, won't be sorry."

But the teacher said she certainly was sorry, most of all because Pippi wouldn't behave decently; and that any girl who acted as badly as Pippi did wouldn't be allowed to go to school even if she wanted to ever so.

"Have I behaved badly?" asked Pippi, much astonished. "Goodness, I didn't know that," she added and looked very sad. And nobody could look as sad as Pippi when she was sad. She stood silent for a while, and then she said in a trembling voice, "You understand, Teacher, don't you, that when you have a mother who's an angel and a father who is a cannibal king, and when you have sailed on the ocean all your whole life, then you don't know just how to behave in school with all the apples and ibexes."

Then the teacher said she understood and didn't feel annoyed with Pippi any longer, and maybe Pippi could come back to school when she was a little older. Pippi positively beamed with delight. "I think you are awfully nice, Teacher. And here is something for you."

Out of her pocket Pippi took a lovely little gold watch and laid it on the desk. The teacher said she couldn't possibly accept such a valuable gift from Pippi, but Pippi replied, "You've got to take it; otherwise I'll come back again tomorrow, and that would be a pretty how-do-you-do."

Then Pippi rushed out to the schoolyard and jumped on her horse. All the children gathered around to pat the horse and see her off.

"You ought to know about the schools in Argentina," said Pippi, looking down at the children. "That's where you should go. Easter vacation begins three days after Christmas vacation ends, and when Easter vacation is over there are three days and then it's summer vacation. Summer vacation ends on the first of November, and then you have a tough time until Christmas vacation begins on November 11. But you can stand that because there are at least no lessons. It is strictly against the law to have lessons in Argentina. Once in a while it happens that some Argentine kid sneaks into a closet and sits there studying a lesson, but it's just too bad for him if his mother finds him. Arithmetic they don't have at all in the schools, and if there is any kid who knows what seven and five are he has to stand in the corner all day—that is, if he's foolish enough to let the teacher know that he knows. They have reading on Friday, and then only if they have some books, which they never have."

"But what do they do in school?" asked one little boy.

"Eat caramels," said Pippi decidedly. "There is a long pipe that goes from a caramel factory nearby directly into the schoolroom, and caramels keep shooting out of it all day long so the children have all they can do to eat them up."

"Yes, but what does the teacher do?" asked one little girl.

"Takes the paper off the caramels for the children, of course," said Pippi. "You didn't suppose they did it themselves, did you? Hardly. They don't even go to school themselves—they send their brothers." Pippi waved her big hat.

"So long, kids," she cried gaily. "Now you won't see me for a while. But always remember how many apples Axel had or you'll be sorry."

With a ringing laugh Pippi rode out through the gate so wildly that the pebbles whirled around the horse's hoofs and the windowpanes rattled in the schoolhouse.

Pippi Sits on the Gate and Climbs a Tree

• •

Outside Villa Villekulla sat Pippi, Tommy, and Annika. Pippi sat on one gatepost, Annika on the other, and Tommy sat on the gate. It was a warm and beautiful day toward the end of August. A pear tree that grew close to the fence stretched its branches so low down that the children could sit and pick the best little red-gold pears without any trouble at all. They munched and ate and spit pear cores out onto the road.

Villa Villekulla stood just at the edge of the little town, where the street turned into a country road. The people in the little town loved to go walking out Villa Villekulla way, for the country out there was so beautiful.

As the children were sitting there eating pears, a girl came walking along the road from town.

When she saw the children she stopped and asked, "Have you seen my papa go by?"

"M-m-m," said Pippi. "How did he look? Did he have blue eyes?"

"Yes," said the girl.

"Medium large, not too tall and not too short?"

"Yes," said the girl.

"Black hat and black shoes?"

"Yes, exactly," said the girl eagerly.

"No, that one we haven't seen," said Pippi decidedly.

The girl looked crestfallen and went off without a word.

"Wait a minute," shrieked Pippi after her. "Was he bald-headed?"

"No, he certainly was not," said the girl crossly.

"Lucky for him!" said Pippi and spit out a pear core.

The girl hurried away, but then Pippi shouted, "Did he have big ears that reached way down to his shoulders?"

"No," said the girl and turned and came running back in amazement. "You don't mean to say that you have seen a man walk by with such big ears?"

"I have never seen anyone who walks with his ears," said Pippi. "All the people I know walk with their feet."

"Oh, don't be silly! I mean have you really seen a man who has such big ears?"

"No," said Pippi, "there isn't anybody with such big ears. It would be ridiculous. How would they look? It isn't possible to have such big ears. At least not in this country," she added after a thoughtful pause. "Of course in China it's a little different. I once saw a Chinese in Shanghai. His ears were so big that he could use them for a cape. When it rained he just crawled in under his ears and was as warm and snug as you please. Of course his ears didn't have it so good. If it was very bad weather he used to invite his friends to camp under his ears. There they sat and sang sad songs while the rain poured down. They liked him a lot because of his ears. His name was Hai Shang. You should have seen Hai Shang run to work in the morning. He always came dashing in at the last minute because he loved to sleep late, and you can't imagine how funny he looked, rushing in with his ears flying behind him like two big golden sails."

The girl had stopped and stood open-mouthed listening to Pippi. And

Tommy and Annika forgot to eat any more pears, they were so utterly absorbed in the story.

"He had more children than he could count, and the littlest one was named Peter," said Pippi.

"Oh, but a Chinese baby can't be called Peter," interrupted Tommy.

"That's just what his wife said to him, 'A Chinese baby can't be called Peter.' But Hai Shang was dreadfully stubborn, and he said that the baby should be called Peter or Nothing. And then he sat down in a corner and pulled his ears over his head and howled. And his poor wife had to give in, of course, and the kid was called Peter."

"Really?" said Annika.

"It was the hatefulest kid in all Shanghai," continued Pippi. "Fussy about his food, so that his mother was most unhappy. You know, of course, that they eat swallows' nests in China? And there sat his mother, with a whole plate full of swallows' nests, trying to feed him. 'Now, little Peter,' she said, 'come, we'll eat a swallow's nest for Daddy.' But Peter just shut his mouth tight and shook his head. At last Hai Shang was so angry that he said that no new food should be prepared for Peter until he had eaten a swallow's nest for Daddy. And when Hai Shang said something, that was that. The same swallow's nest rode in and out of the kitchen from May until October. On the fourteenth of July his mother begged to be allowed to give Peter a couple of meatballs, but Hai Shang said no."

"Nonsense!" said the girl in the road.

"Yes, that's just what Hai Shang said," continued Pippi. "'Nonsense,' he said, 'it's perfectly plain that the child can eat the swallow's nest if he'll only stop being so stubborn.' But Peter kept his mouth shut tight from May to October."

"But how could he live?" asked Tommy, astonished.

"He couldn't live," said Pippi. "He died. Of Plain Common Ordinary Pigheadedness. The eighteenth of October. And was buried the nineteenth.

And on the twentieth a swallow flew in through the window and laid an egg in the nest, which was standing on the table. So it came in handy after all. No harm done," said Pippi happily. Then she looked thoughtfully at the bewildered girl, who still stood in the road.

"Why do you look so funny?" asked Pippi. "What's the matter? You don't really think that I'm sitting here telling lies, do you? Just tell me if you do," said Pippi threateningly and rolled up her sleeves.

"Oh, no, indeed," said the girl, terrified. "I don't really mean that you are lying, but—"

"No?" said Pippi. "But it's just what I'm doing. I'm lying so my tongue is turning black. Do you really think that a child can live without food from May to October? To be sure, I know they can get along without food for three or four months all right. But from May to October! It's just foolish to think that. You must know that's a lie. You mustn't let people fool you so easily."

Then the girl left without turning around again.

"People will believe anything," said Pippi to Tommy and Annika. "From May until October! That's ridiculous!"

Then she called after the girl, "No, we haven't seen your papa. We haven't seen a single bald-headed person all day. But yesterday seventeen of them went by. Arm in arm."

Pippi's garden was really lovely. You couldn't say it was well kept, but there were wonderful grass plots that were never cut, and old rosebushes that were full of white and yellow and pink roses—perhaps not such fine roses, but oh, how sweet they smelled! A good many fruit trees grew there too, and, best of all, several ancient oaks and elms that were excellent for climbing.

The trees in Tommy's and Annika's garden were not very good for climbing, and besides, their mother was always so afraid they would fall and get hurt that they had never climbed much. But now Pippi said, "Suppose we climb up in the big oak tree?"

Tommy jumped down from the gate at once, delighted with the suggestion. Annika was a little hesitant, but when she saw that the trunk had nubbly places to climb on, she too thought it would be fun to try.

A few feet above the ground the oak divided into two branches, and right there was a place just like a little room. Before long all three children were sitting there. Over their heads the oak spread out its crown like a great green roof.

"We could drink coffee here," said Pippi. "I'll skip in and make a little."

Tommy and Annika clapped their hands and shouted, "Bravo!"

In a little while Pippi had the coffee ready. She had made buns the day before. She came and stood under the oak and began to toss up coffee cups. Tommy and Annika caught them. Only sometimes it was the oak that caught them, and so two cups were broken. Pippi ran in to get new ones. Next it was the buns' turn, and for a while the air was full of flying buns. At least they didn't break. At last Pippi climbed up with the coffee pot in one hand. She had cream in a little bottle in her pocket, and sugar in a little box.

Tommy and Annika thought coffee had never tasted so good before. They were not allowed to drink it every day—only when they were at a party. And now they were at a party. Annika spilled a little coffee in her lap. First it was warm and wet, and then it was cold and wet, but that didn't matter to her.

When they had finished, Pippi threw the cups down on the grass. "I want to see how strong the china they make these days is," she said. Strangely enough, one cup and three saucers held together, and only the spout of the coffee pot broke off.

Presently Pippi decided to climb a little higher.

"Can you beat this?" she cried suddenly. "The tree is hollow."

There in the trunk was a big hole, which the leaves had hidden from the children's sight.

"Oh, may I climb up and look too?" called Tommy. But there was no answer.

"Pippi, where are you?" he cried, worried.

Then they heard Pippi's voice, not from above but from way down below. It sounded as if it came from under the ground.

"I'm inside the tree. It is hollow clear down to the ground. If I peek out through a little crack I can see the coffee pot outside on the grass."

"Oh, how will you get up again?" cried Annika.

"I'm never coming up," said Pippi. "I'm going to stay here until I retire and get a pension. And you'll have to throw my food down through that hole up there. Five or six times a day."

Annika began to cry.

"Why be sorry? Why complain?" said Pippi. "You come down here too, and then we can play that we are pining away in a dungeon."

"Never in this world!" said Annika, and to be on the safe side she climbed right down out of the tree.

"Annika, I can see you through the crack," cried Pippi. "Don't step on the coffee pot; it's an old well-mannered coffee pot that never did anyone any harm. It can't help it that it doesn't have a spout any longer."

Annika went up to the tree trunk, and through a little crack she saw the very tip of Pippi's finger. This comforted her a good deal, but she was still worried.

"Pippi, can't you really get up?" she asked.

Pippi's finger disappeared, and in less than a minute her face popped out of the hole up in the tree.

"Maybe I can if I try very hard," she said and parted the foliage with her hands.

"If it's as easy as all that to get up," said Tommy, who was still up in the tree, "then I want to come down and pine away a little too."

"Wait," said Pippi, "I think we'll get a ladder."

She crawled out of the hole and hurried down the tree. Then she ran after a ladder, pushed it up the tree, and let it down into the hole.

Tommy was wild to go down. It was difficult to climb to the hole, because it was so high up, but Tommy was brave. And he wasn't afraid to climb down into the dark hollow in the trunk. Annika watched him disappear and wondered if she would ever see him again. She peeked in through the crack.

"Annika," came Tommy's voice. "You can't imagine how wonderful it is here. You must come in too. It isn't the least bit dangerous when you have a ladder to climb on. If you only do it once, you'll never want to do anything else."

"Are you sure?" asked Annika.

"Absolutely," said Tommy.

With trembling legs Annika climbed up in the tree again, and Pippi helped her with the last hard bit. She drew back a little when she saw how dark it was in the tree trunk, but Pippi

held her hand and kept encouraging her.

"Don't be scared, Annika," she heard Tommy say from down below. "Now I can see your legs, and I'll certainly catch you if you fall."

But Annika didn't fall. She reached Tommy safely, and a moment later Pippi followed.

"Isn't it grand here?" said Tommy.

And Annika had to admit that it was. It wasn't nearly so dark as she had thought, because light came in through the crack. She peeked through and announced that she too could see the coffee pot outside on the grass.

"We'll have this for our secret hiding place," said Tommy. "Nobody will know that we are here. And if they should come and hunt around outside for us, we can see them through the crack. And we'll have a good laugh."

"We can have a little stick and poke it out through the crack and tickle them, and then they'll think the place is haunted," said Pippi.

At this idea the children were so delighted that they hugged each other, all three. Then they heard the "ding-dong" that meant the bell was ringing for dinner at Tommy's and Annika's house.

"Oh, bother!" said Tommy. "Now we've got to go home. But we'll come over tomorrow as soon as we get back from school."

"Do that," said Pippi.

And so they climbed up the ladder, first Pippi, then Annika, and Tommy last. And then they climbed down out of the tree, first Pippi, then Annika, and Tommy last.

Pippi Arranges a Picnic

• •

"We don't have any school today because we're having Scrubbing Vacation," said Tommy to Pippi.

"Scrubbing Vacation? Well, I like that!" said Pippi. "Another injustice! Do I get any Scrubbing Vacation? Indeed I don't, though goodness knows I need one. Just look at the kitchen floor. But for that matter," she added, "now I come to think of it, I can scrub without any vacation. And that's what I intend to do right now, Scrubbing Vacation or no Scrubbing Vacation. I'd like to see anybody stop me! You two sit on the kitchen table, out of the way."

Tommy and Annika obediently climbed up on the kitchen table, and Mr. Nilsson hopped up after them and went to sleep in Annika's lap.

Pippi heated a big kettle of water and without more ado poured it out on the kitchen floor. She took off her big shoes and laid them neatly on the bread plate. She tied two scrubbing brushes on her bare feet and skated over the floor, plowing through the water so that it splashed all around her.

"I certainly should have been a skating princess," she said and kicked her left foot up so high that the scrubbing brush broke a piece out of the overhead light.

45

"Grace and charm I have at least," she continued and skipped nimbly over a chair standing in her way.

"Well, now I guess it's clean," she said at last and took off the brushes.

"Aren't you going to dry the floor?" asked Annika.

"Oh, no, it can dry in the sun," answered Pippi. "I don't think it will catch cold so long as it keeps moving."

Tommy and Annika climbed down from the table and stepped across the floor very carefully so they wouldn't get wet.

Out of doors the sun shone in a clear blue sky. It was one of those radiant September days that make you feel like walking in the woods. Pippi had an idea.

"Let's take Mr. Nilsson and go on a little picnic."

"Oh, yes, let's," cried Tommy and Annika.

"Run home and ask your mother, then," said Pippi, "and I'll be getting the picnic basket ready."

Tommy and Annika thought that was a good suggestion. They rushed home and were back again almost immediately, but Pippi was already wait-ing by the gate with Mr. Nilsson on her shoulder, a walking stick in one hand, and a big basket in the other.

The children walked along the road a little way and then turned into a pasture where a pleasant path wound in and out among the thickets of birch and hazel. Presently they came to a gate on the other side of which was an even more beautiful pasture, but right in front of the gate stood a cow who looked as if nothing would persuade her to move. Annika yelled at her, and Tommy bravely went up and tried to push her away, but she just stood there staring at the children with her big cow eyes. To put an end to the matter, Pippi set down her basket and lifted the cow out of the way. The cow, looking very silly, lumbered off into the hazel bushes.

"How can cows be so bull-headed," said Pippi and jumped over the gate.

"What a lovely, lovely wood!" cried Annika in delight as she climbed up on all the stones she could see. Tommy had brought along a dagger Pippi had given him, and with it he cut walking sticks for Annika and for him-self. He cut his thumb a little too, but that didn't matter.

"Maybe we ought to pick some mushrooms," said Pippi, and she broke off a pretty, rosy one. "I wonder if it's possible to eat it?" she continued. "At any rate, it isn't possible to drink it—that much I know; so there is no choice except to eat it. Maybe it's possible."

She took a big bite and swallowed it. "It was possible," she announced, delighted. "Yes sirree, we'll certainly stew the rest of this sometime," she said and threw it high over the treetops.

"What have you got in your basket?" asked Annika. "Is it something good?"

"I wouldn't tell you for a thousand dollars," said Pippi. "First we must find a good picnic spot."

The children eagerly began to look for such a place. Annika found a large flat stone that she thought was satisfactory, but it was covered with red ants. "I don't want to sit with them," said Pippi, "because I'm not acquainted with them."

"And besides, they bite," said Tommy.

"Do they?" said Pippi. "Bite back then."

Then Tommy found a little clearing among the hazel bushes, and he thought that would be a good place.

"Oh, no, that's not sunny enough for my freckles," said Pippi, "and I do think freckles are so attractive."

Farther on they came to a hill that was easy to climb. On one side of the hill was a nice sunny rock just like a little balcony, and there they sat down.

"Now shut your eyes while I set the table," said Pippi. Tommy and Annika squeezed their eyes as tightly shut as possible. They heard Pippi opening the basket and rattling paper.

"One, two, nineteen—now you may look," said Pippi at last.

They looked, and they squealed with delight when they saw all the good things Pippi had spread on the bare rock. There were good sandwiches with meatballs and ham, a whole pile of sugared pancakes, several little brown sausages, and three pineapple puddings. For, you see, Pippi had learned cooking from the cook on her father's ship.

"Aren't Scrubbing Vacations grand?" said Tommy with his mouth full of pancakes. "We ought to have them every day."

"No, indeed, I'm not that anxious to scrub," said Pippi. "It's fun, to be sure, but not every day. That would be too tiresome."

At last the children were so full they could hardly move, and they sat still in the sunshine and just enjoyed it.

"I wonder if it is hard to fly," said Pippi and looked dreamily over the edge of the rock. The rock sloped down very steeply below them, and it was a long way to the ground.

"*Down* at least one ought to be able to learn to fly," she continued. "It must be harder to fly up. But you could begin with the easiest way. I do think I'll try."

"No, Pippi," cried both Tommy and Annika. "Oh, dear, Pippi, don't do that!"

But Pippi was already standing at the edge.

"Fly, you foolish fly, fly, and the foolish fly flew," she said, and just as she said "flew" she lifted her arms and took off into the air. In half a second there was a thud. It was Pippi hitting the ground. Tommy and Annika lay on their stomachs and looked down at her, terrified.

Pippi got up and brushed off her knees. "I forgot to flap," she said joyfully, "and I guess I had too many pancakes in my stomach."

At that moment the children noticed that Mr. Nilsson had disappeared. He had evidently gone off on a little expedition of his own. They remembered that they had last seen him contentedly chewing the picnic basket to pieces, but during Pippi's flying experiment they had forgotten him. And now he was gone.

Pippi was so angry that she threw her shoe into a big deep pool of water. "You should never take monkeys with you anywhere," she said. "He should have been left at home to pick fleas off the horse. That would have served him right," she continued, wading out into the pool to get her shoe. The water reached up to her waist.

"I might as well take advantage of this and wash my hair," said Pippi and ducked her head under the water and kept it there so long that the water began to bubble.

"There now, I've saved a visit to the hairdresser," she said contentedly when at last she

49

came up for air. She stepped out of the pool and put on her shoe. Then they went off to hunt for Mr. Nilsson.

"Hear how it squishes when I walk," laughed Pippi. "It says 'klafs, klafs' in my dress and 'squish, squish' in my shoes. Isn't that jolly? I think you ought to try it too," she said to Annika, who was walking along beside her, with her lovely flaxen hair, pink dress, and little white kid shoes.

"Some other time," said the sensible Annika.

They walked on.

"Mr. Nilsson certainly can be exasperating," said Pippi. "He's always doing things like this. Once in Arabia he ran away from me and took a position as a maidservant to an elderly widow. That last was a lie, of course," she added after a pause.

Tommy suggested they all three go in different directions and hunt. At first Annika didn't want to because she was a little afraid, but Tommy said, "You aren't a 'fraidy cat, are you?" And, of course, Annika couldn't tolerate such an insult, so off they all went.

Tommy went through a field. Mr. Nilsson he did not find, but he did find something else. A bull! Or to be more exact, the bull found Tommy. And the bull did not like Tommy, for he was a very cross bull who was not at all fond of children. With his head down he charged toward Tommy, bellowing fearfully. Tommy let out a terrified shriek that could be heard all through the woods. Pippi and Annika heard it and came running to see what was the matter. By that time the bull had almost reached Tommy who had fallen head over heels over a stump.

"What a stupid bull!" said Pippi to Annika, who was crying uncontrollably. "He ought to know he can't act like that. He'll get Tommy's white sailor suit all dirty. I'll have to go and talk some sense into the stupid animal."

And off she started. She ran up and pulled the bull by the tail. "Forgive me for breaking up the party," she said. Since she had given his tail a good hard pull, the bull turned around and saw a new child to catch on his horns.

"As I was saying," went on Pippi, "forgive me for breaking up, and also forgive me for breaking off," and with that she broke off one of the bull's horns. "It isn't the style to have two horns this year," she said. "All the better bulls have just one horn—if any." And she broke off the other horn too.

As bulls have no feeling in their horns, this one didn't know what she had done. He charged at Pippi, and if she had been any other child there would have been nothing left but a grease spot.

"Hey, hey, stop tickling me!" shrieked Pippi. "You can't imagine how ticklish I am! Hey, stop, stop, or I'll die laughing!"

But the bull didn't stop, and at last Pippi jumped up on his back to get a little rest. To be sure, she didn't get much, because the bull didn't in the least approve of having Pippi on his back. He dodged about madly to get her off, but she clamped her knees and hung on. The bull dashed up and down the field, bellowing so hard that smoke came out of his nostrils. Pippi laughed and shrieked and waved at Tommy and Annika, who stood a little distance away, trembling like aspen leaves. The bull whirled round and round, trying to throw Pippi.

"See me dancing with my little friend!" cried Pippi and kept her seat. At last the bull was so tired that he lay down on the ground and wished that he'd never seen such a thing as a child. He had never thought children amounted to much anyway.

"Are you going to take a little nap now?" asked Pippi politely. "Then I won't disturb you."

She got off his back and went over to Tommy and Annika. Tommy had cried a little. He had a cut on one arm, but Annika had bandaged it with her handkerchief so that it no longer hurt.

"Oh, Pippi!" cried Annika excitedly.

"Sh, sh," whispered Pippi. "Don't wake the bull. He's sleeping. If we wake him he'll be fussy."

But the next minute, without paying any attention to the bull and his nap, she was shrieking at the top of her voice, "Mr. Nilsson, Mr. Nilsson, where are you? We've got to go home."

And, believe it or not, there sat Mr. Nilsson up in a pine tree, sucking his tail and looking very lonely. It wasn't much fun for a little monkey to be left all alone in the woods. He skipped down from the pine and up on Pippi's shoulder, waving his little straw hat as he always did when he was very happy.

"Well, well, so you aren't going to be a maidservant this time?" said Pippi, stroking his back. "Oh, that was a lie, that's true," she continued. "But still, if it's true, how can it be a lie?" she argued. "You wait and see, it's going to turn out that he was a maidservant in Arabia after all, and if that's the case, I know who's going to make the meatballs at our house hereafter!"

And then they strolled home, Pippi's dress still going "klafs, klafs," and her shoes "squish, squish."

Tommy and Annika thought they had had a wonderful day in spite of the bull, and they sang a song they had learned at school. It was really a summer song, but they thought it fitted very well even if it was now nearly autumn:

> *In the jolly summertime*
> *Through field and wood we make our way.*
> *Nobody's sad, everyone's gay.*
> *We sing as we go, hol-lá, hol-ló!*
>
> *You who are young,*
> *Come join in our song.*
> *Don't sit home moping all the day long.*
> *Our song will swell*

Through wood and dell
And up to the mountaintop as well.
In the jolly summertime
We sing as we go, hol-lá, hol-ló.

Pippi sang too, but with slightly different words:

In the jolly summertime
Through field and wood I make my way.
I do exactly as I wish,
And when I walk it goes squish, squish,
Squish, squish. Squish, squish.

And my old shoe—
It's really true—
Sometimes says "chip" and sometimes "choo."
For the shoe is wet.
The bull sleeps yet.
And I eat all the rice pudding I can get.
In the jolly summertime
I squish wherever I go. Squish-oh! Squish-oh!

Pippi Goes to the Circus

A circus had come to the little town, and all the children were begging their mothers and fathers for permission to go. Of course Tommy and Annika asked to go too, and their kind father immediately gave them some money.

Clutching it tightly in their hands, they rushed over to Pippi's. She was on the porch with her horse, braiding his tail into tiny pigtails and tying each one with red ribbon.

"I think it's his birthday today," she announced, "so he has to be all dressed up."

"Pippi," said Tommy, all out of breath because they had been running so fast, "Pippi, do you want to go with us to the circus?"

"I can go with you most anywhere," answered Pippi, "but whether I can go to the surkus or not I don't know, because I don't know what a surkus is. Does it hurt?"

"Silly!" said Tommy. "Of course it doesn't hurt; it's fun. Horses and clowns and pretty ladies that walk the tightrope."

"But it costs money," said Annika, opening her small fist to see if the shiny half-dollar and the quarters were still there.

"I'm rich as a troll," said Pippi, "so I guess I can buy a surkus all right. But it'll be crowded here if I have more horses. The clowns and the pretty ladies I could keep in the laundry, but it's harder to know what to do with the horses."

"Oh, don't be so silly," said Tommy, "you don't buy a circus. It costs money to go and look at it—see?"

"Preserve us!" cried Pippi and shut her eyes tightly. "It costs money to *look?* And here I go around goggling all day long. Goodness knows how much money I've goggled up already!"

Then, little by little, she opened one eye very carefully, and it rolled round and round in her head. "Cost what it may," she said, "I must take a look!"

At last Tommy and Annika managed to explain to Pippi what a circus really was, and she took some gold pieces out of her suitcase. Then she put on her hat, which was as big as a millstone, and off they all went.

There were crowds of people outside the circus tent and a long line at the ticket window. But at last it was Pippi's turn. She stuck her head through the window and stared at the dear old lady sitting there.

"How much does it cost to look at you?" Pippi asked.

But the old lady was a foreigner who did not understand what Pippi meant and answered in broken Swedish.

"Little girl, it costs a dollar and a quarter in the grandstand and seventy-five cents on the benches and twenty-five cents for standing room."

Now Tommy interrupted and said that Pippi wanted a seventy-five-cent ticket. Pippi put down a gold piece and the old lady looked suspiciously at it. She bit it too, to see if it was genuine. At last she was convinced that it really was gold and gave Pippi her ticket and a great deal of change in silver.

"What would I do with all those nasty little white coins?" asked Pippi disgustedly. "Keep them and then I can look at you twice. In the standing room."

As Pippi absolutely refused to accept any change, the lady changed her ticket to one for the grandstand and gave Tommy and Annika grandstand tickets too without their having to pay a single penny. In that way Pippi, Tommy, and Annika came to sit on some beautiful red chairs right next to the ring. Tommy and Annika turned around several times to wave to their schoolmates, who were sitting much farther away.

"This is a remarkable place," said Pippi, looking around in astonishment. "But, see, they've spilled sawdust all over the floor! Not that I'm overfussy myself, but that does look careless to me."

Tommy explained that all circuses had sawdust on the floor for the horses to run around in.

On a platform nearby the circus band suddenly began to play a thundering march. Pippi clapped her hands wildly and jumped up and down with delight.

"Does it cost money to hear too?" she asked. "Or can you do that for nothing?"

At that moment the curtain in front of the performers' entrance was drawn aside, and the ringmaster in a black frock coat, with a whip in his hand, came running in, followed by ten white horses with red plumes on their heads.

The ringmaster cracked his whip, and all the horses galloped around the ring. Then he cracked it again, and all the horses stood still with their front feet up on the railing around the ring.

One of them had stopped directly in front of the children. Annika didn't like to have a horse so near her and drew back in her chair as far as she could, but Pippi leaned forward and took the horse's right foot in her hands.

"Hello, there," she said, "my horse sent you his best wishes. It's his birthday today too, but he has bows on his tail instead of on his head."

Luckily she dropped the foot before the ringmaster cracked his whip again, because then all the horses jumped away from the railing and began to run around the ring.

When the act was over, the ringmaster bowed politely and the horses ran out. In an instant the curtain opened again for a coal-black horse. On its back stood a beautiful lady dressed in green silk tights. The program said her name was Miss Carmencita.

The horse trotted around in the sawdust, and Miss Carmencita stood calmly on his back and smiled. But then something happened; just as the horse passed Pippi's seat, something came swishing through the air—and it was none other than Pippi herself. And there she stood on the horse's back, behind Miss Carmencita. At first Miss Carmencita was so astonished that she nearly fell off the horse. Then she got mad. She began to strike out with her hands behind her back to make Pippi jump off. But that didn't work.

"Take it easy," said Pippi. "Do you think you're the only one who can have any fun? Other people have paid too, haven't they?"

Then Miss Carmencita tried to jump off herself, but that didn't work either, because Pippi was holding her tightly around the waist. At that the audience couldn't help laughing. They thought it was funny to see the lovely Miss Carmencita held against her will by a little red-headed youngster who stood there on the horse's back in her enormous shoes and looked as if she had never done anything except perform in a circus.

But the ringmaster didn't laugh. He turned toward an attendant in a red uniform and made a sign to him to go and stop the horse.

"Is this act already over," asked Pippi in a disappointed tone, "just when we were having so much fun?"

"Horrible child!" hissed the ringmaster between his teeth. "Get out of here!"

Pippi looked at him sadly. "Why are you mad at me?" she asked. "What's the matter? I thought we were here to have fun."

She skipped off the horse and went back to her seat. But now two huge guards came to throw her out. They took hold of her and tried to lift her up.

They couldn't do it. Pippi sat absolutely still, and it was impossible to budge her although they tried as hard as they could. At last they shrugged their shoulders and went off.

Meanwhile the next act had begun. It was Miss Elvira about to walk the tightrope. She wore a pink tulle skirt and carried a pink parasol in her hand. With delicate little steps she ran out on the rope. She swung her legs gracefully in the air and did all sorts of tricks. It looked so pretty. She even showed how she could walk backward on the narrow rope. But when she got back to the little platform at the end of the rope, there stood Pippi.

"What are you going to do now?" asked Pippi, delighted when she saw how astonished Miss Elvira looked.

Miss Elvira said nothing at all but jumped down from the rope and threw her arms around the ringmaster's neck, for he was her father. And the ringmaster once more sent for his guards to throw Pippi out. This time he sent for five of them, but all the people shouted, "Let her stay! We want to see the red-headed girl." And they stamped their feet and clapped their hands.

Pippi ran out on the rope, and Miss Elvira's tricks were as nothing compared with Pippi's. When she got to the middle of the rope she stretched one leg straight up in the air, and her big shoe spread out like a roof over her head. She bent her foot a little so that she could tickle herself with it back of her ear.

The ringmaster was not at all pleased to have Pippi performing in his circus. He wanted to get rid of her, and so he stole up and loosened the mechanism that held the rope taut, thinking surely Pippi would fall down.

But Pippi didn't. She set the rope a-swinging instead. Back and forth it swayed, and Pippi swung faster and faster, until suddenly she leaped out into the air and landed right on the ringmaster. He was so frightened he began to run.

"Oh, what a jolly horse!" cried Pippi. "But why don't you have any pom-poms in your hair?"

Now Pippi decided it was time to go back to Tommy and Annika. She jumped off the ringmaster and went back to her seat. The next act was about to begin, but there was a brief pause because the ringmaster had to go out and get a drink of water and comb his hair.

Then he came in again, bowed to the audience, and said, "Ladies and gentlemen, in a moment you will be privileged to see the Greatest Marvel of all time, the Strongest Man in the World, the Mighty Adolf, whom no one has yet been able to conquer. Here he comes, ladies and gentlemen, Allow me to present to you THE MIGHTY ADOLF."

And into the ring stepped a man who looked as big as a giant. He wore flesh-colored tights and had a leopard skin draped around his stomach. He bowed to the audience and looked very pleased with himself.

"Look at these muscles," said the ringmaster and squeezed the Mighty Adolf's arm where the muscles stood out like balls under the skin.

"And now, ladies and gentlemen, I have a very special invitation for you. Who will challenge the Mighty Adolf in a wrestling match? Which of you dares to try his strength against the World's Strongest Man? A hundred dollars for anyone who can conquer the Mighty Adolf! A hundred dollars, ladies and gentlemen! Think of that! Who will be the first to try?"

Nobody came forth.

"What did he say?" asked Pippi.

"He says that anybody who can lick that big man will get a hundred dollars," answered Tommy.

"I can," said Pippi, "but I think it would be too bad to, because he looks nice."

"Oh, no, you couldn't," said Annika, "he's the strongest man in the world."

"*Man,* yes," said Pippi, "but I am the strongest *girl* in the world, remember that."

Meanwhile the Mighty Adolf was lifting heavy iron weights and bending thick iron rods in the middle just to show how strong he was.

"Oh, come now, ladies and gentlemen," cried the ringmaster, "is there really nobody here who wants to earn a hundred dollars? Shall I really be forced to keep this myself?" And he waved a bill in the air.

"No, that you certainly won't be forced to do," said Pippi and stepped over the railing into the ring.

The ringmaster was absolutely wild when he saw her. "Get out of here! I don't want to see any more of you," he hissed.

"Why do you always have to be so unfriendly?" said Pippi reproachfully. "I just want to fight with Mighty Adolf."

"This is no place for jokes," said the ringmaster. "Get out of here before the Mighty Adolf hears your impudent nonsense."

But Pippi went right by the ringleader and up to Mighty Adolf. She took his hand and shook it heartily.

"Shall we fight a little, you and I?" she asked.

Mighty Adolf looked at her but didn't understand a word.

"In one minute I'll begin," said Pippi.

And begin she did. She grabbed Mighty Adolf around the waist, and before anyone knew what was happening she had thrown him on the mat. Mighty Adolf leaped up, his face absolutely scarlet.

"Atta girl, Pippi!" shrieked Tommy and Annika, so loudly that all the people at the circus heard it and began to shriek, "Atta girl, Pippi!" too. The ringmaster sat on the railing, wringing his hands. He was mad, but Mighty Adolf was madder. Never in his life had he experienced anything so humiliating as this. And he certainly intended to show that red-headed girl what kind of a man Mighty Adolf really was. He rushed at Pippi and caught her round the waist, but Pippi stood firm as a rock.

"You can do better than that," she said to encourage him. Then she wriggled out of his grasp, and in the twinkling of an eye Mighty Adolf was on the mat again. Pippi stood beside him, waiting. She didn't have to wait long. With a roar he was up again, rushing at her.

"Tiddelipom and piddeliday," said Pippi.

All the people in the tent stamped their feet and threw their hats in the air and shouted, "Hurrah, Pippi!"

When Mighty Adolf came rushing at her for the third time, Pippi lifted him high in the air and, with her arms straight above her, carried him clear around the ring. Then she laid him down on the mat again and held him there.

"Now, little fellow," said she, "I don't think we'll bother about this any more. We'll never have any more fun than we've had already."

"Pippi is the winner! Pippi is the winner!" cried all the people.

Mighty Adolf stole out as fast as he could, and the ringmaster had to go up and hand Pippi the hundred dollars, although he looked as if he'd much prefer to eat her.

"Here you are, young lady, here you are," he said. "One hundred dollars."

"That thing!" said Pippi scornfully. "What would I want with that old piece of paper. Take it and use it to fry herring on if you want to." And she went back to her seat.

"This is certainly a long surkus," she said to Tommy and Annika. "I think I'll take a little snooze, but wake me if they need my help with anything else."

And then she lay back in her chair and went to sleep at once. There she lay and snored while the clowns, the sword swallowers, and the snake charmers did their tricks for Tommy and Annika and all the rest of the people at the circus.

"Just the same, I think Pippi was best of all," whispered Tommy to Annika.

Pippi Entertains Two Burglars

After Pippi's performance at the circus there was not a single person in all the little town who did not know how strong she was. There was even a piece about her in the paper. But people who lived in other places, of course, didn't know who Pippi was.

One dark autumn evening two tramps came walking down the road past Villa Villekulla. They were two bad thieves wandering about the country to see what they could steal. They saw that there was a light in the windows of Villa Villekulla and decided to go in to ask for a sandwich.

That evening Pippi had poured out all her gold pieces on the kitchen floor and sat there counting them. To be sure, she couldn't count very well, but she did it now and then anyway, just to keep everything in order.

"... sixty-five, sixty-six, sixty-seven, sixty-eight, sixty-nine, sixty-ten, sixty-eleven, sixty-twelve, sixty-thirteen, sixty-sixteen—whew, it makes my throat feel like sixty! Goodness, there must be *some* more numbers in the arithmetic—oh, yes, now I remember—one hundred four, one thousand. That certainly is a lot of money," said Pippi.

There was a loud knock on the door.

"Walk in or stay out, whichever you choose!" shouted Pippi. "I never force anyone against his will."

The door opened and the two tramps came in. You can imagine that they opened their eyes when they saw a little red-headed girl sitting all alone on the floor, counting money.

"Are you all alone at home?" they asked craftily.

"Of course not," said Pippi. "Mr. Nilsson is at home too."

The thieves couldn't very well know that Mr. Nilsson was a monkey sleeping in a little green bed with a doll's quilt around his stomach. They thought the man of the house must be named Mr. Nilsson and they winked at each other. "We can come back a little later" is what they meant, but to Pippi they said, "We just came in to ask what your clock is."

They were so excited that they had forgotten all about the sandwich.

"Great, strong men who don't know what a clock is!" said Pippi. "Where in the world were you brought up? The clock is a little round thingamajig that says 'tick tack, tick tack,' and that goes and goes but never gets to the door. Do you know any more riddles? Out with them if you do," said Pippi encouragingly.

The tramps thought Pippi was too little to tell time, so without another word they went out again.

"I don't demand that you say 'tack'" [thanks in Swedish], shouted Pippi after them, "but you could at least make an effort and say 'tick.' You haven't even as much sense as a clock has. But by all means go in peace." And Pippi went back to her counting.

No sooner were the tramps outside than they began to rub their hands with delight. "Did you see all that money? Heavenly day!" said one of them.

"Yes, once in a while luck is with us," said

the other. "All we need to do is wait until the kid and that Nilsson are asleep. Then we'll sneak in and grab the dough."

They sat down under an oak tree in the garden to wait. A drizzling rain was falling; they were very hungry, so they were quite uncomfortable, but the thought of all that money kept their spirits up.

From time to time lights went out in other houses, but in Villa Villekulla they shone on. It so happened that Pippi was learning to dance the schottische, and she didn't want to go to bed until she was sure she could do it. At last, however, the lights went out in the windows of Villa Villekulla too.

The tramps waited quite a while until they were sure Mr. Nilsson would have gone to sleep. At last they crept quietly up to the kitchen door and prepared to open it with their burglar tools. Meanwhile one of them—his name, as a matter of fact, was Bloom—just happened to feel the doorknob. The door was not locked!

"Well, some people *are* smart!" he whispered to his companion. "The door is open!"

"So much the better for us," answered his companion, a black-haired man called Thunder-Karlsson by those who knew him. Thunder-Karlsson turned on his pocket flashlight, and they crept into the kitchen. There was no one there. In the next room was Pippi's bed, and there also stood Mr. Nilsson's little doll bed.

Thunder-Karlsson opened the door and looked around carefully. Everything was quiet as he played his flashlight around the room. When the light touched Pippi's bed the two tramps were amazed to see nothing but a pair of feet on the pillow. Pippi, as usual, had her head under the covers at the foot of the bed.

"That must be the girl," whispered Thunder-Karlsson to Bloom. "And no doubt she sleeps soundly. But where in the world is Nilsson, do you suppose?"

"*Mr.* Nilsson, if you please," came Pippi's calm voice from under the covers. "*Mr.* Nilsson is in the little green doll bed."

The tramps were so startled that they almost rushed out at once, but then it suddenly dawned on them what Pippi had said. That Mr. Nilsson was lying in a *doll's* bed! And now in the light of the flashlight they could see the little bed and the tiny monkey lying in it.

Thunder-Karlsson couldn't help laughing. "Bloom," he said, "Mr. Nilsson is a monkey. Can you beat that?"

"Well, what did you think he was?" came Pippi's calm voice from under the covers again. "A lawn mower?"

"Aren't your mother and father at home?" asked Bloom.

"No," said Pippi. "They're gone. Completely gone."

Thunder-Karlsson and Bloom chuckled with delight.

"Listen, little girl," said Thunder-Karlsson, "come out so we can talk to you."

"No, I'm sleeping," said Pippi. "Is it more riddles you want? If so, answer this one. What is it that goes and goes and never gets to the door?"

Now Bloom went over and pulled the covers off Pippi.

"Can you dance the schottische?" asked Pippi, looking at him gravely in the eye. "I can."

"You ask too many questions," said Thunder-Karlsson. "Can we ask a few too? Where, for instance, is the money you had on the floor a little while ago?"

"In the suitcase on top of the wardrobe," answered Pippi truthfully.

Thunder-Karlsson and Bloom grinned.

"I hope you don't have anything against our taking it, little friend," said Thunder-Karlsson.

"Certainly not," said Pippi. "Of course I don't."

Whereupon Bloom lifted down the suitcase.

"I hope you don't have anything against my taking it back, little friend," said Pippi, getting out of bed and stepping over to Bloom.

Bloom had no idea how it all happened, but suddenly the suitcase was in Pippi's hand.

"Here, quit your fooling!" said Thunder-Karlsson angrily. "Hand over the suitcase." He took Pippi firmly by the hand and tried to snatch back the booty.

"Fooling, fooling, too much fooling," said Pippi and lifted Thunder-Karlsson up on the wardrobe. A moment later she had Bloom up there too. Then the tramps were frightened; they began to see that Pippi was no ordinary girl. However, the suitcase tempted them so much they forgot their fright.

"Come on now, both together," yelled Thunder-Karlsson, and they jumped down for the wardrobe and threw themselves on Pippi, who had the suitcase in her hand. Pippi gave each one a little poke with her finger, and they shrank away into a corner. Before they had a chance to get up again, Pippi had fetched a rope and quick as a flash had bound the arms and

legs of both burglars. Now they sang a different tune.

"Please, please, miss," begged Thunder-Karlsson, "forgive us. We were only joking. Don't hurt us. We are just two tramps who came in to ask for food."

Bloom even began to cry a bit.

Pippi put the suitcase neatly back on the wardrobe. Then she turned to her prisoners. "Can either of you dance the schottische?"

"Why, yes," said Thunder-Karlsson, "I guess we both can."

"Oh, what fun!" cried Pippi, clapping her hands. "Can't we dance a little? I've just learned, you know."

"Well, certainly, by all means," said Thunder-Karlsson, a bit confused.

Pippi took some large scissors and cut the ropes that bound her guests.

"But we don't have any music," she said in a worried voice. Then she had an idea. "Can't you blow on a comb?" she said to Bloom. "And I'll dance with him." She pointed to Thunder-Karlsson.

Oh, yes, Bloom could blow on a comb, all right. And blow he did, so that you could hear it all through the house. Mr. Nilsson sat up in bed, wide awake, just in time to see Pippi whirling around with Thunder-Karlsson. She was dead serious and danced as if her life depended on it.

At last Bloom said he couldn't blow on the comb any longer because it tickled his mouth unmercifully. And Thunder-Karlsson, who had tramped the roads all day, began to feel tired.

"Oh, please, just a little longer," begged Pippi, dancing on, and Bloom and Thunder-Karlsson could do nothing but continue.

At three in the morning Pippi said, "I could keep on dancing until Thursday, but maybe you're tired and hungry."

That was exactly what they were, though they hardly dared to say so. Pippi went to the pantry and took out bread and cheese and butter, ham and cold roast and milk; and they sat around the kitchen table—Bloom and

Thunder-Karlsson, and Pippi—and ate until they were almost four-cornered.

Pippi poured a little milk into her ear. "That's good for earache," she said.

"Poor thing, have you got an earache?" asked Bloom.

"No," said Pippi, "but I might get one."

Finally the two tramps got up, thanked Pippi for the food, and begged to be allowed to say good-by.

"It was awfully jolly that you came. Do you really have to go so soon?" said Pippi regretfully. "Never have I seen anyone who can dance the schottische the way you do, my sugar pig," she said to Thunder-Karlsson. And to Bloom, "If you keep on practicing on the comb, you won't notice the tickling."

As they were going out of the door Pippi came running after them and gave them each a gold piece. "These you have honestly earned," she said.

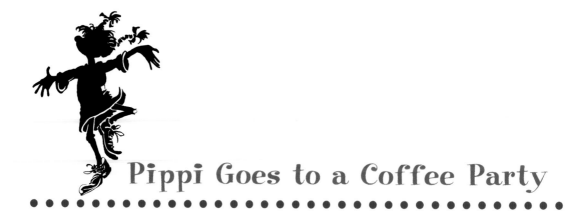

Pippi Goes to a Coffee Party

Tommy's and Annika's mother had invited a few ladies to a coffee party, and as she had done plenty of baking, she thought Tommy and Annika might invite Pippi over at the same time. The children would entertain each other and give no trouble to anyone.

Tommy and Annika were overjoyed when their mother told them and immediately dashed over to Pippi's to invite her. Pippi was in the garden, watering the few flowers still in bloom with an old rusty watering can. As it was raining cats and dogs that day Tommy told Pippi her watering seemed hardly necessary.

"Yes, that's what you say," said Pippi grudgingly, "but I've lain awake all night thinking what fun it was going to be to get up and water, and I'm not going to let a little rain stand in my way."

Now Annika came forth with the delightful news about the coffee party.

"A coffee party! *Me!*" cried Pippi, and she was so excited that she began to water Tommy instead of the rosebush she intended to sprinkle. "Oh, what will happen? Oh, I'm so nervous. What if I can't behave myself?"

"Of course you can," said Annika.

"Don't you be too certain about that," said Pippi. "You can be sure I'll

72

try, but I have noticed several times that people don't think I know how to behave even when I'm trying as hard as I can. At sea we were never so fussy about things like that. But I promise that I'll take special pains today so you won't have to be ashamed of me."

"Good," said Tommy, and he and Annika hurried home again in the rain.

"This afternoon at three o'clock, don't forget," cried Annika, peeking out from under the umbrella.

At three o'clock a very stylish young lady walked up the steps of the Settergrens' house. It was Pippi Longstocking. For this special occasion she had unbraided her pigtails, and her red hair hung like a lion's mane around her. With red crayon she had painted her mouth fiery red, and she had blackened her eyebrows so that she looked almost dangerous. With the crayon she had also painted her fingernails, and she had put big green rosettes on her shoes.

"I should imagine I'll be the most stylish person of all at this party," she said contentedly to herself as she rang the doorbell.

In the Settergrens' living room sat three fine ladies, and with them Tommy, Annika, and their mother. A wonderful coffee table had been spread, and in the fireplace a fire was burning brightly. The ladies were talking quietly with one another, and Tommy and Annika were sitting on the sofa, looking at an album. Everything was so peaceful.

Suddenly the peace was shattered.

"Atten-shun!" A piercing cry came from the hall, and the next minute Pippi Longstocking stood in the doorway. She had cried out so loudly and so unexpectedly that the ladies had jumped in their seats.

"Forward march!" came the next command, and Pippi, with measured steps, walked up to Mrs. Settergren.

"Halt!" She stopped. "Arms forward, one, *two*," she cried and with both hands gripped one of Mrs. Settergren's and shook it heartily.

"Knees bend!" she shrieked and curtsied prettily. Then she smiled at Mrs. Settergren and said in her ordinary voice, "You see, I am really very shy, so if I didn't give myself some commands I'd just stand in the hall and not dare to come in."

Then she rushed up to the other ladies and kissed them on the cheek.

"Charming, charming, upon my honor!" said she, for she had once heard a stylish gentleman say that to a lady. Then she sat down in the best chair she could find. Mrs. Settergren had intended the children to have their party up in Tommy's and Annika's room, but Pippi stayed calmly in her chair, slapped herself on the knee, and said, looking at the coffee table, "That certainly looks good. When do we begin?"

At that moment Ella, the maid, came in with the coffee pot, and Mrs. Settergren said, "Please come and have some coffee."

"*First!*" cried Pippi and was up by the table in two skips. She heaped as many cakes as she could onto a plate, threw five lumps of sugar into a cof-

fee cup, emptied half the cream pitcher into her cup, and was back in her chair with her loot even before the ladies had reached the table.

Pippi stretched her legs out in front of her and placed the plate of cakes between her toes. Then she merrily dunked cakes in her coffee cup and stuffed so many in her mouth at once that she couldn't have uttered a word no matter how hard she tried. In the twinkling of an eye she had finished all the cakes on the plate. She got up, struck the plate as if were a tambourine, and went up to the table to see if there were any cakes left. The ladies looked disapprovingly at her, but that didn't bother her. Chatting gaily, she walked around the table, snatching a cake here and a cake there.

"It certainly was nice of you to invite me," she said. "I've never been to a coffee party before."

On the table stood a large cream pie, decorated in the center with a piece of red candy. Pippi stood with her hands behind her back and looked at it. Suddenly she bent down and snatched the candy with her teeth. But she dived down a little too hastily, and when she came up again her whole face was covered with whipped cream.

"Goody!" laughed Pippi. "Now we can play blindman's buff, for we've certainly got a blind man all made to order! I can't see a thing!"

She stuck out her tongue and licked away the cream. "This was indeed a dreadful accident," said she. "And the pie is all ruined now anyway, so I may as well eat it all up at once."

She dug into it with the pie server, and in a few minutes the whole pie had disappeared. Pippi patted her stomach contentedly. Mrs. Settergren had gone out into the kitchen so she knew nothing about the accident to the cream pie, but the other ladies looked very sternly at Pippi. No doubt they would have liked a little pie too. Pippi noticed that they looked disappointed and decided to cheer them up.

"Now you mustn't feel bad about such a little accident," she said comfortingly. "The main thing is that we have our health. And at a coffee party you should have fun."

She then picked up a sugar bowl and tipped all the lump sugar in it out on the floor. "Well, my goodness!" she cried. "Now look what I've done! How could I make such a mistake? I thought this was the granulated sugar. Bad luck seems to follow me today."

Thereupon she took a sugar spoon out of another bowl and began to sprinkle granulated sugar all over the floor. "I hope you notice," she said, "that this is the kind of sugar you sprinkle on things. So it's perfectly all right for me to do this. Because why should there be the kind of sugar to sprinkle on things if somebody doesn't go and sprinkle it?—that's what I'd like to know.

"Have you ever noticed what fun it is to walk on a floor that has had sugar sprinkled all over it?" she asked the ladies. "Of course it's even more fun when you're barefoot," she added as she pulled off her shoes and stockings. "You ought to try it too, because nothing's more fun, believe me!"

At that moment Mrs. Settergren came in, and when she saw the sugar all over the floor she took Pippi firmly by the arm and led her over to the sofa to Tommy and Annika. Then she went over to the ladies and invited them to have more coffee. That the cream pie had disappeared only made her happy, because she thought the ladies had liked it so much that they had eaten it all.

Pippi, Tommy, and Annika sat talking quietly on the sofa. The fire crackled on the hearth. The ladies drank their coffee, and all was quiet and peaceful again. And as so often happens at coffee parties, the ladies began to talk about their servant problems. Apparently they had not been able to get very good servants, for they were not at all satisfied with them, and they agreed that it really was better not to have any servants at all. It was much more satisfactory to do things yourself because then you at least knew that things were done right.

Pippi sat on the sofa listening, and after the ladies had been talking a while she said, "Once my grandmother had a servant named Malin. She had chilblains on her feet, but otherwise there was nothing wrong with her. The only annoying thing was that as soon as company came she would rush at them and bite their legs. And bark! Oh, how she would bark! You could hear it all through the neighborhood, but it was only because she was playful. Only, of course, strangers didn't always understand that. The dean's wife, an elderly woman, came to see Grandmother once soon after Malin first came, and when Malin came dashing at her and bit her in the ankle, the dean's wife screamed so loudly that it scared Malin, so that her teeth clamped together and she couldn't get them apart. There she sat, stuck to the dean's wife's ankle until Friday. And Grandmother had to peel the potatoes herself. But at least it was well done. She peeled so well that when she was done there were no potatoes left—only peelings. But after that Friday the dean's wife never came to call on Grandmother again. She just never could take a joke. And poor Malin who was always so good-natured and happy! Though for that matter she was a little touchy at times, there's no denying that. Once when Grandmother poked a fork in her ear she howled all day."

Pippi looked around and smiled pleasantly. "Yes, that was Malin for you," she said and twiddled her thumbs.

The ladies acted as if they had heard nothing. They continued to talk.

"If my Rosa were only clean," said Mrs. Berggren, "then maybe I could keep her. But she's a regular pig—"

"Say, you ought to have seen Malin," Pippi interrupted. "Malin was so outrageously dirty that it was a joy to see her, Grandmother said. For the longest time Grandmother thought she had a very dark complexion but, honest and true, it was nothing but dirt that would wash off. And once at a bazaar at the City Hotel she got first prize for the dirt under her nails. Mercy me, how dirty that girl was!" said Pippi happily. Mrs. Settergren looked at her sternly.

77

"Can you imagine!" said Mrs. Granberg. "The other evening when Britta was going out she borrowed my blue satin dress without even asking for it. Isn't that dreadful?"

"Yes, indeed," said Pippi, "she certainly seems to be cut from the same piece of cloth as Malin, from what you say. Grandmother had a pink undershirt that she was specially fond of. But the worst of it was that Malin liked it too. And every morning Grandmother and Malin argued about who was to wear the undershirt. At last they decided it would be fair to take turns and each wear it every other day. But imagine how tricky Malin could be! Sometimes she'd come running in when it wasn't her turn at all and say, 'No mashed turnip today if I can't wear the pink woolen undershirt!' Well, what was Grandmother to do? Mashed turnip was her very favorite dish. There was nothing for it but to give Malin the shirt. As soon as Malin got the shirt she went out into the kitchen as nice as could be and began to mash turnip so that it spattered all over the walls."

There was silence for a little while, and then Mrs. Alexandersson said, "I'm not absolutely certain but I strongly suspect that my Hulda steals. In fact I've noticed that things disappear."

"Malin," began Pippi, but Mrs. Settergren interrupted her. "Children," she said decidedly, "go up to the nursery immediately!"

"Yes, but I was only going to tell that Malin stole too," said Pippi. "Like a raven! Everything she could lay her hands on. She used to get up in the middle of the night and steal; otherwise she couldn't sleep well, she said. Once she stole Grandmother's piano and tucked it into her own top bureau drawer. She was very clever with her hands, Grandmother said."

Tommy and Annika took hold of Pippi and pulled her out of the room and up the stairs. The ladies began on their third cups of coffee, and Mrs. Settergren said, "It's not that I want to complain about my Ella, but she does break the china."

A red head appeared over the stair rail.

"Speaking of Malin," said Pippi, "maybe you are wondering if she used to break any china. Well, she did. She set apart one day a week just to break china. It was Tuesday, Grandmother said. As early as five o'clock on Tuesday morning you could hear this jewel of a maid in the kitchen, breaking china. She began with the coffee cups and glasses and little things like that and then went on to the soup bowls and dinner plates, and she finished up with platters and soup tureens. There was such a crash bang in the kitchen all morning that it was a joy to hear it, Grandmother said. And if Malin had any spare time late in the afternoon, she would go into the drawing room with a little hammer and knock down the antique East Indian plates that were hanging on the walls. Grandmother bought new china every Wednesday," said Pippi and disappeared up the stairs as quickly as a jack-in-the-box.

But now Mrs. Settergen's patience had come to an end. She ran up the stairs, into the nursery, and up to Pippi, who had just begun to teach Tommy to stand on his head.

"You must never come here again," said Mrs. Settergren, "if you can't behave any better than this."

Pippi looked at her in astonishment and her eyes slowly filled with tears. "That's just what I was afraid of," she said. "That I couldn't behave properly. It's no use to try; I'll never learn. I should have stayed on the ocean."

She curtsied to Mrs. Settergren, said good-by to Tommy and Annika, and went slowly down the stairs.

The ladies were now getting ready to go home too. Pippi sat down in the hall near the shelf where rubbers were kept and watched the ladies putting on their hats and coats.

"Too bad you don't like your maids," said she. "You should have one like Malin! Grandmother always said there was nobody like her. Imagine! One Christmas when Malin was going to serve a little roast pig, do you know what she did? She had read in the cookbook that roast pig must be served with frilled paper in the ears and an apple in the mouth. But poor Malin didn't understand that it was the pig who was supposed to have the apple. You should have seen her when she came in on Christmas Eve with her best apron on and a big Gravenstein apple in her mouth. 'Oh, Malin, you're crazy!' Grandmother said to her, and Malin couldn't say a word in her own defense, she could only wiggle her ears until the frilled paper rustled. To be sure, she tried to say something, but it just sounded like blubb, blubb, blubb. And of course she couldn't bite people in the leg as she usually did, and it *would* be a day when there was a lot of company. Poor little Malin, it wasn't a very happy Christmas Eve for her," said Pippi sadly.

The ladies were now dressed and said a last good-by to Mrs. Settergren. And Pippi ran up to her and whispered, "Forgive me because I couldn't behave myself. Good-by!"

Then she put on her large hat and followed the ladies. Outside the gate their ways parted. Pippi went toward Villa Villekulla and the ladies in the other direction.

When they had gone a little way they heard someone panting behind them. It was Pippi who had come racing back.

"You can imagine that Grandmother mourned when she lost Malin. Just think, one Tuesday morning when Malin had had time to break only about a dozen teacups she ran away and went to sea. And Grandmother had to break the china herself that day. She wasn't used to it, poor thing, and she got blisters all over her hands. She never saw Malin again. And that was a shame because she was such an excellent maid, Grandmother said."

Pippi left, and the ladies hurried on, but when they had gone a couple of hundred feet, they heard Pippi, from far off, yelling at the top of her lungs, "SHE NEVER SWEPT UNDER THE BEDS!"

Pippi Acts as a Lifesaver

One Sunday afternoon Pippi sat wondering what to do. Tommy and Annika had gone to a tea party with their mother and father, so she knew she couldn't expect a visit from them.

The day had been filled with pleasant tasks. She had got up early and served Mr. Nilsson fruit juice and buns in bed. He looked so cute sitting there in his light blue nightshirt, holding the glass in both hands. Then she had fed and groomed the horse and told him a long story of her adventures at sea. Next she had gone into the parlor and painted a large picture on the wallpaper. The picture represented a fat lady in a red dress and a black hat. In one hand she held a yellow flower and in the other a dead rat. Pippi thought it a very beautiful picture; it dressed up the whole room. Then she had sat down in front of her chest and looked at all her birds' eggs and shells, and thought about the wonderful places where she and her father had collected them, and about all the pleasant little shops all over the world where they had bought the beautiful things that were now in the drawers of her chest. Then she had tried to teach Mr. Nilsson to dance the schottische, but he didn't want to learn. For a while she had thought of trying to teach the horse, but instead she had crept down into the woodbox and pulled the cover down. She had pretended she was a sardine in a sardine box, and it was a shame Tommy and Annika weren't there so they could have been sardines too.

Now it had begun to grow dark. She pressed her little pug nose against the windowpane and looked out into the autumn dusk. She remembered that she hadn't been riding for a couple of days and decided to go at once. That would be a nice ending to a pleasant Sunday.

Accordingly she put on her big hat, fetched Mr. Nilsson from a corner where he sat playing marbles, saddled the horse, and lifted him down from the porch. And off they went, Mr. Nilsson on Pippi and Pippi on the horse.

It was quite cold and the roads were frozen, so there was a good crunchy sound as they rode along. Mr. Nilsson sat on Pippi's shoulder and tried to catch hold of some of the branches of the trees as they went by, but Pippi rode so fast that it was no use. Instead, the branches kept boxing him in the ears, and he had a hard time keeping his straw hat on his head.

Pippi rode through the little town, and people pressed anxiously up against the walls when she came storming by.

The town had a market square, of course. There were several charming old one-story buildings and a little yellow-painted town hall. And there was also an ugly wretch of a building, newly built and three stories high. It was called "The Skyscraper" because it was taller than any of the other houses in town.

On a Sunday afternoon the little town was always quiet and peaceful, but suddenly the quiet was broken by loud cries. "The Skyscraper's burning! Fire! Fire!"

People came running excitedly from all directions. The fire engine came clanging down the street, and the little children who usually thought fire engines were such fun now cried from fright because they were sure their own houses would catch fire too. The police had to hold back the crowds of people gathering in the square so that the fire engine could get through. The flames came leaping out of the windows of the Skyscraper, and smoke and sparks enveloped the firemen who were courageously trying to put out the fire. The fire had started on the first floor but was quickly spreading to the upper stories.

Suddenly the crowd saw a sight that made them gasp with horror. At the top of the house was a gable, and in the gable window, which a little child's hand had just opened, stood two little boys calling for help. "We can't get out because somebody has built a fire on the stairs," cried the older boy.

He was five and his brother a year younger. Their mother had gone out on an errand, and there they stood, all alone. Many of the people in the square began to cry, and the fire chief looked worried. There was, of course, a ladder on the fire truck, but it wouldn't reach anywhere near to the little boys. To get into the house to save the children was impossible. A wave of despair swept over the crowd in the square when they realized there was no way to help the children. And the poor little things just stood up there and cried. It wouldn't be long now before the fire reached the attic.

In the midst of the crowd in the square sat Pippi on her horse. She looked with great interest at the fire engine and wondered if she should buy one like it. She liked it because it was red and because it made such a fearful noise as it went through the streets. Then she looked at the fire and she thought it was fun when a few sparks fell on her.

Presently she noticed the little boys up in the attic. To her astonishment they looked as if they weren't enjoying the fire at all. That was more than she could understand, and at last she had to ask the crowd around her, "Why are the children crying?"

First she got only sobs in answer, but finally a stout gentleman said, "Well, what do you think? Don't you suppose you'd cry yourself if you were up there and couldn't get down?"

"I never cry," said Pippi. "But if they want to get down, why doesn't somebody help them?"

"Because it isn't possible, of course," said the stout gentleman.

Pippi thought for a while. Then she asked, "Can anybody bring me a long rope?"

"What good would that do?" asked the stout gentleman. "The children are too small to get down the rope, and, for that matter, how would you ever get the rope up to them?"

"Oh, I've been around a bit," said Pippi calmly. "I want a rope."

There was not a single person who thought it would do any good, but somehow or other Pippi got her rope.

Not far from the gable of the Skyscraper grew a tall tree. The top of it was almost level with the attic window, but between the tree and the window was a distance of almost three yards. And the trunk of the tree was smooth and had no branches for climbing on. Even Pippi wouldn't be able to climb it.

The fire burned. The children in the window screamed. The people in the square cried.

Pippi jumped off the horse and went up to the tree. Then she took the rope and tied it tightly to Mr. Nilsson's tail.

"Now you be Pippi's good boy," she said. She put him on the tree trunk and gave him a little push. He understood perfectly what he was supposed to do. And he climbed obediently up the tree trunk. Of course it was no trouble at all for a little monkey to do that.

The people in the square held their breath and watched Mr. Nilsson. Soon he had reached the top of the tree. There he sat on a branch and looked down at Pippi. She beckoned to him to come down again. He did so at once, climbing down on the other side of the branch, so that when he reached the ground the rope was looped over the branch and hung down double with both ends on the ground.

"Good for you, Mr. Nilsson," said Pippi. "You're so smart you can be a professor any time you wish." She untied the knot that had fastened the rope to Mr. Nilsson's tail.

Nearby, a house was being repaired, and Pippi ran over and got a long board. She took the board in one hand, ran to the tree, grasped the rope in her free hand, and braced her feet against the trunk of the tree. Quickly and nimbly she climbed up the trunk, and the people stopped crying in astonishment. When she reached the top of the tree she placed the board over a stout branch and then carefully pushed it over to the window sill. And there lay the board like a bridge between the top of the tree and the window.

The people down in the square stood absolutely silent. They were so tense they couldn't say a word. Pippi stepped out on the board. She smiled pleasantly at the two boys in the gabled window. "Why do you look so sad?" she asked. "Have you got a stomach-ache?"

She ran across the board and hopped in at the window. "My, it seems warm in here," she said. "You don't need to make any more fire in here today, that I can guarantee. And at the most four sticks in the stove tomorrow, I should think."

Then she took one boy under each arm and stepped out on the board again.

"Now you're really going to have some fun," she said. "It's almost like walking the tight rope."

When she got to the middle of the board she lifted one leg in the air just as she had done at the circus. The crowd below gasped, and when a little later Pippi lost one of her shoes several old ladies fainted. However, Pippi reached the tree safely with the little boys. Then the crowd cheered so loudly that the dark night was filled with noise and the sound drowned out the crackling of the fire.

Pippi hauled up the rope, fastened one end securely to a branch and tied

the other around one of the boys. Then she let him down slowly and care-fully into the arms of his waiting mother, who was beside herself with joy when she had him safe. She held him close and hugged him, with tears in her eyes.

But Pippi yelled, "Untie the rope, for goodness' sake! There's another kid up here, and he can't fly either."

So the people helped to untie the rope and free the little boy. Pippi could tie good knots, she could indeed. She had learned that at sea. She pulled up the rope again, and now it was the second boy's turn to be let down.

Pippi was alone in the tree. She sprang out on the board, and all the people looked at her and wondered what she was going to do. She danced back and forth on the narrow board. She raised and lowered her arms gracefully and sang in a hoarse voice that could barely be heard down in the square:

> *The fire is burning,*
> *It's burning so bright,*
> *The flames are leaping and prancing.*
> *It's burning for you,*
> *It's burning for me,*
> *It's burning for all who are dancing!*

As she sang she danced more and more wildly until many people cov-ered their eyes in horror for they were sure she would fall down and kill herself. Flames came leaping out of the gable window, and in the firelight people could see Pippi plainly. She raised her arms to the night sky, and while a shower of sparks fell over her she cried loudly, "Such a jolly, jolly fire!"

She took one leap and caught the rope. "Look out!" she cried and came sliding down the rope like greased lightning.

"Three cheers for Pippi Longstocking! Long may she live!" cried the fire chief.

"Hip, hip, hurray! Hip, hip, hurray! Hip, hip, hurray!" cried all the people—three times. But there was one person there who cheered four times.

It was Pippi Longstocking.

Pippi Celebrates Her Birthday

One day Tommy and Annika found a letter in their mailbox.

It was addressed to TMMY and ANIKA, and when they opened it they found a card which read:

TMMY AND ANIKA ARE INVITED TO PIPPI'S TOMORO TO
HER BERTHDAY PARTY. DRES: WARE WATEVER YOU LIK.

Tommy and Annika were so happy they began to skip and dance. They understood perfectly well what was printed on the card although the spelling was a little unusual. Pippi had had a great deal of trouble writing it. To be sure, she had not recognized the letter *i* in school the day she was there, but all the same she could write a little. When she was sailing on the ocean one of the sailors on her father's ship used to take her up on deck in the evening now and then and try to teach her to write. Unfortunately Pippi was not a very patient pupil. All of a sudden she would say, "No, Fridolf"—that was his name—"no, Fridolf, bother all this learning! I can't study any more now because I must climb the mast to see what kind of weather we're going to have tomorrow."

So it was no wonder the writing didn't go so well now. One whole night

89

she sat struggling with that invitation, and at dawn, just as the stars were paling in the sky over Villa Villekulla, she tiptoed over to Tommy's and Annika's house and dropped the letter into their mailbox.

As soon as Tommy and Annika came home from school they began to get all dressed up for the party. Annika asked her mother to curl her hair, and her mother did, and tied it with a big pink satin bow. Tommy combed his hair with water so that it would lie all nice and smooth. He certainly didn't want any curls. Then Annika wanted to put on her very best dress, but her mother thought she'd better not for she was seldom neat and clean when she came home from Pippi's; so Annika had to be satisfied with her next best dress. Tommy didn't care what suit he wore so long as he looked nice.

Of course they had bought a present for Pippi. They had taken the money out of their own piggy banks, and on the way home from school had run into the toy shop on Main Street and bought a very beautiful—well, what they had bought was a secret for the time being. There it lay, wrapped in green paper and tied with a great deal of string, and when they were ready Tommy took the package, and off they went, followed by their mother's warning to take good care of their clothes. Annika was to carry the package part of the way, and they were both to hold it when they handed it to Pippi—that they had agreed upon.

It was already November, and dusk came early. When Tommy and Annika went in through the gate of Villa Villekulla they held each other's hands tightly, because it was quite dark in Pippi's garden and the wind sighed mournfully through the bare old trees. "Seems like fall," said Tommy. It was so much pleasanter to see the lighted windows in Villa Villekulla and to know that they were going to a birthday party.

Ordinarily Tommy and Annika rushed in through the kitchen door, but this time they went to the front door. The horse was not on the porch. Tommy gave a lively knock on the door.

From inside came a low voice:

Who comes in the dark night
On the road to my house?
Is it a ghost or just
A poor little mouse?

"No, no, Pippi, it's us," shrieked Annika. "Open the door!"

Pippi opened the door.

"Oh, Pippi, why did you say that about a ghost? I was so scared," said Annika and completely forgot to congratulate Pippi.

Pippi laughed heartily and opened the door to the kitchen. How good it was to come in where it was light and warm! The birthday party was to be in the kitchen, because that was the pleasantest room in the house. There were only two other rooms on the first floor, the parlor—in which there was only one piece of furniture—and Pippi's bedroom. The kitchen was large and roomy, and Pippi had scrubbed it until it shone. She had put rugs on the floor and a large new cloth on the table. She had embroidered the cloth herself with flowers that certainly looked most remarkable, but Pippi declared that such flowers grew in Farthest India, so of course that made them all right. The curtains were drawn and the fire burned merrily. On the woodbox sat Mr. Nilsson, banging pot lids together. In a corner stood the horse, for he too had been invited to the party.

Now at last Tommy and Annika remembered that they were supposed to congratulate Pippi. Tommy bowed and Annika curtsied, and then they handed Pippi the green package and said, "May we congratulate you and wish you a happy birthday?" Pippi thanked them and eagerly tore the package open. And there was a music box! Pippi was wild with delight. She patted Tommy and she patted Annika and she patted the music box and she patted the wrapping paper. She wound up the music box, and with much

91

plinking and plonking out came a melody that was probably supposed to be "Ack, du käre Augustin."

Pippi wound and wound and seemed to forget everything else. But suddenly she remembered something. "Oh, my goodness, you must have your birthday presents too!" she said.

"But it isn't our birthday," said Tommy and Annika.

Pippi stared at them in amazement. "No, but it's my birthday, isn't it? And so I can give birthday presents too, can't I? Or does it say in your schoolbooks that such a thing can't be done? Is it something to do with that old pluttifikation that makes it impossible?"

"Oh, of course it's possible," said Tommy. "It just isn't customary. But for my part, I'd be very glad to have a present."

"Me too," said Annika.

Pippi ran into the parlor and brought back two packages from the chest. When Tommy opened his he found a little ivory flute, and in Annika's package was a lovely brooch shaped like a butterfly. The wings of the butterfly were set with blue and red and green stones.

When they had all had their birthday presents it was time to sit down at the table, where there were all sorts of cakes and buns. The cakes were rather peculiar in shape, but Pippi declared they were just the kind of cakes they had in China.

Pippi served hot chocolate with whipped cream, and the children were just about to begin their feast when Tommy said, "When Mamma and Papa have a party the gentlemen always get cards telling them what ladies to take in to dinner. I think we ought to have cards too."

"Okay," said Pippi.

"Although it will be kind of hard for us because I'm the only gentleman here," added Tommy doubtfully.

"Fiddlesticks," said Pippi. "Do you think Mr. Nilsson is a lady, maybe?"

"Oh, of course not, I forgot Mr. Nilsson," said Tommy, and he sat down on the woodbox and wrote on a card:

MR. SETTERGREN WILL HAVE THE PLEASURE OF
TAKING MISS LONGSTOCKING IN TO DINNER.

"Mr. Settergren, that's me," said he with satisfaction and showed Pippi
the card. Then he wrote on the next card:

MR. NILSSON WILL HAVE THE PLEASURE OF
TAKING MISS SETTERGREN IN TO DINNER.

"Okay, but the horse must have a card too," said Pippi decidedly, "even
if he can't sit at the table."

So Tommy, at Pippi's dictation, wrote:

THE HORSE WILL HAVE THE PLEASURE OF
REMAINING IN THE CORNER WHERE
HE WILL BE SERVED CAKES AND SUGAR.

Pippi held the card under the horse's nose and said, "Read this and see
what you think of it."

As the horse had no objection to make, Tommy offered Pippi his arm,
and they walked to the table. Mr. Nilsson showed no intention of offering
his arm to Annika, so she took a firm hold of him and lifted him up to the
table. But he didn't want to sit on a chair; he insisted on sitting right on the
table. Nor did he want any chocolate with whipped cream, but when Pippi
poured water in his cup he took it in both his hands and drank.

Annika and Tommy and Pippi ate and ate, and Annika said that if these
cakes were the kind they had in China, then she intended to move to China
when she grew up.

When Mr. Nilsson had emptied his cup he turned it upside down and
put it on his head. When Pippi saw that, she did the same, but as she had

not drunk quite all her chocolate a little stream ran down her forehead and over her nose. She caught it with her tongue and lapped it all up.

"Waste not, want not," she said.

Tommy and Annika licked their cups clean before they put them on their heads.

When everybody had had enough and the horse had had his share, Pippi took hold of all four corners of the tablecloth and lifted it up so that the cups and plates tumbled over each other as if they were in a sack. Then she stuffed the whole bundle in the woodbox.

"I always like to tidy up a little as soon as I have eaten," she said.

Then it was time for games. Pippi suggested that they play a game called "Don't touch the floor." It was very simple. The only thing one had to do was walk all around the kitchen without once stepping on the floor. Pippi skipped around in the twinkling of an eye, and even for Tommy and Annika it was quite easy. You began on the drain-board, and if you stretched your legs enough it was possible to step onto the back of the stove. From the stove to the woodbox, and from the woodbox to the hat shelf, and down onto the table, and from there across two chairs to the corner cupboard. Between the corner cupboard and the drainboard was a distance of several feet, but, luckily, there stood the horse, and if you climbed up on him

at the tail end and slid off at the head end, making a quick turn at exactly the right moment, you landed exactly on the drainboard.

When they had played this game for a while, and Annika's dress was no longer her next-best dress but her next-next-next-best one, and Tommy had become as black as a chimney sweep, then they decided to think up something else.

"Suppose we go up in the attic and visit the ghosts," suggested Pippi.

Annika gasped. "A-a-are there really ghosts in the attic?" she asked.

"Are there ghosts? Millions!" said Pippi. "It's just swarming with all sorts of ghosts and spirits. You trip over them wherever you walk. Shall we go up?"

"Oh, Pippi!" said Annika and looked reproachfully at her.

"Mamma says there aren't any such things as ghosts and goblins," said Tommy boldly.

"And well she might," said Pippi, "because there aren't any anywhere else. All the ghosts in the world live in my attic. And it doesn't pay to try to make them move. But they aren't dangerous. They just pinch you in the arm so you get black and blue, and they howl, and they play ninepins with their heads."

"Do—do—do they really play n-n-ninepins with their heads?"

"Sure, that's just what they do," said Pippi. "Come on, let's go up and talk with them. I'm good at playing n-n-ninepins."

Tommy didn't want to show that he was frightened, and in a way he really did want to see a ghost. That would be something to tell the boys at school! Besides, he consoled himself with the thought that the ghosts probably wouldn't dare to hurt Pippi. He decided to go along. Poor Annika didn't want to go under any circumstances, but then she happened to think that a little tiny ghost might sneak downstairs while she was sitting alone in the kitchen. That decided the matter. Better to be with Pippi and

Tommy among thousands of ghosts than alone in the kitchen with even the tiniest little ghost child.

Pippi went first. She opened the door to the attic stairs. It was pitch-dark there. Tommy took a firm grip on Pippi, and Annika took an even firmer grip on Tommy, and so they went up. The stairs creaked and squeaked with every step. Tommy began to wonder if it wouldn't have been better to stay down in the kitchen, and Annika didn't need to wonder—she was sure of it. At last they came to the top of the stairs and stood in the attic. It was pitch-dark there too, except where a little moonbeam shone on the floor. There were sighs and mysterious noises in every corner when the wind blew in through the cracks.

"Hi, all you ghosts!" shrieked Pippi.

But if there was any ghost there he certainly didn't answer.

"Well, I might have known," said Pippi, "they've gone to a council meeting of the Ghost and Goblin Society."

Annika sighed with relief and hoped that the meeting would last a long time. But just then an awful sound came from one of the comers of the attic.

"Who-ooo-ooo!" it said, and a moment later Tommy saw something come rushing toward him in the dimness. He felt it brush his forehead and saw something disappear through a little window that stood open.

He shrieked to high heaven, "A ghost! A ghost!"

And Annika shrieked with him.

"That poor thing will be late for the meeting," said Pippi. "If it was a ghost. And not an owl. For that matter, there aren't any ghosts," she continued after a while. "If anybody insists that there are ghosts, I'll tweak him in the nose."

"Yes, but you said so yourself," said Annika.

"Is that so? Did I?" said Pippi. "Well, then I'll certainly tweak my own nose."

And she took a firm grip on her nose and tweaked it.

After that Tommy and Annika felt a little calmer. In fact they were now so courageous that they ventured to go up to the window and look out over the garden. Big dark clouds sailed through the sky and did their best to hide the moon. And the wind sighed in the trees.

Tommy and Annika turned around. But then—oh, horrors—they saw a white figure coming toward them.

"A ghost!" shrieked Tommy wildly.

Annika was so scared she couldn't even shriek. The ghost came nearer and nearer. Tommy and Annika hugged each other and shut their eyes.

But then they heard the ghost say, "Look what I found! Papa's night-shirt in an old sea chest over here. If I hem it up around the bottom I can wear it."

Pippi came up to them with the nightshirt dangling around her legs.

"Oh, Pippi, I could have died of fright," said Annika.

"But nightshirts aren't dangerous," Pippi assured her. "They don't bite anybody except in self-defense."

Pippi now decided to examine the sea chest thoroughly. She lifted it up and carried it over to the window and opened the cover, so that what little moonlight there was fell on the contents of the chest. There were a great many old clothes, which she threw out on the attic floor. There were a tele-scope, a few books, three pistols, a sword, and a bag of gold pieces.

"Tiddelipom and piddeliday," said Pippi contentedly.

"It's so exciting!" said Tommy.

Pippi gathered everything in the nightshirt, and down they went into the kitchen again. Annika was perfectly satisfied to leave the attic.

"Never let children handle firearms," said Pippi and took a pistol in each hand and prepared to fire. "Otherwise some accident can easily hap-pen," she said, shooting off both pistols at once. "That was a good bang," she announced and looked up in the ceiling. The bullets had made two holes.

"Who knows?" she said hopefully. "Perhaps the bullets have gone right through the ceiling and hit some ghosts in the legs. That will teach them to think twice before they set out to scare any innocent little children again. Because even if there aren't any ghosts, they don't need to go round scaring folks out of their wits, I should think. Would you each like a pistol?" she asked.

Tommy was enchanted, and Annika also very much wanted a pistol, provided it wasn't loaded.

"Now we can organize a robber band if we want to," said Pippi. She held the telescope up to her eyes. "With this I can almost see the fleas in South America, I think," she continued. "And it'll be good to have if we do organize a robber band."

Just then there was a knock at the door. It was Tommy's and Annika's father, who had come to take them home. It was long past their bedtime, he said. Tommy and Annika hurried to say thank you, bid Pippi good-by, and collect all their belongings, the flute, the brooch, and the pistols.

Pippi followed her guests out to the porch and watched them disappear through the garden. They turned around to wave. The light from inside shone on her. There she stood with her stiff red braids, dressed in her father's nightshirt which billowed around her feet. In one hand she held a pistol and in the other the sword. She saluted with it.

When Tommy and Annika and their father reached the gate they heard her calling. They stopped to listen. The wind whistled through the trees so they could just barely hear what she said.

"I'm going to be a pirate when I grow up," she cried. "Are you?"

PIPPI GOES ON BOARD

translated by Florence Lamborn

CONTENTS

Pippi at Home in Villa Villekulla

If a stranger should come to a certain little Swedish town and should happen one day to find himself at a certain spot on the edge of it, he would see Villa Villekulla. Not that the cottage is much to look at—it's rather a ramshackle old place with a tangled garden around it. But it would be natural for a stranger to pause and wonder who lived there, and why there was a horse on the porch. If it was evening and beginning to get dark, and if he caught a glimpse of a little girl strolling around in the garden looking as if she had no idea of going to bed, he might think, "Now I wonder why that little girl's mother doesn't see that she goes to bed? All the other children are fast asleep by this time of night."

If the little girl came to the gate—as she would almost certainly do, because she liked talking to people—then he would be able to take a good look at her. And he would very likely think, "She's one of the most freckled and red-haired children I've ever seen." Later on he would probably think, "Freckles and red hair are really very nice—that is, if the person who has them looks as happy as this child does."

Any stranger would probably be interested to know the name of this little redhead sauntering around by herself in the twilight, and he would ask, "What's your name?"

103

And she'd answer gaily, "My name's Pippilotta Delicatessa Window-shade Mackrelmint Efraim's Daughter Longstocking, daughter of Captain Efraim Longstocking, formerly the Terror of the Sea, now a cannibal king. But everybody calls me Pippi."

She really believed it when she said her father was a cannibal king, because he had once been blown overboard and had vanished from sight when he and Pippi were sailing on the sea. Pippi's father was rather stout, so she was sure he couldn't have drowned. It was perfectly reasonable to think that he had been washed up on an island and become king of the cannibals there. This is what Pippi was sure must have happened.

If the stranger went on talking with Pippi, he would learn that Pippi lived all alone at Villa Villekulla—alone, that is, except for the horse on the porch and a monkey called Mr. Nilsson. If he was a kindhearted man, he would naturally wonder, How does this poor youngster live?

But he needn't have worried. "I'm rich as a troll," Pippi used to say. And she was. She had a whole suitcase full of gold pieces that her father had given her, and she got along beautifully with neither a father nor a mother. Because there was nobody there to tell her when to go to bed, Pippi told herself. Sometimes, to be sure, she didn't tell herself until around ten o'clock, because she had never been able to see why children *should* go to bed at seven. After seven was when you could have the most fun. So the stranger shouldn't have been surprised to see Pippi roaming around the garden even after the sun had gone down and the air was getting cold and Tommy and Annika had been tucked into bed long ago.

Tommy and Annika were the children Pippi played with. They lived next door. They had both a father and a mother, and both father and mother thought it was a good thing for children to go to bed at seven.

If the stranger stayed after Pippi had said good night and gone away from the gate, and if he saw Pippi go up on the porch and pick up the horse in her strong arms and carry him out into the garden, he would certainly rub his eyes and wonder if he were dreaming.

"What an extraordinary child this is!" he would say to himself. "Why, she can actually lift that horse! She's the most extraordinary child I've ever seen!"

He'd be right, too. Pippi *was* the most extraordinary child—in that town, at any rate. There *may* be more extraordinary children in other places, but in that little town there was no one to compare with Pippi Longstocking. And nowhere in the world, in that town or any other, was there anyone half so strong as she was.

Pippi Goes Shopping

One lovely spring day when the sun was shining, the birds were singing, and water was running in all the ditches, Tommy and Annika came skipping over to Pippi's. Tommy had brought along a couple of lumps of sugar for Pippi's horse, and both he and Annika stopped on the porch to pat the horse before they went into the house. Pippi was asleep with her feet on the pillow and her head way under the covers. That was the way she always slept.

Annika pinched Pippi's big toe and said, "Wake up!"

Mr. Nilsson was already awake and had jumped up and seated himself on the overhead light. Something began to stir under the quilts, and suddenly a red head popped out. Pippi opened her bright eyes and smiled broadly. "Oh, it's you pinching my toes? I thought it was my father, the cannibal king, looking to see if I had any corns."

She sat down on the edge of the bed and pulled on her stockings—one brown and one black.

"No, sir, you'll never get corns as long as you wear these," she said, and thrust her feet into her large black shoes, which were exactly twice as long as her feet.

"Pippi," said Tommy, "what shall we do today? Annika and I don't have any school."

"Well, now, that's worth thinking about," said Pippi. "We can't dance around the Christmas tree because we threw it out three months ago. Otherwise we could have dashed around on the ice all morning long. Gold-digging would be fun, but we can't do that either because we don't know where to dig. Furthermore, most of the gold is in Alaska, where there are so many gold-diggers already that there wouldn't be room for us. No, we'll have to think of something else."

"Yes, something jolly," said Annika.

Pippi braided her hair into two tight braids that stuck straight out. She considered.

"How would it be if we went into town and did some shopping?" she said at last.

"But we haven't any money," said Tommy.

"I have," said Pippi, and to prove it she opened her suitcase, which of course was chock full of gold pieces. She carefully scooped up a good handful and put them into her apron pocket, which was just exactly in the middle of her stomach.

"If I only had my hat now, I'd be all ready to start," she said. The hat was nowhere to be seen. Pippi looked first in the woodbox, but, remarkable as it may seem, the hat was not there. Then she looked in the bread crock in the pantry, but there were only a garter, a broken alarm clock, and a little bread. At last she even looked on the hat shelf, but there was nothing there except a frying pan, a screwdriver, and a piece of cheese.

"There's no order here at all, and you can't find a single thing," said Pippi disgustedly, "though to be sure I have missed this piece of cheese for a long time and it's lucky it turned up at last.

"Hey, Hat," she shrieked, "are you going shopping or aren't you? If you don't come out this minute it will be too late."

No hat came out.

"Well, then, it can blame itself if it's so stupid, but when I get home I don't want to hear any complaining," she said sternly.

A few minutes later they were marching down the road to town—Tommy, Annika, and Pippi with Mr. Nilsson on her shoulder. The sun was shining so gloriously, the sky was so blue, and the children were so happy! And in the gutter along the roadside the water flowed merrily by. It was a very deep gutter with a great deal of water in it.

"I love gutters," said Pippi and without giving much thought to the matter, she stepped into the water. It reached way over her knees, and if she skipped along briskly it splattered Tommy and Annika.

"I'm making believe I'm a boat," she said, plowing through the water. Just as she spoke she stumbled and went under.

"Or, to be more exact, a submarine," she continued calmly when she got her nose in the air again.

"Oh, Pippi, you're absolutely soaked," said Annika anxiously.

"And what's wrong with that?" asked Pippi. "Is there a law that children should always be dry? I've heard it said that cold showers are very good for the health. It's only in this country that people have got the notion that children shouldn't walk in gutters. In America the gutters are so full of children that there is no room for the water. They stay there the year round. Of course in the winter they freeze in and their heads stick up through the ice. Their mothers have to carry fruit soup and meatballs to them because they can't come home for dinner. But they're sound as nuts, you can be sure of that."

The little town looked pleasant and comfortable in the spring sunshine. The narrow cobblestone streets wound in and out every which way among the houses. Almost every house was surrounded by a little yard in which snowdrops and crocuses were peeping up. There were a good many shops in the town, and on this lovely spring day so many people were running in and out that the bells on the shop doors tinkled unceasingly. The ladies came with baskets on their arms to buy coffee and sugar and soap and butter. Some of the children were also out to buy candy or chewing gum. Most of them, however, had no money for shopping, and the poor dears had to stand outside the shops and just look in at all the good things in the windows.

When the day was at its sunniest and brightest, three little figures appeared on Main Street. They were Tommy and Annika and Pippi—a very wet Pippi, who left a little trickle of water in her path.

"Aren't we lucky, though?" said Annika. "Look at all the shops, and we have a whole apron pocket full of gold pieces!"

Tommy was so happy when he thought of this that he gave a high skip.

"Well, let's get going," said Pippi. "First of all I want to buy myself a piano."

"But, Pippi," said Tommy, "you can't play the piano, can you?"

"How can I tell," said Pippi, "when I've never tried? I've never had any piano to try on. And this much I can tell you, Tommy—to play the piano without any piano, that takes a powerful lot of practicing."

There didn't seem to be any piano store. Instead the children came to a perfume shop. In the show window was a large jar of freckle salve, and beside the jar was a sign which read: DO YOU SUFFER FROM FRECKLES?

"What does the sign say?" ask Pippi. She couldn't read very well because she didn't want to go to school as other children did.

"It says, 'Do you suffer from freckles?'" said Annika.

"Does it indeed?" said Pippi thoughtfully. "Well, a civil question deserves a civil answer. Let's go in."

She opened the door and entered the shop, closely followed by Tommy and Annika. An elderly lady stood back of the counter. Pippi went right up to her. "No!" she said decidedly.

"What is it you want?" asked the lady.

"No," said Pippi once more.

"I don't understand what you mean," said the lady.

"No, I don't suffer from freckles," said Pippi.

Then the lady understood, but she took one look at Pippi and burst out, "But, my dear child, your whole face is covered with freckles!"

"I know it," said Pippi, "but I don't suffer from them. I love them. Good morning."

She turned to leave, but when she got to the door she looked back and cried, "But if you should happen to get in any salve that gives people more freckles, then you can send me seven or eight jars."

Next to the perfume store was a shop that sold ladies' clothes.

"So far we haven't done much shopping," said Pippi. "Now we must really get going."

And they tramped into the store—first Pippi, then Tommy, and then

Annika. The first thing they saw was a very beautiful dummy representing a fashionable lady dressed in a blue satin dress.

Pippi went up to the dummy and grasped it cordially by the hand. "How do you do, how do you do!" she said. "You are the lady who owns this store, I presume. So nice to meet you!" she continued and shook the dummy's hand even more cordially.

Then a dreadful accident happened—the dummy's arm came off and slid out of its satin sleeve, and there stood Pippi with a long white arm in her hand. Tommy gasped with terror, and Annika was beginning to cry when a clerk came rushing up to Pippi and began to scold her most dreadfully.

"Here, here, hold your horses," said Pippi after she had been listening a few minutes. "I thought this was a self-service store, and I was planning to buy this arm."

Then the clerk was angrier than ever and said that the dummy was not for sale, and in any case one couldn't sell just a single arm. But Pippi would certainly have to pay for the whole dummy because she had spoiled it.

"Well, that's very strange," said Pippi. "It's a good thing they aren't so foolish as all that in every store. Just imagine if next time I am going to have mashed turnip for dinner I go to the butcher to buy a shinbone to cook the turnip with, and he makes me take a whole pig!"

While she was speaking she casually pulled out a few gold pieces from her apron pocket and threw them down on the counter. The clerk was struck dumb with amazement.

"Does the lady cost more than that?" asked Pippi.

"No, certainly not, it doesn't cost nearly that much," said the clerk and bowed politely.

"Well, keep the change and buy something for your children," said Pippi and started toward the door. The clerk ran after her, bowing continually, and asked where she should send the dummy.

"I just want this arm and I'll take it with me," said Pippi. "The rest you can portion out among the poor. Good day!"

"But what are you going to use the arm for?" asked Tommy when they had come out on the street.

"That?" said Pippi. "What am I going to use it for? Don't people have false teeth and false hair, maybe? And even false noses sometimes? Why can't I have a little false arm? For that matter, let me tell you that it's very handy to have three arms. I remember that once when Papa and I were sailing around the world we came to a city where all the people had three arms. Wasn't that smart? Imagine, when they were sitting at the table and had a fork in one hand and a knife in the other and suddenly needed to scratch their ears—well, then it wasn't so foolish to pull out a third arm. They saved a lot of time that way, let me tell you."

Pippi looked thoughtful. "Oh, dear, now I'm lying again," she said. "It's funny, but every now and then so many lies come bubbling up inside me that I just can't help it. To tell the truth, they didn't have three arms at all in that city. They had only two."

She was silent for a minute, thinking.

"For that matter, a whole lot of them had only one arm. Well, if the truth were known, there were even some who didn't have any, and when they were going to eat they had to lie right down on their plates and lap. Scratch themselves on the ear—that they couldn't do at all; they had to ask their mothers to! That's the way it really was."

Pippi shook her head sadly. "The fact is, I've never seen a place where they had so few arms as they did in that city. But that's just like me—always trying to make myself important and wonderful and pretend that people have more arms than they have."

Pippi walked on with her false arm slung jauntily over one shoulder. She stopped in front of a candy shop. A whole row of children was standing there, gazing in at the wonderful things in the window. There were large jars full of red and blue and green candies, long rows of cakes of chocolate, mounds of chewing gum, and the most tempting lollipops. Yes, it was no wonder that the little children who stood there looking in the window now and then gave a deep sigh, for they had no money, not even the tiniest penny.

"Pippi, are we going into that store?" asked Tommy eagerly, tugging at Pippi's dress.

"That store we are going into," said Pippi, "far in!"

And in they went.

"Please, may I have thirty-six pounds of candy," said Pippi, waving a gold piece.

The clerk in the store merely stared, open-mouthed. She wasn't used to having anyone buy so much candy at once. "You mean you want thirty-six candies?" she said.

"I mean that I want thirty-six *pounds* of candy," said Pippi and put the gold piece on the counter. And then the clerk had to hurry and measure out candy in big bags. Tommy and Annika pointed out the kinds that were best. There were some red candies that were wonderful. When you had sucked them for a while you came suddenly to a wonderful creamy center. Then there were some sour green ones that weren't so bad either. Jellied raspberries and licorice boats were good too.

"We'll take six pounds of each," suggested Annika, and that is what they did.

"Then if I could have sixty lollipops and seventy-two packages of caramels, I don't think I'll need any more today except one hundred and three chocolate cigarettes," said Pippi. "There really ought to be a little cart somewhere in which I could put all this."

The clerk told Pippi she could no doubt buy a cart in the toy store next door.

Meanwhile a large crowd of children had gathered outside the candy store. They stood looking in the window and nearly fainted with excitement when they saw the scale on which Pippi did her shopping.

Pippi ran into the toy shop next door, bought a cart, and loaded all her bags on it. She looked around. Then she cried, "If there are any children here who don't eat candy, will they kindly step forward?"

Nobody stepped forward.

"Very strange," said Pippi. "Well, then, is there any child here who does eat candy?"

Twenty-three children stepped forward, and among them were, of course, Tommy and Annika.

"Tommy, open the bags," said Pippi.

Tommy did. And then began a candy-eating party the like of which had never been seen in the little town. All the children stuffed their mouths full of candies—the red ones with the delicious creamy centers, the sour green

ones, the licorice boats, and the jellied raspberries. And a chocolate cigarette you could always keep in the corner of your mouth, because the chocolate flavor and the jellied-raspberry flavor were terrifically good together.

From all directions children came running, and Pippi dealt out candy by the handful. "I think I'll have to go and buy thirty-six more pounds," she said, "or we shan't have any left for tomorrow."

She bought thirty-six pounds more, and there wasn't much left for tomorrow anyway.

"Now we'll go to the next store," said Pippi and stepped into the toy shop. All the children followed her. In the toy shop were all sorts of delightful things—railroad trains and automobiles you could wind up, sweet little dolls in pretty dresses, dolls' dinner sets, cap pistols and tin soldiers, and dogs and elephants made out of cloth, and bookmarks and jumping jacks.

"What can I do for you?" asked the clerk.

"We'd like a little of everything," answered Pippi, looking searchingly around the shelves. "We are very short of jumping jacks, for example," she continued, "and of cap pistols, but you can remedy that, I hope."

Pippi pulled out a fistful of gold pieces, and the children were allowed to pick out whatever they thought they most needed. Annika decided on a wonderful doll with light curly hair and a pink satin dress. It could say "Mama" when you pressed it on the stomach. Tommy wanted a popgun and a steam engine—and he got them. All the other children pointed out what they wanted too, and when Pippi had finished her shopping there wasn't very much left in the store—only a few bookmarks and building blocks. Pippi didn't buy a single thing for herself, but Mr. Nilsson got a mirror.

Just before they went out, Pippi bought each child a cuckoo whistle, and when the children got out on the street they all played on their cuckoo whistles, and Pippi beat time with her false arm. One little boy complained that his cuckoo whistle wouldn't blow. Pippi took the whistle and examined it.

"No wonder, when there's a big wad of gum in front of the hole. Where did you get hold of this treasure?" she asked and threw away a big white chunk. "As far as I know, I haven't bought any gum."

"I've had it since Friday," said the boy.

"And you aren't worried that your windpipe will grow together? I thought that was the usual end to gum-chewers."

She handed the whistle to the boy, who now could blow as merrily as all the others. There was such a racket on Main Street that at last a policeman came to see what it was all about.

"What's all this noise?" he cried.

"It is the Dress Parade March of Kronoberg's Regiment," said Pippi, "but I am not sure that all the kids realize that. Some of them seem to think we are playing 'Let your song resound like thunder!'" (This is a famous Swedish song which begins, "Thunder like the thunder, brothers!" Only in Swedish the verb for "thunder" and the noun for "thunder" are different words.)

"Stop, this minute!" roared the policeman and held his hands over his ears.

Pippi patted his back comfortingly with her false arm. "Be thankful we didn't buy bassoons," she said.

Gradually the cuckoo whistles were silenced, one after another, until at last it was only from Tommy's whistle that there was a little peep now and then.

The policeman said emphatically that crowds were not to gather on Main Street, and all the children must go home. The children really didn't object to this at all; they wanted very much to try their new toy trains and play with their automobiles a little and put their new dolls to bed. So they all went home, happy and contented. Not one of them ate any supper that night.

Pippi and Tommy and Annika also started for home, Pippi drawing the little cart after her. She looked at all the advertisements they went by and spelled them out as well as she could.

"D-R-U-G S-T-O-R-E. Isn't that where you buy meduseen?"

"Yes, that's where you buy med-i-cine," said Annika.

"Oh, then I must go right in and buy some," said Pippi.

"Yes, but you aren't sick, are you?" said Tommy.

"What one isn't one may become," said Pippi.

"There are millions of people who get sick and die just because they don't buy meduseen in time. And you are mistaken if you think such a thing is going to happen to me."

In the drug store stood the druggist, filling capsules; he was planning to fill only a few more because it was almost closing time. Then Pippi and Tommy and Annika stepped up to the counter.

"I should like to buy eight quarts of meduseen," said Pippi.

"What kind of medicine?" asked the druggist impatiently.

"Preferably some that is good for sickness," said Pippi.

"What kind of sickness?" said the druggist still more impatiently.

"Oh, let's have one that's good for whooping cough and blistered heels and belly ache and a charley horse and if you've happened to push a bean up your nose and a few little things like that. And it would be good if it was possible to polish furniture with it too. It must be really good meduseen."

The druggist said there was no medicine that was as good as all that. He claimed that different kinds of sicknesses required different kinds of medicine, and when Pippi had mentioned about ten other troubles that she wanted to cure, he put a whole row of bottles on the counter. On some of them he wrote "For External Use Only." That meant that the medicine in those bottles should only be rubbed on, and not drunk.

Pippi paid, took her bottles, thanked him, and left. Tommy and Annika followed her. The druggist looked at the clock and realized that it was closing time. He locked the door carefully and thought how good it would be to get home and have a bite to eat.

Pippi put her bottles down outside the door. "Oh, I almost forgot the most important thing of all," she said.

As the door was now locked, she put her finger on the bell and pushed long and hard. Tommy and Annika could hear how clearly it sounded inside the drug store.

After a while a little window in the door opened—it was the window where you could buy medicine if you happened to be taken ill in the night. The druggist stuck his head out. His face was quite red. "What do you want now?" he asked Pippi angrily.

"Oh, dear sir, please excuse me," said Pippi, "but I just happened to think of something. Sir, you understand sickness so well; which is better when you have a stomach-ache—to eat a hot pancake or to put your whole stomach to soak in cold water?"

The druggist's face grew redder still. "Get out," he screamed, "and be quick about it, or else—" He slammed the window.

"Gee, what a temper he's got," said Pippi. "You'd certainly think I'd done something."

She rang the bell once more, and in a few seconds the druggist's head appeared in the window again. His face was dreadfully red now.

"Pancake really is a little hard to digest, isn't it?" said Pippi and looked up at him with her friendly eyes. The druggist did not answer but shut the window again with a bang.

Pippi shrugged her shoulders. "Oh, well," she said. "I'll try warm pancake anyway. He'll have only himself to blame if anything goes wrong."

She calmly sat down on the step in front of the drug store and lined up her bottles. "How impractical grownups can be!" she said. "Here I have—

let me see—eight bottles, and everything could perfectly well have gone into this one that's more than half empty anyway. It's lucky I have a little common sense myself."

With these words she pulled the corks out of the bottles and poured all the medicine into one bottle. She shook it vigorously, lifted the bottle to her mouth, and drank two good swallows.

Annika, who knew that some of the medicine was to be used only to rub on, was a little worried. "But, Pippi," she said, "how do you know that some of that medicine isn't poison?"

"I'll find out," said Pippi happily. "I'll find out by tomorrow at the latest. If I'm still alive, then we'll know that it isn't poison and the smallest child can drink it."

Tommy and Annika thought this over. After a while Tommy said doubtfully in a rather frightened voice, "Yes, but what if it is poison? Then what?"

"Then you can have what's left in the bottle to polish the dining-room furniture with," said Pippi. "Poison or not, this meduseen was not bought in vain."

She took the bottle and put it in the cart, along with the false arm, Tommy's steam engine and pop-gun, and Annika's doll and a bag with five little red candies in it—that was all that was left of the seventy-two pounds. Mr. Nilsson was in the cart too. He was tired and wanted to ride.

"For that matter, let me tell you that I think it is very good meduseen. I feel much better already. I feel especially healthy and happy in my tail," said Pippi, and she swung her little backside back and forth. Then off she went with the cart, home to Villa Villekulla. Tommy and Annika walked beside her and felt as if they had just a little stomach-ache.

Pippi Writes a Letter and Goes to School— But Only a Little Bit

"Today," said Tommy, "Annika and I wrote a letter to our grandmother."

"Did you?" said Pippi, stirring something in a kettle with the handle of her umbrella. "This is going to be a wonderful dinner," she continued, putting her nose down for a good smell. "Boil one hour, stirring vigorously, and serve immediately without ginger. What was it you said—that you wrote to your grandmother?"

"Yes," answered Tommy, who was sitting, dangling his legs, on Pippi's woodbox, "and pretty soon we'll be sure to have an answer from her."

"I never get any letters," complained Pippi.

"But you never write any either," said Annika. "You can't expect to get any unless you write some yourself."

"And that's just because you won't go to school," said Tommy. "You can't ever learn to write if you don't go to school."

"I can too write," said Pippi. "I know a whole lot of letters. Fridolf, who was a sailor on my father's ship, taught me a great many letters. And if I run out of letters I can always fall back on the numbers. Yes sirree, I certainly can write, but I don't know what to write about. What do you usually say in letters?"

"Oh," said Tommy, "first I usually ask Grandmother how she is, and then I tell her I'm feeling well, and then I usually talk a little about the weather and things like that. Today I also told her that I had killed a big rat in our cellar."

Pippi stirred and considered. "It's a shame that I never get any letters. All the other children get them. This state of affairs can't go on. And since I haven't any grandmother to write to me, I can write to myself. I'll do it at once."

She opened the oven door and looked in. "There ought to be a pencil in here, if I remember correctly."

There was a pencil. Pippi took it out. Then she tore in two a big white paper bag and sat down by the kitchen table. She frowned deeply, chewing on the end of her pencil.

"Don't disturb me! I'm thinking," she said.

Tommy and Annika decided to play with Mr. Nilsson while Pippi was writing. They took turns dressing and undressing him. Annika also tried to put him into the little green doll's bed where he slept. She wanted to play nurse; Tommy was to be the doctor and Mr. Nilsson the sick child. But Mr. Nilsson didn't want to lie still. He persisted in getting out of bed and hopping up and hanging by his tail from the overhead light.

Pippi raised her eyes from her writing. "Stupid Mr. Nilsson!" she said. "Sick children don't hang by the tail from the lights in the ceiling. At least not in this country. I've heard it said that they do in South Africa. There they hang a kid up on the overhead light as soon as he gets a little fever and let him hang there until he gets well again. But we aren't in South Africa now; you ought to realize that."

At last Tommy and Annika left Mr. Nilsson and went out to curry the horse. The horse was very happy when they came out on the porch. He nosed around in their hands to see if they had brought him any sugar. They hadn't, but Annika ran right back into the house and got a couple of pieces.

Pippi wrote and wrote. At last the letter was ready. She didn't have any envelopes, but Tommy ran home for one for her. He gave her a stamp too. Pippi printed her name carefully on the envelope. "Miss Pippilotta Longstocking, Villa Villekulla."

"What does it say in the letter?" asked Annika.

"How do I know?" said Pippi. "I haven't received it yet."

Just then the mailman came by Villa Villekulla.

"Well, sometimes one does have good luck," exclaimed Pippi, "and meets a mailman just when one needs him!"

She ran out onto the street. 'Will you please be so kind as to deliver this to Miss Pippi Longstocking at once?" she said. "It's urgent."

The mailman looked first at the letter and then at Pippi. "Aren't you Pippi Longstocking yourself?" he asked.

"Sure. Who did you think I was, the Empress of Abyssinia?"

"But why don't you take the letter yourself?"

"Why don't I take the letter myself?" said Pippi. "Should I be delivering the letter myself? No, that's going too far. Do you mean to say that people have to deliver their letters themselves nowadays? What do we have mailmen for, then? We might as well get rid of them. I've never in my life heard anything so foolish. No, my lad, if that's the way you do your work, they'll never make a postmaster out of you, you can be sure of that."

The mailman decided it was just as well to do what she wished, so he dropped the letter in the mailbox at Villa Villekulla. It had scarcely landed before Pippi eagerly pulled it out again.

"Oh, how curious I am!" she said to Tommy and Annika. "This is the first letter I ever got in my life."

All three children sat down on the porch steps, and Pippi slit open the envelope. Tommy and Annika looked over her shoulder and read.

DARLING PIPPI,

I SIRTINLEE HOP U R NOT SIK. IT WOOD BE 2 BAD 4 U 2 BE SIK. MYSELF I AM JUST FIN. THER IS 0 RONG WTH THE WETHER ETHER. YESTERDAY TOMY KILT 1 BIG RAT. YES.

      THAT IS WHAT HE DID.

BEST WISHIS FORM

PIPPI

"Oh," said Pippi, delighted, "it says exactly the same things in my letter that it does in the one you wrote to your grandmother, Tommy. So you can be sure it is a real letter. I'll keep it as long as I live."

She put the letter in the envelope and the envelope in one of the little drawers in the big chest in the parlor. Tommy and Annika thought it was almost more fun than anything to be allowed to look at all the treasures in Pippi's chest. Every now and then Pippi would give them a little present from the chest, and still the drawers were never empty.

"Anyway," said Tommy when Pippi had put away the letter, "there were an awful lot of words spelled wrong in it."

"Yes, you really ought to go to school and learn to write a little better," said Annika.

"Thank you," said Pippi. "I went once for a whole day, and I got so much learning that it's still plopping around in my head."

"But we're going to have a picnic someday soon," said Annika. "The whole class."

"Alas!" said Pippi, biting one of her braids. "Alas! And of course I can't come just because I don't go to school. Seems as if people think they can treat you just any way if you haven't been to school and learned pluttification."

"Multiplication," said Annika emphatically.

"Yes, isn't that what I said?—'pluttification.'"

"We're going to walk about seven miles—way, way out into the woods. And then we're going to play there," said Tommy.

"Alas," said Pippi once again.

The next day was so warm and beautiful that all the school children in the little town found it very hard to sit still in their seats. The teacher opened all the windows and let the sun come streaming in. Just outside the school window stood a birch tree, and high up in it sat a little starling, singing so cheerily that the children just listened to him and didn't care at all that nine times nine equals eighty-one.

Suddenly Tommy jumped up in amazement. "Look, Teacher," he cried, pointing out of the window, "there's Pippi!" All the children turned to look and, sure enough, there sat Pippi on a branch of the birch tree. She was sitting very close to the window, for the branch reached almost down to the window sill.

"Hi, Teacher!" she cried. "Hi, kids!"

"Good morning, little Pippi," said the teacher. Once Pippi had come to school for a whole day, so the teacher knew her very well. Pippi and the teacher had agreed that Pippi might come back to school when she grew a little older and more sensible.

"What do you want, little Pippi?" asked the teacher.

"Oh, I was just going to ask you to throw a little pluttification out of the window," said Pippi, "as much as would be necessary for me to be allowed to go to the picnic with you. And if you have discovered any new letters, you might throw them out at the same time."

"Don't you want to come in for a little while?" asked the teacher.

"I'd rather not," said Pippi honestly, leaning back comfortably on the branch. "I just get dizzy. The knowledge in there is so thick you can cut it with a knife. But don't you think, Teacher," she continued hopefully, "that a little of that knowledge might fly out through the window and stick to me—just enough so that I could go with you on the picnic?"

"It might," said the teacher, and then went on with the arithmetic lesson. All the children thought it was very pleasant to have Pippi sitting in a tree outside. She had given them all candy and toys that day when she went shopping. Pippi had Mr. Nilsson with her, of course, and the children thought it was fun to see how he threw himself from one branch to another. Sometimes he even hopped down into the window, and once he took a long jump and landed right on Tommy's head and began to scratch his hair. But then the teacher told Pippi she'd have to call Mr. Nilsson because Tommy was just going to figure out how much 315 divided by 7 is, and you can't do that when you have a monkey in your hair. But anyway, lessons just wouldn't go right that morning. The spring sunshine, the starling, and Pippi and Mr. Nilsson—all this was just too much for the children.

"I don't know what's got into you, children," said the teacher.

"Do you know what, Teacher?" said Pippi out in the tree. "To tell the truth, I don't think this is the right kind of a day for pluttification."

"We're doing division," said the teacher.

"On this kind of day you shouldn't have any kind of 'shun,'" said Pippi, "unless of course it's recreation."

Teacher gave up. "Maybe you can furnish some recreation, Pippi," she said.

"No, I'm not very good at recreation," said Pippi, suddenly hanging over the branch by her knee joints so that her red braids almost touched the ground. "But I know a school where they don't have anything but recreation. 'All Day: Recreation' is what it says on the school program."

"Is that so?" said the teacher. "And where is that school?"

"In Australia," said Pippi. "In a little village in Australia. Way down in the southern part." She sat up on the branch again, and her eyes began to sparkle.

"What kind of recreation do they have?" asked the teacher.

"Oh, all kinds," said Pippi. "Usually they begin by jumping out of the window, one after another. Then they give a terrific yell and rush into the schoolroom again and skip around on the seats as fast as ever they can."

"But what does their teacher say then?" asked the teacher.

"She?" said Pippi. "Oh, she skips too—faster than anyone else. Then the children usually fight for half an hour or so, and the teacher stands near and cheers them on. When the weather is rainy all the kids take off their clothes and rush out into the rain and dance and jump. The teacher plays a march on the organ for them so that they can keep time. Some of them stand under the rainspout so that they can have a real shower."

"Do they indeed?" said the teacher.

"They certainly do," said Pippi, "and it's an awfully good school, one of the better ones in Australia. But it is very far down in the south."

"Yes, I can imagine so," said the teacher. "But I don't think we'll have as much fun as all that in this school."

"Too bad," said Pippi. "If it was only a matter of skipping around on the seats I'd dare to come in for a while."

"You'll have to wait to skip until we have the picnic," said the teacher.

"Oh, may I really go to the picnic?" cried Pippi, and was so happy that she turned a somersault backward right out of the tree. "I'll certainly write and tell them about that in Australia. Then they can keep on with their recreation as much as they want to. Because a picnic is certainly more fun."

Pippi Goes to the School Picnic

••

There was a tramping of many feet on the ground, and much talk and laughter. There was Tommy with a knapsack on his back, and Annika in a brand-new cotton dress, and their teacher and all their classmates except one poor child who had the misfortune to get a sore throat on the very day of the picnic. And there in front of all the others was Pippi, riding on her horse. Back of her sat Mr. Nilsson with his pocket mirror in his hand. Yes, there he sat, catching the sun's light in the mirror and looking extraordinarily pleased when he managed to reflect it right in Tommy's eye.

Annika had been absolutely sure it would rain on this important day. In fact, she had been so sure of it that she had almost been angry at the weather in advance. But just think how lucky you can be sometimes—the sun continued to shine just as usual, even if it was picnic day, and Annika's heart almost jumped for joy as she walked along the road in her brand-new cotton dress. For that matter, all the children looked happy and eager. Pussy willows were growing everywhere along the roadside, and in one place there was a whole field of wild flowers. All the children decided to pick big bunches of pussy willows and bouquets of yellow wild flowers on the way home.

"Such a glorious, glorious day," said Annika with a sigh, looking up at Pippi, who sat on her horse as straight as a general.

"Yes, I haven't had so much fun since I fought with the champion boxer in San Francisco," said Pippi. "Would you like to ride a little while?"

Annika would indeed, so Pippi lifted her up onto the horse's back, and there she rode, right in front of Pippi. When the other children saw her, of course they all wanted to ride too. And Pippi let them, each in turn. But Tommy and Annika were allowed to ride a little longer than most of the others. There was one girl who had a blister on her heel. She was allowed to sit behind Pippi and ride all the way. Mr. Nilsson pulled her braids whenever he could get hold of them.

The picnic was to be held in a wood which was called the Monsters' Forest—probably, Pippi thought, because it was so monstrously beautiful. When they were almost there Pippi jumped out of the saddle, patted her horse, and said, "Now you've carried us for such a long time that you must be tired. It isn't right for one person to do all the work."

And she lifted the horse up in her strong arms and carried him until they came to a little clearing in the woods and the teacher said, "We'll stop here."

Pippi looked around and screamed, "Come out now, all you monsters, and let's see who is the strongest."

The teacher explained that there were no monsters in the woods, and Pippi was much disappointed.

"A Forest of Monsters without any monsters! What will folks think of next? Soon they'll invent fires without any fire and a Christmas-tree gift party without any Christmas tree—just out of stinginess. But on the day they begin having candy stores without any candy, I'll go and tell them a thing or two. Oh, well, I'll have to be a monster myself, I suppose. I don't see any other way out of it."

She let out such a terrific roar that the teacher had to hold her hands over her ears, and several of the children were scared almost to death.

"Oh, yes, we'll play that Pippi is a monster," cried Tommy, enchanted, and clapped his hands. All the children thought that was a fine idea. The Monster then went into a deep crevice between the rocks, which was to be its den, and all the children ran around outside, teasing and yelling, "Stupid, stupid Monster! Stupid, stupid Monster!"

Out rushed the Monster, bellowing and chasing the children, who ran in all directions to hide. Those who were captured were dragged home to the den in the rocks, and the Monster said they were to be cooked for dinner. Sometimes they managed to escape while the Monster was out hunting for more children, although in order to get away they had to climb up a steep rock and that was hard work. There was only one little pine tree to get hold of, and it was difficult to know where to put one's feet. But it was very exciting, and the children thought it was the best game they had ever played.

The teacher lay in the green grass, reading a book and casting a glance at the children every now and then. "That's the wildest monster I ever saw," she mumbled to herself.

131

And it certainly was. The Monster jumped around and bellowed and threw three or four boys over its shoulder at once and dragged them down into the den. Sometimes the Monster climbed furiously up into the highest treetops and skipped from branch to branch, just as if it were a monkey. Sometimes it threw itself upon the horse's back and chased a whole crowd of children who were trying to escape through the trees. With the horse still in full gallop, the Monster would lean down from the saddle, snatch up the children, place them in front of itself on the horse, and gallop madly back to the den, yelling, "Now I'm going to cook you for dinner!"

It was such fun the children thought they'd never want to stop. But suddenly everything was quiet, and when Tommy and Annika came running to see what was the matter they found the Monster sitting on a stone with a very strange expression on its face, looking at something in its hand.

"He's dead. Look, he's absolutely dead," said the Monster.

It was a little baby bird that was dead. It had fallen out of the nest and killed itself.

"Oh, what a shame!" said Annika. The Monster nodded.

"Pippi, you're crying," said Tommy suddenly.

"Crying? Me?" said Pippi. "Of course I'm not crying."

"Yes, but your eyes are all red," insisted Tommy.

"My eyes red?" said Pippi, and borrowed Mr. Nilsson's pocket mirror to see. "Do you call that red? Then you ought to have been with Father and me in Batavia. There was a man there whose eyes were so red that the police refused to allow him on the streets."

"Why?" asked Tommy.

"Because people thought he was a stop sign, of course. And there was a dreadful traffic jam every time he came out. Red eyes? Me? No sirree, you needn't think I'd cry for a little scrap of a bird like this," said Pippi.

"Stupid, stupid Monster! Stupid, stupid Monster!" From all directions the children came running to see where the Monster was hiding. The Monster took the little scrap of a bird and laid it down very carefully on a bed of soft moss.

"If I could, I'd bring you to life again," she said with a deep sigh.

Then she let out a terrific yell. "Now I'll cook you for dinner," she shrieked. And with happy shouts the children disappeared into the bushes.

One of the girls in the class—her name was Ulla—lived right near the Forest of Monsters. Ulla's mother had promised her that she could invite her teacher and her classmates—and Pippi, too, of course—for refreshments in the garden. So when the children had played the monster game for a long time, and climbed about among the rocks for a while, and sailed their birch-bark boats on a large pool, and seen how many of them dared to jump off a high stone, then Ulla said that it must be time to go to her house to have their fruit punch. And the teacher, who had read her book from cover to cover, agreed. She gathered the children together and they left the Forest of the Monsters.

Out on the road they met a man with a wagon-load of sacks. They were heavy sacks and there were many of them, and the man's horse was tired. All of a sudden one of the wagon wheels went down into the ditch. The man, whose name was Mr. Blomsterlund, became terrifically angry. He thought it was the horse's fault. He got out his whip and immediately began to beat the horse fast and furiously. The horse pulled and tugged and tried with all its might to pull the load up onto the road again, but it couldn't do it. Mr. Blomsterlund grew angrier and angrier and beat harder and harder. Then the teacher noticed him and was almost overcome with sympathy for the poor horse.

"How can you bear to beat an animal that way?" she said to Mr. Blomsterlund.

He let the whip rest a moment and spat before he answered. "Don't interfere with what doesn't concern you," said he. "Otherwise it might just happen that I'll give you a taste of the whip too, the whole lot of you."

He spat once more and picked up the whip again. The poor horse trembled through its whole body. Then something came dashing through the crowd of children like a flash of lightning, It was Pippi. She was absolutely white around the nose, and when Pippi was white around the nose she was *angry*. Tommy and Annika knew that. She rushed at Mr. Blomsterlund, caught him around the waist, and threw him high up in the air. When he came down, she caught him and threw him up again. Four, five, six times he had to take a trip up into the air. He didn't know what had happened to him.

"Help! Help!" he cried, terrified. At last he landed with a thump on the road. He had lost the whip.

Pippi went and stood in front of him with her hands on her hips. "You are not to hit that horse any more. You are not to do it, I tell you. Once down in Cape Town I met another man who was whipping his horse. He had on such a beautiful uniform, that man, and I told him that if he ever whipped his horse again I'd scratch and claw him so that there wouldn't be one single thread left whole in his beautiful uniform. Just imagine, a week later he did whip his horse again. Wasn't it too bad about such a nice uniform?"

Mr. Blomsterlund was still sitting in the road, completely bewildered.

"Where are you going with your load?" asked Pippi.

Mr. Blomsterlund, still frightened, pointed at a cottage a little way down the road. "Home, over there," he said.

Then Pippi unhitched the horse, which stood there trembling with weariness and fright. "There, there, little horsie!" she said. "Now you'll see another kettle of fish!"

With that she lifted it up in her strong arms and carried it home to its stall. The horse looked just as astonished as Mr. Blomsterlund did.

All the children were standing with the teacher, waiting for Pippi. And Mr. Blomsterlund stood by his load, scratching his head. He didn't know how he was going to get it home.

Then Pippi came back. She took one of the big, heavy sacks and hung it on Mr. Blomsterlund's back.

"There now!" she said. "Let's see if you're as good at carrying as you were at whipping." She picked up the whip. "I really ought to give you a few whacks with this since you seem to be so fond of whippings. But the whip is beginning to wear out," she added and broke off a piece of it. "Completely worn out, sad to say," she continued, and broke the whole whip into tiny, tiny pieces.

Mr. Blomsterlund with his sack was trudging along the road without saying a word. He only puffed a little. And Pippi took hold of the wagon shafts and pulled the wagon home for him.

"There, that won't cost you a cent," she said when she had deposited the wagon outside Mr. Blomsterlund's barn. "I was glad to do it. The trips up into the air were free too."

Then she went away. Mr. Blomsterlund stood staring after her for a long time.

"Three cheers for Pippi," cried the children when she came back.

The teacher too was much pleased with Pippi and praised her. "That was well done," said she. "We should always be kind to animals—and to people too, of course."

Pippi sat on her horse, looking perfectly satisfied. "Well, I certainly was good to Mr. Blomsterlund, anyway," she said. "All that flying in the air for nothing!"

"That is why we are here," said the teacher, "to be good and kind to other people."

Pippi stood on her head on the horse's back and waved her legs in the air. "Heigh-ho," said she, "then why are the other people here?"

❀ ❀ ❀

A large table had been set in Ulla's garden. There were so many buns and cakes on it that they made the children's mouths water, and they all hurried to find places at the table. Pippi sat down at one end. The first thing she did was to snatch two buns and cram them into her mouth. She looked like a cherub with her puffed-out cheeks.

"Pippi, it is customary to wait until one is invited to have something," said the teacher reproachfully.

"Oh, you don't need to shtand on sheremony on my account," said Pippi with her mouth full. "I don't mind if everything is informal."

Just then Ulla's mother came up to Pippi. She had a pitcher of fruit punch in one hand and a pot of chocolate in the other. "Punch or chocolate?" she asked.

"Punch *and* chocolate," said Pippi. "I'll send punch after one bun and chocolate after the other." Without waiting to be urged, she took from Ulla's mother both the punch pitcher and the chocolate pot and drank a deep draught from each.

"She has been at sea all her life," the teacher explained in a whisper to Ulla's mother, who looked much astonished.

"Oh, I see." She nodded and decided to pay no attention to Pippi's bad manners. "Will you have molasses cookies?" she asked and passed the plate of them to Pippi.

"Well, it looks as if I would," said Pippi, giggling happily at her own joke. "To be sure, you didn't have very good luck cutting them out, but I hope they'll taste good anyway," she continued, taking a handful.

Suddenly she noticed some pretty pink cakes a little way down on the table. She pulled Mr. Nilsson lightly by the tail. "Look, Mr. Nilsson, skip over and get me one of those pink thingamajigs. You might as well take two or three while you're about it."

And Mr. Nilsson dashed away, right across the table so that the punch glasses splashed over.

"I hope you have had enough?" asked Ulla's mother when Pippi came up to say thank you after the party.

"No, I haven't. I'm thirsty," said Pippi, scratching her ear.

"Well, we didn't have so very much to treat you on," said Ulla's mother.

"No, but at least you had something," said Pippi pleasantly.

After this, the teacher decided to have a little talk with Pippi about her behavior. "Listen, little Pippi," she said in a friendly voice, "you want to be a really fine lady when you grow up, don't you?"

"You mean the kind with a veil on her nose and three double chins under it?" asked Pippi.

"I mean a lady who always knows how to behave and is always polite and well bred. You want to be that kind of a lady, don't you?"

"It's worth thinking about," said Pippi, "but you see, Teacher, I had just about decided to be a pirate when I grow up." She thought a while. "But don't you think, Teacher, one could be a pirate and a really fine lady too? Because then—"

The teacher didn't think one could.

"Oh, dear, oh, dear, which one shall I decide on?" said Pippi unhappily.

The teacher said that whatever Pippi decided to do when she grew up, it would not hurt her to learn how to behave—because Pippi's behavior at the table was really impossible.

"To think it should be so hard to know how to behave." Pippi sighed. "Can't you tell me the most important rules?"

The teacher did the best she could, and Pippi listened attentively. One mustn't help oneself until one was invited; one mustn't take more than one cake at a time; one mustn't eat with a knife; one mustn't scratch oneself while talking with other people; one mustn't do this and one mustn't do that.

Pippi nodded thoughtfully. "I'll get up an hour earlier every morning and practice," she said, "so I'll get the hang of it in case I decide not to be a pirate."

Now the teacher said it was time to go home. All the children stood in line except Pippi. She sat still on the lawn with a tense face, as if she were listening to something.

"What's the matter, little Pippi?" asked the teacher.

"Teacher," asked Pippi, "does a really fine lady's stomach ever rumble?" She sat quiet, still listening.

"Because if it doesn't," she said at last, "I might just as well decide to be a pirate."

Pippi Goes to the Fair

Once every year a fair was held in the little town, and all the children were simply wild with joy that anything so nice could happen. The town looked quite different on Fair Day. There were big crowds in the streets, flags were flying, and in the marketplace were booths where you could buy the most wonderful things. There was so much commotion that it was exciting just to walk in the streets. Best of all, down by the city gate there was a carnival with a merry-go-round and shooting galleries and a tent show and all kinds of things. And there was a menagerie—a menagerie with wild animals: tigers and giant snakes and monkeys and trained seals! You could stand outside the menagerie and hear the strangest growling and roaring you ever heard in all your life, and if you had money you could, of course, go in and see everything too.

No wonder that even the bow in Annika's hair trembled with excitement when she had finished dressing on the morning of the fair. Or that Tommy swallowed his cheese sandwich almost whole. Tommy's and Annika's mother asked them if they didn't want to go to the fair with her, but they squirmed and wiggled and said if she didn't mind, they would rather go with Pippi.

"For you see," explained Tommy to Annika as they ran through the garden gate at Villa Villekulla, "I think more funny things will happen where Pippi is."

Annika thought so too.

Pippi was all dressed up and standing right in the middle of the kitchen floor, waiting for them. She had at last found her big cartwheel hat in the woodshed.

"I forgot that I used it to carry wood in the other day," she said, and pulled the hat down over her eyes. "Don't I look nice?"

Tommy and Annika had to admit that she did. She had blackened her eyebrows with a piece of charcoal and had painted her lips and her nails red, and then she had put on a very fine evening dress that reached to the floor. It was cut low in the back and showed her red flannel underwear. Her big black shoes stuck out from under her skirt, and they were even finer than usual, for she had tied on them the big green rosettes she wore only on special occasions.

"I think one should look like a really fine lady when one goes to the fair," she said, and she tripped down the road as daintily as was possible in such big shoes. She lifted up the edge of her skirt and, holding it away from her, said in a voice that didn't sound at all like her own, "Chawming, chawming."

"What is it that's so charming?" asked Tommy.

"Me!" said Pippi happily.

Tommy and Annika thought that everything was charming when there was a fair in town. It was charming to mingle with the crowd and to go from one booth to another on the square and look at all the things displayed there. Pippi bought a red silk scarf for Annika as a souvenir of the fair, and for Tommy a visor cap which he had always longed for but which his mother didn't want him to have. In another booth Pippi bought two glass bells filled with pink and white candies.

"Oh, how kind you are, Pippi!" said Annika, hugging her bell.

"Oh, yes, chawming," said Pippi. "Chawming," she said, lifting her skirt gracefully.

A stream of people moved slowly down the street from the square to the carnival. Pippi, Tommy, and Annika went along.

"Gee, isn't this great!" said Tommy.

The organ grinder played, the merry-go-round went round and round, the people laughed joyously. The dart-throwing and china-breaking were in full swing. People crowded around the shooting galleries to show their skill.

"I'd like to look a little closer at that," said Pippi and pulled Tommy and Annika with her to a shooting gallery.

Just then there was no one at that particular gallery, and the lady who was supposed to be handing out guns and taking in money was cross. She didn't think three children would make very good customers, and so she paid no attention to them. Pippi looked at the target with great interest. It was a cardboard man with a round face, dressed in a blue coat. Right in the middle of his face was a red nose, which you were supposed to hit. If you couldn't hit his nose, you should at least come close to it. Shots that didn't hit his face weren't counted.

It annoyed the lady to see the children standing there. She wanted customers who could both shoot and pay.

"Are you still hanging around here?" she said angrily.

"No," said Pippi seriously, "we're sitting in the middle of the square cracking nuts."

"What are you glaring at?" asked the lady, still more angrily. "Are you waiting for someone to come and shoot?"

"No," said Pippi, "we're waiting for you to start turning somersaults."

Just then a customer came up, a very fine gentleman with a big gold chain over his stomach. He took a gun and weighed it in his hand.

141

"I think I'll take a few shots just to show how it's done," he said.

He looked around to see if he had any audience, but there was no one except Pippi, Tommy, and Annika.

"Look here, children," he said. "Watch me and I'll give you your first lesson in the art of shooting."

He lifted the gun to his cheek. The first shot was way off, the second shot also; the third and fourth were still farther from the nose. The fifth shot hit the cardboard man on the bottom of his chin.

"The gun's no good!" said the fine gentleman and threw it down.

Pippi picked it up and loaded it. "My, how well you shoot!" she said. "Another time I'll shoot just as you taught us, and not like this."

Pang, pang, pang, pang, pang! Five shots had hit the cardboard man right in the middle of his nose. Pippi gave the lady a gold piece and walked off.

The merry-go-round was so marvelous that Tommy and Annika held their breath in awe when they saw it. There were black and white and brown wooden horses to ride on. They had real manes and tails and looked almost alive. They also had saddles and reins. You could choose any horse you wanted. Pippi bought a whole gold piece's worth of tickets. She got so many there was hardly room for them in her big purse.

"If I had given them another gold coin, I think I would have got the whole whirling thingamajig," she said to Tommy and Annika, who stood waiting for her.

Tommy decided on a black horse, and Annika took a white one. Pippi placed Mr. Nilsson on a black horse that looked very wild. Mr. Nilsson immediately began to scratch the horse's mane to see if it had fleas.

"Is Mr. Nilsson going to ride the merry-go-round too?" asked Annika, surprised.

"Of course," said Pippi. "If I'd thought about it I would have brought my horse too. He really needed a bit of entertainment, and a horse who rides on a horse—that would have been really horsy."

Pippi threw herself into the saddle of a brown horse, and the next second the merry-go-round started, and the music played "Do you remember our childhood days, with all their jolly fun?"

Tommy and Annika thought it was wonderful to ride the merry-go-round, and Pippi looked as though she were enjoying herself too. She stood on her head on her horse with her legs straight up in the air. Her long evening dress fell down around her neck. The people who were watching saw only a red flannel shirt and a pair of green pants, Pippi's long, thin legs with one black and one brown stocking, and her large black shoes playfully waving back and forth.

"That's the way a really fine lady rides the merry-go-round!" exclaimed Pippi at the end of the first ride.

The children rode the merry-go-round a whole hour, but at last Pippi was dizzy and said that she saw three merry-go-rounds instead of one.

"It's so hard to decide which one to ride on," she said, "so I think we'll go some other place."

She had a whole lot of tickets left, and these she gave to some little children who hadn't ridden at all because they didn't have any money for tickets.

Outside a tent nearby, a man was shouting, "New show starts in five minutes. Don't miss this wonderful opportunity to see 'The Murder of the Countess Aurora' or 'Who's Sneaking Around in the Bushes?' Right this way, folks, right this way for the big show!"

"If there's someone sneaking around in the bushes we'll have to go in and find out who it is, and immediately!" said Pippi to Tommy and Annika. "Come on, let's go in!"

She walked up to the ticket window. "Can't I go in for half price if I promise to look with just one eye?" she asked with a sudden attack of economy.

But the ticket seller wouldn't hear of anything like that.

"I don't see any bushes, and no one to sneak around in them either," said Pippi disgustedly when she and Tommy and Annika had seated themselves on the front bench.

"It hasn't started yet," said Tommy.

Just then the curtain went up, and the Countess Aurora was seen walking back and forth on the stage. She wrung her hands and looked worried. Pippi followed every move with breathless interest.

"She must feel sad," she said to Tommy and Annika, "or maybe she has a safety pin that is sticking her some place."

Countess Aurora *was* feeling sad. She raised her eyes to the ceiling and said in a plaintive voice, "Is there anyone as unhappy as I? My children taken away from me, my husband disappeared, and I myself surrounded by villains and bandits who want to kill me."

"Oh, how terrible it is to hear this," said Pippi, whose eyes were getting red.

"I wish I were dead already," said the Countess Aurora.

Pippi burst out crying. "Please don't talk like that!" She sniffed. "Things will be brighter for you. The children will find their way home, and you can always get another husband. There are so many me-e-en," she gasped between her sobs.

The manager of the show—the one who had stood outside—came up to Pippi and told her that if she didn't keep absolutely quiet she would have to leave the theater at once.

"I'll try," said Pippi, wiping her eyes.

The play was terribly exciting. Tommy sat through it all twisting and turning his cap from sheer nervousness. Annika held her hands tightly clasped in her lap. Pippi's bright eyes didn't leave Countess Aurora a minute.

Things were growing worse and worse for the poor countess. She walked in the palace garden, suspecting nothing. Suddenly there was a loud cry. It was Pippi. She had seen a man hiding behind a tree, and he didn't look like a kind man.

Countess Aurora must have heard something rustling, for she said in a frightened voice, "Who's sneaking around in the bushes?"

"I can tell you!" said Pippi excitedly. "It's a horrible man with a black mustache. Run into the woodshed and lock the door, quick!"

The manager came up to Pippi and said she would have to leave at once.

"And leave the Countess Aurora alone with that horrid man! You don't know me, mister," answered Pippi.

On the stage the play went on. Suddenly the "horrid man" sprang from the bushes and threw himself at the Countess Aurora.

"Ha! Your last hour has come," he hissed.

"Oh, it has, has it?" cried Pippi. "We'll see about that!" And with one jump she was on the stage. Grabbing the villain around the waist, she threw him across the footlights onto the floor of the auditorium. She was still crying.

"How can you?" she sobbed. "What have you against the countess anyway? Remember that her children and her husband have left her and she's all alo-o-one."

She went up to the countess, who had sunk down on the garden seat, completely exhausted.

"You can come and live with me in Villa Villekulla if you want to," Pippi said comfortingly.

Sobbing loudly, Pippi stumbled out of the theater, followed by Tommy and Annika—and the manager. He shook his fist after Pippi, but the people in the audience clapped their hands and thought she had given a good performance.

Outside, Pippi blew her nose and, quickly regaining her composure, said, "Come, we'll have to cheer up. This was too sad."

"The menagerie," said Tommy. "We haven't been to the menagerie."

On their way to the menagerie they stopped at a sandwich stand, and Pippi bought six sandwiches for each of them and three big bottles of soda.

"Crying always makes me so hungry," explained Pippi.

There were many things to see inside the menagerie—an elephant and two tigers in a cage, and several large trained seals that were throwing a ball to one another, and a whole lot of monkeys and a hyena and two giant snakes. Pippi took Mr. Nilsson over to the monkey cage so that he could speak to his relatives. An old chimpanzee sat there, looking very sad.

"Come on, Mr. Nilsson," said Pippi, "speak up nicely now. I imagine this is your grandfather's cousin's aunt's mother-in-law's nephew."

Mr. Nilsson doffed his straw hat and spoke as politely as he knew how, but the chimpanzee didn't bother to answer.

The two giant snakes lay in a big box. Every hour the beautiful snake charmer, Mademoiselle Paula, took them from their box and did an act with them on the stage. The children were lucky, for they came in just in time for the performance. Annika was so afraid of snakes that she held tightly to Pippi's arm.

Mademoiselle Paula lifted one of the snakes up—a big, ugly thing—and put it around her neck like a scarf.

"That looks like a boa constrictor," whispered Pippi to Tommy and Annika. "I wonder what kind the other one is."

She went over to the box and lifted up the other snake. It was still larger and uglier. Pippi put it around her neck just as Mademoiselle Paula had done. All the people in the menagerie cried out in horror. Mademoiselle Paula threw her snake into the box and rushed over to try to save Pippi from certain death. Pippi's snake was frightened and angry from the noise, and he couldn't at all understand why he should be hanging around the neck of a little redheaded girl instead of around Mademoiselle Paula's neck as he was used to doing. He decided to teach the little redheaded girl a lesson and contracted his body in a grip that would ordinarily choke an ox.

"Don't try that old trick on me," said Pippi. "I've seen larger snakes than you, you know, in Farthest India."

She pulled the snake away from her throat and put him back into the box. Tommy and Annika stood there, pale with fright.

"That was a boa constrictor too," said Pippi, fastening one of her garters that had come loose, "just as I thought."

Mademoiselle Paula scolded her for several minutes in some foreign language, and all the people in the menagerie drew a long breath in relief, but their relief was short-lived, for this was evidently a day when THINGS happened.

Afterward no one knew just how the next thing had happened. The tigers had been fed large red chunks of meat, and the keeper said he was sure he had locked the door of the cage, but a minute later a terrible cry was heard—"A tiger is loose!"

It was. There, outside the cage, lay the yellow striped beast, ready to spring. The people fled in all directions—all but one little girl who stood squeezed into a corner right next to the tiger.

"Stand perfectly still," the people called to her. They hoped the tiger would not touch her if she didn't move. "What shall we do?" they cried, wringing their hands.

"Run for the police!" someone suggested.

"Call the fire department!" cried another.

"Bring Pippi Longstocking!" cried Pippi, and stepped forward. She squatted a couple of yards from the tiger and called to him. "Pussy, pussy, pussy!"

The tiger growled ferociously and showed his enormous teeth. Pippi held up a warning finger. "If you bite me, I'll bite you. You can be sure of that!"

Then the tiger sprang right at her.

"What's this? Don't you understand a joke?" cried Pippi and pushed the tiger away.

With a loud snarl that made cold shivers go up and down everyone's back, the tiger threw himself at Pippi a second time. You could plainly see that he intended to bite her throat.

"So you want to fight, eh?" said Pippi. "Well, just remember that it was you who started it."

With one hand she pressed together the huge jaws of the tiger, picked him up, and, cradling him in her arms, tenderly carried him back to the cage, singing a little song. "Have you seen my little pussy, little pussy, little pussy?"

The people drew a sigh of relief for a second time, and the little girl who had stood squeezed into the corner ran to her mother and said she never wanted to go to a menagerie again.

The tiger had torn the hem of Pippi's dress. Pippi looked at the rags and said, "Does anyone have a pair of scissors?"

Mademoiselle Paula had a pair, and she wasn't angry with Pippi any more.

"Here you are, you brave little girl," she said and gave Pippi the scissors. Pippi cut her dress off a few inches above the knees.

"There!" she said happily. "Now I'm finer than ever. My dress is cut low at the neck and high at the knees; you really couldn't find a finer dress."

She tripped off so elegantly that her knees hit each other at each step. "Chawming!" she said.

You would have thought that there had been enough excitement for one day at the fair, but fairs are never very quiet places, and it was soon evident that the people had again drawn their breath in relief too soon.

In the little town lived a very bad man—a very strong bad man. All the children were afraid of him—and not only the children but everyone else too. Even the policemen preferred to stay out of the way when the bad man, Laban, was on the warpath.

He wasn't angry all the time, only when he had drunk ale, and he had had quite a bit of ale the day of the fair. Yelling and bellowing, he came down Main Street, swinging his huge arms.

"Out of the way," he cried, "for here comes Laban!"

The people anxiously backed up against the walls, and many children cried in terror. There was no policeman in sight. Laban made his way toward the carnival. He was terrible to look at with his long black hair hanging down over his forehead, his big red nose, and one yellow tooth sticking out of his mouth. The crowd at the carnival thought that he looked even more ferocious than the tiger.

A little old man stood in a booth, selling hot dogs. Laban went up to the booth, struck his fist on the counter, and yelled, "Give me a hot dog and be quick about it!"

The old man gave him a hot dog at once. "That will be fifty cents," he said timidly.

"Do you charge for a hot dog when you serve it to such a fine gentleman as Laban? Aren't you ashamed of yourself? Hand over another one."

The old man said that first he must have the money for the one that Laban had already eaten. Then Laban took hold of the old man's ears and shook him.

"Hand over another hot dog," he demanded, "this instant!"

The old man didn't dare disobey, but the people who stood around couldn't help muttering disapprovingly. One was even brave enough to say, "It's disgraceful to treat a poor old man like that."

Laban turned around. He looked at the crowd with his bloodshot eyes. "Did someone sneeze?" he sneered.

The crowd sensed trouble and wanted to leave.

"Stand still!" shouted Laban. "I'll bash in the head of the first one who moves. Stand still, I say, for Laban will now give a little show."

He took a whole handful of hot dogs and began to juggle them. He threw them into the air and caught some of them in his mouth and some in his hands, but several fell on the ground. The poor old hot dog man almost cried.

Suddenly a little form darted out of the crowd. Pippi stopped right in front of Laban.

"Whose little boy can this be?" she asked sweetly. "And what will his Mommy say when he throws his breakfast around like this?"

Laban gave a terrifying growl. "Didn't I say that everyone should stand still?" he shouted.

"Do you always turn on the loudspeaker?" wondered Pippi.

Laban raised a threatening fist and yelled, "Brat!!! Do I have to make hash out of you before you shut up?"

Pippi stood with her hands at her sides and looked at him with interest. "What was it you did to the hot dogs? Was it this?" She threw Laban high up into the air and juggled with him for a few minutes. The people cheered.

The old man clapped his hands and smiled.

When Pippi had finished, a very much frightened and confused Laban sat on the ground, looking around.

"Now I think the bad man should go home," said Pippi.

Laban had no objection.

"But before you go there are some hot dogs to be paid for," said Pippi.

Laban stood up and paid for eighteen hot dogs, and then he left without a word. He was never quite himself after that day.

"Three cheers for Pippi!" cried the people.

"Hurrah for Pippi!" cried Tommy and Annika.

"We don't need a policeman in this town," somebody said, "as long as we have Pippi Longstocking."

"No, sir!" said someone else. "She takes care of both tigers and bad men."

"Of course we have to have a policeman," said Pippi. "Someone has to see to it that the bicycles stand decently parked in the wrong places."

"Oh, Pippi, you were wonderful!" said Annika as the children walked home from the fair.

"Oh, yes, chawming!" said Pippi.

She held up her skirt—which already came only halfway to her knees. "Really, most chawming!"

Pippi Is Shipwrecked
• •

Every day as soon as school was out Tommy and Annika rushed over to Villa Villekulla. They didn't even want to do their homework at their own house but took their books over to Pippi's instead.

"That's good," said Pippi. "Sit here and study, and no doubt a little knowledge will soak into me. Not that I really think I need it, but I suppose I can never be a really fine lady unless I know how many Hottentots there are in Australia."

Tommy and Annika sat at the kitchen table with their geographies in front of them. Pippi sat in the middle of the table with her legs tucked under her.

"Just think," said Pippi thoughtfully, pressing her finger on the end of her nose. "Suppose I did learn how many Hottentots there are in Australia and then one of them should go and get pneumonia and die, my count would be wrong; I would have had all that trouble for nothing, and I still wouldn't be a really fine lady."

She thought about it a few minutes. "Someone ought to tell the Hottentots to behave themselves so there wouldn't be any mistakes in your schoolbooks."

When Tommy and Annika were through with their homework the fun began. If the weather was nice they played in the garden, rode horseback a little, or clambered up on the laundry roof and sat there drinking coffee, or climbed up into the old hollow oak tree and let themselves down into the trunk. Pippi said that it was a very remarkable tree, for soda grew in it. That seemed to be true, for every time the children climbed down into their hiding place inside the oak they found three bottles of soda waiting for them. Tommy and Annika couldn't understand what happened to the empty bottles, but Pippi said they wilted away as soon as they were emptied. Yes, it was indeed a strange tree, thought both Tommy and Annika. Sometimes chocolate bars grew there too, but Pippi said that was only on Thursdays. Tommy and Annika were very careful to go there and pick chocolate bars every Thursday. Pippi said that if you just gave yourself time to water the tree decently you could probably get French bread to grow there too, and perhaps even a small roast of veal.

If it rained they had to stay in the house, and that wasn't bad either. They could look at all the fine things in Pippi's chest, or sit in front of the stove and watch Pippi make waffles or fry apples, or climb into the woodbox and sit there listening to Pippi telling exciting stories about the time when she sailed the seas.

"Goodness, how it stormed!" Pippi would say. "Even the fishes were seasick and wanted to go ashore. I saw a shark that was absolutely green in the face and an octopus that sat holding his head in all his many arms. My, my, what a storm that was!"

"Oh, weren't you afraid, Pippi?" asked Annika.

"Yes, just suppose you had been shipwrecked!" said Tommy.

"Oh, well," said Pippi, "I've been more or less shipwrecked so many times that I wasn't exactly afraid—not at first, anyway. I wasn't afraid when the raisins blew out of the fruit soup at dinner, and not when the cook's false teeth blew out either. But when I saw that only the skin was left on the ship's cat, and that he himself was flying off completely naked toward the Far East, I began to feel a little unpleasant."

154

"I have a book about a shipwreck," said Tommy. "It's called *Robinson Crusoe.*"

"Oh, yes, it's so good," said Annika. "Robinson—*he* came to a desert island."

"Have you ever been shipwrecked," asked Tommy, making himself a little more comfortable in the woodbox, "and landed on a desert island?"

"I should say I have!" said Pippi emphatically. "You'd have to hunt far and wide to find anyone as shipwrecked as I. Robinson's got nothing on me. I should think that there are only about eight or ten islands in the Atlantic and the Pacific that I have *not* landed on after shipwrecks. They are in a special blacklist in the tourists' books."

"Isn't it wonderful to be on a desert island?" asked Tommy. "I'd so much like to be shipwrecked just once!"

"That's easily arranged," said Pippi. "There's no shortage of islands."

"No—I know one not at all far away from here," said Tommy.

"Is it in a lake?" asked Pippi.

"Sure," said Tommy.

"Swell!" said Pippi. "For if it had been on dry land it would have been no good."

Tommy was wild with excitement. "Let's get shipwrecked!" he cried. "Let's go now, right away!"

In two days Tommy's and Annika's summer vacation was to begin, and at the same time their mother and father were going away. You couldn't find a better time to play Robinson Crusoe!

"If you're going to be shipwrecked you first have to have a boat," said Pippi.

"And we haven't any," said Annika.

"I saw an old, broken rowboat lying at the bottom of the river," said Pippi.

"But that has already been shipwrecked," said Annika.

"So much the better," said Pippi. "Then it knows what to do."

It was a simple matter for Pippi to pull out the sunken rowboat. She spent a whole day down by the river, mending the boat with boards and tar, and one rainy morning in the woodshed, making a pair of oars.

Tommy's and Annika's vacation began, and their parents went away.

"We'll be home in two days," said the children's mother. "Now be very good and obedient and remember that you must do just as Ella says."

Ella was the maid, and she was going to look after Tommy and Annika while their mother and father were away. But when the children were alone with Ella, Tommy said, "You don't need to look after us at all, because we're going to be with Pippi the whole time."

"We can look after ourselves," said Annika. "Pippi never has anyone to look after her. Why can't we be left alone for two days at least?"

Ella had no objection to having a couple of days off, and when Tommy and Annika had begged and teased long enough, Ella said she would go home and visit with her mother a while. But the children must promise to eat and sleep properly and not run out at night without putting on warm sweaters. Tommy said he would gladly put on a dozen sweaters, if only Ella would leave them alone.

So Ella left, and two hours later Pippi, Tommy and Annika, the horse, and Mr. Nilsson started on their trip to the desert island.

It was a mild evening in early summer. The air was warm, although the sky was cloudy. They had to walk quite a way before they came to the lake where the desert island was. Pippi carried the boat on her head. She had loaded an enormous sack and a tent on the horse's back.

"What's in the sack?" asked Tommy.

"Food and firearms, a blanket and an empty bottle," said Pippi, "for I think we ought to have quite a comfortable shipwreck, since it's your first one. Otherwise when I'm shipwrecked I usually shoot an antelope or a

156

llama and eat the meat raw, but there might not be any antelopes or llamas on this island, and it would be a shame if we should have to starve to death just on account of a little thing like that."

"What are you going to use the empty bottle for?" asked Annika.

"What am I going to use the empty bottle for? How can you ask anything so stupid? A boat is, of course, the most important thing when you're going to be shipwrecked, but next comes an empty bottle. My father taught me that when I was still in the cradle. 'Pippi,' he said, 'it doesn't matter if you forget to wash your feet when you're going to be presented at Court, but if you forget the empty bottle when you're going to be shipwrecked, you might as well give up.'"

"Yes, but what are you going to use it for?" insisted Annika.

"Haven't you ever heard of a bottle letter? You write a letter and ask for help," said Pippi. "Then you stuff it in the bottle, put the stopper in, and throw the bottle into the water. And then it floats to someone who can come and save you. How on earth do you think you could be saved otherwise? Leave everything to chance? No, sir!"

"Oh, I see," said Annika.

Soon they came to the edge of the little lake, and there in the middle of the lake was the desert island. The sun was just breaking through the clouds, throwing a warm glow over the early summer foliage.

"Really," said Pippi, "this is one of the nicest desert islands I've ever seen."

She quickly launched the boat onto the lake, lifted the pack off the horse, and stuffed everything into the bottom of the boat. Annika and Tommy and Mr. Nilsson jumped in.

Pippi patted the horse. "My dear horse, no matter how much I would like it, I cannot ask you to sit in the bottom of the boat. I hope you can swim. It's very simple. Look!"

Pippi jumped into the lake with all her clothes on and swam a few strokes. "It's lots of fun, you know, and if you want to have still more fun you can play whale, like this."

Pippi filled her mouth with water, lay on her back, and squirted like a fountain. The horse didn't look as if he thought it would be much fun, but when Pippi crawled into the boat, took the oars, and rowed off, the horse threw himself into the water and swam after her. He didn't play whale, though.

When they had almost reached the island, Pippi yelled, "Man all the pumps!"

And the next second: "In vain! We'll have to leave the ship. Every man for himself!"

She stepped up on the back seat of the boat and dived head first into the water. Soon she came up again, took hold of the rope on the boat, and swam for shore.

"I have to save the provisions anyway, so the crew might as well stay on board," she said.

She tied the rope around a stone and helped Tommy and Annika ashore. Mr. Nilsson rescued himself.

"A miracle has happened!" cried Pippi. "We are saved—at least for the time being, unless there are cannibals and lions on this island."

Even the horse had now reached the island. He got out of the water and shook himself.

"Good! here comes the first mate too," said Pippi. "Let us all hold a council of war."

Out of the sack she took a pistol which she had once found in a sea chest up in the attic. Holding the pistol straight in front of her, ready

to fire, she sneaked about, looking carefully in all directions.

"What's the matter, Pippi?" asked Annika worriedly.

"I thought I heard the growling of a cannibal," said Pippi. "You can never be careful enough. What would be the use of saving yourself from drowning only to be served with stewed vegetables for a cannibal's dinner?"

No cannibals were to be seen.

"Aha! they have retreated and taken cover," said Pippi. "Or perhaps they are sitting looking through their cookbooks to learn how they could cook us. And I'll tell you this, if they serve me with stewed carrots I'll never forgive them—I *hate* carrots."

"Oh, Pippi, don't talk like that!" said Annika, shivering.

"Oh, don't you like carrots either? Well, anyway, let's put up the tent now."

Pippi put up the tent in a sheltered place, and Tommy and Annika crept in and out of it and were perfectly happy. A short distance from the tent, Pippi placed some stones in a ring, and on top of these sticks and pine cones.

"Oh! how wonderful! Are we going to have a fire?" asked Annika.

"Yes, sirree!" said Pippi. She took two pieces of wood and started to rub them together.

Tommy was much interested. "Oh, Pippi!" he said, delighted. "Are you going to make a fire the way they do in the jungles?"

"No, but my fingers are cold," said Pippi, "and this is a good way to warm them. Let me see, where did I put the matches?"

Soon a bright fire was burning, and Tommy said he thought it was awfully cozy.

"Yes, and besides, it will keep the wild animals away," said Pippi.

Annika drew in her breath sharply. "What wild animals?" she asked with a tremor in her voice.

"The mosquitoes," said Pippi and thoughtfully scratched a large mosquito bite on her leg.

Annika sighed with relief.

"Yes, and the lions too, of course," continued Pippi. "I don't think it will help against pythons or against the American buffalo."

She patted her pistol. "But don't worry, Annika," she said. "With this I'll surely be able to defend us even if we should be attacked by a field mouse."

Then Pippi got out coffee and sandwiches, and the children sat around the fire and ate and enjoyed themselves immensely. Mr. Nilsson sat on Pippi's shoulder and ate too, and the horse stuck out his nose from time to time and got a piece of bread and a lump of sugar. There was also lots of tender green grass for him to eat.

The sky was cloudy and it began to grow dark. Annika moved up as near to Pippi as she could get. The flames threw strange shadows. It seemed as if the darkness were alive outside the little circle that was lighted by the fire. Annika shivered. Just suppose a cannibal was standing behind that bush, or a lion hiding behind the big stone over there!

Pippi put down her coffee cup. "Fifteen men on a dead man's chest, yo, ho, ho! and a bottle of rum," she sang in her deep, hoarse voice. Annika shivered more than ever.

"I have that song in another one of my books—a pirate book," said Tommy eagerly.

"Really?" said Pippi. "Then it must be Fridolf who wrote that book, for he taught me the song. How often I've sat on the after deck of my father's ship on starlit nights, with the Southern Cross right over my head, and Fridolf beside me, singing. Fifteen men on a dead man's chest, yo, ho, ho! and a bottle of rum" sang Pippi once more with an even hoarser voice.

"Pippi, I feel so funny inside me when you sing like that," said Tommy.

"It feels so terrible and so wonderful at the same time."

"It feels almost only terrible inside me," said Annika, "but a little wonderful too."

"I'm going to sea when I get big," said Tommy decidedly. "I'm going to be a pirate just like you, Pippi."

"Swell!" said Pippi. "The Terror of the Caribbean! That'll be you and me, Tommy. We'll plunder gold and jewels and precious stones and we'll have a hiding place for our treasures way in a cave on a desert island in the Pacific Ocean, and three skeletons to watch the cave. We'll have a flag with a skull and crossbones, and we'll sing 'Fifteen men on a dead man's chest' so that you can hear it from one end of the Atlantic to the other, and all seafaring men will turn pale when they hear us and think about throwing themselves into the sea to avoid our bloody, bloody revenge."

"But what about me?" asked Annika complainingly. "I don't dare become a pirate. What'll I do then?"

"Oh, you can come along anyway," said Pippi, "and dust the grand piano."

After a while the fire died down. "Time to go to bed," said Pippi. She had put spruce boughs on the ground under the tent, and on top of the spruce boughs several thick blankets.

"Do you want to sleep with us in the tent," Pippi asked the horse, "or would you rather stand out here under a tree with a blanket over you? Oh, so you always feel sick when you sleep in a tent? Okay, just as you like!" Pippi gave him a friendly pat.

Soon all three children and Mr. Nilsson lay rolled up in blankets in the tent. Outside the waves lapped against the shore.

"Hear the ocean breakers!" said Pippi dreamily.

It was as dark as pitch, and Annika held Pippi's hand, for everything

seemed less dangerous then. Suddenly it began to rain. The raindrops splashed on the tent, but inside everything was warm and dry, and it seemed very pleasant to hear the pitter-patter of the raindrops. Pippi went out and put another blanket on the horse. He stood under a thick spruce tree, so he kept pretty dry.

"Isn't this wonderful?" Tommy sighed when Pippi came in again.

"Sure!" said Pippi. "And look what I found under a stone—three chocolate bars!"

Three minutes later Annika was asleep with her mouth full of chocolate and her hand in Pippi's.

"We forgot to brush our teeth tonight," said Tommy, and then he too fell asleep.

When Tommy and Annika woke up, Pippi had disappeared. They hurried to crawl out of the tent. The sun was shining brightly. In front of the tent a new fire was burning and Pippi was squatting by the fire, frying ham and boiling coffee.

"Congratulations and Happy Easter!" she called when she saw Tommy and Annika.

"Oh, it's not Easter now," said Tommy.

"Isn't it? Save the wish until next year, then," Pippi replied.

The good smell of ham and coffee tickled the children's nostrils. They squatted around the fire, and Pippi passed around ham and eggs and potatoes, after which they drank coffee and ate molasses cookies and never had a breakfast tasted so wonderful.

"I think we have it better than Robinson Crusoe," said Tommy.

"Yes, and if we could only get a little fresh fish for dinner I'm afraid Robinson Crusoe would be green with envy," said Pippi.

"Ugh! I don't like fish," said Tommy.

"I don't either," said Annika.

But Pippi cut off a long, narrow branch, tied a string to one end, made a hook out of a pin, and put a piece of bread on the hook and herself on a large stone down near the water's edge.

"Now we'll see," she said.

"What will you fish for?" asked Tommy.

"Octopus," said Pippi. "That's a delicacy beyond compare."

She sat there a whole hour, but no octopus bit. A perch came up and sniffed at the piece of bread, but Pippi quickly drew up the hook.

"No, thank you, my boy," she said. "When I say octopus I mean octopus, and you shouldn't come stealing the bait."

After a while Pippi threw the fishpole into the lake. "You were lucky," she said. "We'll have to eat pancakes. The octopuses are stubborn today." Tommy and Annika were satisfied.

The water glistened invitingly in the sun. "Shall we go for a swim?" asked Tommy.

Pippi and Annika were game. The water was quite cold. Tommy and Annika stuck their big toes in, but quickly pulled them out again.

"I know a better way," said Pippi. There was a rock quite near the shore, and on top of the rock was a tree. The branches of the tree stretched themselves out over the water. Pippi climbed up into the tree and tied a rope around a branch. "Like this—see?"

She took hold of the rope, swung herself out, and dropped into the water.

"You get ducked all over at once, this way," she cried as her head came up out of the water.

Tommy and Annika were a little doubtful at first, but it looked like so much fun that they decided to try it, and when they had tried it once they never wanted to stop, for it was even more fun than it looked. Mr. Nilsson wanted to try too. He slid down the rope, but just before he reached the water he turned and scampered back up at a terrific pace. He did this each time, although the children called to him and told him that he was a coward. Then Pippi found that you could sit on a piece of board and slide down into the water, and that was fun too, for it made a terrific splash when you landed.

"That Robinson Crusoe, did he slide down a piece of board too? I wonder," said Pippi as she sat at the top of the rock ready to take off.

"No—it doesn't say so in the book, at least," said Tommy.

"Well, that's what I thought. I don't think there was much to his shipwreck. What did he do all day, cross-stitch embroidery? Here I come!"

Pippi slid down into the water, with her red braids streaming out behind her.

After their swim the children decided to explore the desert island thoroughly. All three got on the horse, and he jogged off good-naturedly. Up hill and down dale they rode, through the underbrush and between clumps of spruce, through marshes and over pretty little clearings where the grass was thick with wild flowers. Pippi sat with the pistol ready, and from time

to time she fired a shot so that the horse jumped high into the air with fright.

"There! I shot a lion!" she said with satisfaction.

Or: "Now that cannibal has planted his last potato."

"I think this island should be ours forever," said Tommy when they returned to the camp and Pippi had started to make pancakes. Pippi and Annika thought so too.

The pancakes tasted wonderful when you ate them steaming hot. There were no plates and no knives or forks, and Annika asked, "May we eat with our fingers?"

"It's all right with me if you do," said Pippi, "but for my part I'll stick to the old method of eating with my mouth."

"Oh, you know what I mean, silly!" said Annika. She took a pancake in her hand and put it in her mouth with great enjoyment.

And then night came again. The fire burned down. Snuggled close to each other, their faces smeared with pancake, the children lay in their blankets. A big star shone through a crack in the tent. The "ocean breakers" lulled them to sleep.

"We have to go home today," said Tommy sadly the next morning.

"Isn't it a shame!" said Annika. "I would like to stay here all summer, but Mommy and Daddy are coming home today."

After breakfast Tommy went exploring down by the shore. Suddenly he gave a loud cry. The boat! It was gone!

Annika was much upset. How would they ever be able to get away from there? She did want to be on the island all summer, but it was different when you knew that you couldn't go home. And what would poor Mommy say when she found that Tommy and Annika had disappeared? Annika's eyes filled with tears when she thought about it.

"What's the matter with you, Annika?" asked Pippi. "What is your idea of a shipwreck anyway? What do you think Robinson Crusoe would have said if a ship had come along and picked him up when he had been on the desert island only two days? 'Here you are, Mr. Crusoe, please come aboard and be saved and bathed and shaved and get your toenails cut.' No, thank you. I think surely Mr. Crusoe would have run and hidden behind a bush. For if you've at last landed on a desert island you would like to stay there at least seven years."

"Seven years!" Annika shivered, and Tommy looked thoughtful.

"Well I don't mean that we should stay here forever," said Pippi comfortingly. "When Tommy has to go to military school we'll have to let folks know where we are, I guess, but perhaps he can get a year or two's postponement."

Annika became more and more desperate. Pippi looked at her searchingly. "Well, if you're going to take it like that, there's nothing for us to do but send off the bottle letter."

She dug the empty bottle out of the sack. She also managed to find some paper and a pencil. Putting these on a stone in front of Tommy, she said, "You know more about the art of writing than I do."

"But what shall I write?" asked Tommy.

"Let me think a moment." Pippi pondered. "You can write this: 'Help us before we perish—we have been on this island for two days without snuff.'"

"Oh, but Pippi, we can't write that!" said Tommy reproachfully. "It isn't true."

"What isn't true?"

"We can't write 'without snuff,'" said Tommy.

"Oh, we can't?" said Pippi. "Have you any snuff?"

"No," said Tommy.

"Has Annika any snuff?"

"No, of course not—but—"

"Have I any snuff?" continued Pippi.

"No, maybe you haven't," said Tommy, "but we don't use snuff."

"Well, that's just what I want you to write: 'We've been without snuff for two days.'"

"Yes, but if we write that people will think we use snuff," insisted Tommy.

"Now look here, Tommy," said Pippi, "will you just answer this. Which people are more often without snuff—the ones who use it or the ones who don't?"

"The ones who don't, of course," said Tommy.

"Well, what are you fussing about, then?" asked Pippi. "Write it as I tell you."

So Tommy wrote: "Help us before we perish—we have been on this island for two days without snuff."

Pippi took the paper, stuffed it into the bottle, put the stopper in, and threw the bottle into the water.

"Now we should soon be rescued," she said.

The bottle floated off but shortly came to rest, caught in some tree roots near the shore.

"We'll have to throw it out farther," said Tommy.

"That would be the most stupid thing we could do," said Pippi, "for if it floats far away our rescuers won't know where to look for us. But if it lies here we can call to them when they have found it, and then we'll be rescued right away."

Pippi sat down by the shore. "It's best that we keep our eyes on the bottle the whole time," she said.

Tommy and Annika sat down beside her. After ten minutes Pippi said impatiently, "People must think that we haven't anything else to do but sit here and wait to get rescued. Where can they be, anyway?"

"What people?" asked Annika.

"The ones who are going to rescue us," said Pippi. "It's unforgivable when you consider that human lives are at stake."

Annika began to believe that they really were going to perish on the island, but suddenly Pippi raised her finger in the air and cried, "My goodness, but I'm thoughtless! How could I forget it?"

"What?" asked Tommy.

"The boat!" said Pippi: "I carried it up on shore last night after you had gone to sleep."

"But why did you do that?" asked Annika reproachfully.

"I was afraid that it might get wet," said Pippi.

In a jiffy she had fetched the boat, which lay well hidden under a spruce. She shoved it into the lake and said grimly, "There! Now the rescuers can come! For when they come to rescue us they'll come in vain, because now we are rescuing ourselves, and that will just be a good one on them. It will teach them to hurry up the next time."

"I hope we'll get home before Mommy and Daddy," said Annika when they were in the boat and Pippi was rowing toward shore with strong strokes. "How worried Mommy will be otherwise!"

"I don't think she will," said Pippi.

Mr. and Mrs. Settergren got home half an hour before the children. No Tommy and Annika were in sight, but in the mailbox was a piece of paper on which was printed

FOR GUDNES SAK DONT TINK YUR CHILDRUN R DED R LOS THEY R NT ATAL THEY R JUS ALITTAL SHIPREKED AN WIL SUN CUM HOM I SWER.

GRITINS FRUM

PIPPI

Pippi Gets Unexpected Company

One summer evening Pippi, Tommy, and Annika sat on the steps of Pippi's porch, eating wild strawberries which they had picked that morning. It was a lovely evening, with birds singing and the perfume of the flowers—and the strawberries. Everything was peaceful. The children ate and said hardly a word. Tommy and Annika were thinking how lovely it was that it was summer and how nice that school wouldn't start for a long time. What Pippi thought about, no one knows.

"Pippi, now you have lived here in Villa Villekulla a whole year," said Annika suddenly, hugging Pippi's arm.

"Yes, time flies and one begins to grow old," said Pippi. "This autumn I'll be ten, and then I guess I'll have seen my best days."

"Do you think you will live here always?" asked Tommy. "I mean until you're old enough to become a pirate?"

"No one knows," said Pippi. "I don't suppose my father will stay on that island forever. As soon as he gets a boat made he'll surely come for me."

Tommy and Annika sighed.

Suddenly Pippi sat upright on the steps. "Look, there he comes now!" she exclaimed, pointing toward the gate. She covered the garden walk in three leaps. Tommy and Annika followed her hesitatingly, just in time to see her throw herself on the neck of a very fat gentleman with a short red mustache and blue sailor pants.

"Papa Efraim!" cried Pippi, waving her legs so eagerly as she hung around his neck that her big shoes fell off. "Papa Efraim, how you have grown!"

"Pippilotta Delicatessa Windowshade Mackrelmint Efraim's Daughter Longstocking, my beloved child! I was just going to say that you have grown."

"I knew that," said Pippi. "That's why I said it first. Ha, ha!"

"My child, are you just as strong as you used to be?"

"Stronger," said Pippi. "Shall we Indian wrestle?"

"Go ahead!" said Papa Efraim.

There was a table in the garden, and there Pippi and her father sat down to lock arms while Tommy and Annika looked on. There was only one person in the world who was as strong as Pippi, and that was her father. There they sat, bending with all their might, but neither succeeded in bending the other's arm.

At last Captain Longstocking's arm began to tremble a little, and Pippi said, "When I'm ten I'll bend your arm, Papa Efraim."

Papa Efraim thought so too.

"Oh, my goodness!" said Pippi. "I forgot all about introducing you. This is Tommy and Annika, and this is my father, the Captain and His Majesty, Efraim Longstocking, because you are a cannibal king, aren't you, Papa?"

"That's right," said Captain Longstocking. "I am king over the Kurre-kurredutt natives on an island known as the Kurrekurredutt Island. I float-ed ashore there after I had been blown into the water, you remember."

"Well, that's just what I knew all along. I never believed that you were drowned."

"Drowned! I should say not! It's just as impossible for me to drown as for a camel to thread a needle. I float on my fat."

Tommy and Annika looked at Captain Longstocking wonderingly. "Why aren't you wearing cannibal king clothes?" asked Tommy.

"Oh, I have them here in my bag," said Captain Longstocking.

"Oh, put them on, please put them on!" cried Pippi. "I want to see my father in royal robes."

They all went into the kitchen. Captain Longstocking disappeared into Pippi's bedroom, and the children sat on the woodbox, waiting.

"It's just like at the theater," said Annika, excitedly.

Then—*pang!*—the door opened and there stood the cannibal king! He had a grass skirt around his middle, and on his head he wore a crown of gold! Around his neck hung many strands of big colored beads. In one hand he held a spear, and in the other a shield. Under the grass skirt a couple of fat, hairy legs stuck out, with thick gold bracelets on the ankles.

"*Ussamkussor mussor filibussor,*" said Captain Longstocking, frowning threateningly.

"Oh, he speaks native language!" said Tommy, delighted. "What does that mean, Uncle Efraim?"

"It means 'Tremble, my enemies!'"

"Listen, Papa Efraim," said Pippi. "Weren't the people surprised when you floated ashore on their island?"

"Yes, terribly surprised," answered Captain Longstocking. "First they wanted to eat me, but when I had torn down a palm tree with my bare hands they changed their minds and made me king. After that I ruled in the mornings and built my boat in the afternoons. It took a long time to finish it, as I had to do everything all by myself. It was just a little sailboat, of course. When it was finished I told the people I had to leave them for a little while but that I would soon come back and then I would have a princess with me, whose name was Pippilotta. Then they beat on their shields and shouted, '*Ussomplussor, ussomplussor!*'"

"What does that mean?" asked Annika.

"It means 'Bravo, bravo!' Then I ruled hard for two weeks so that it would last during the whole time I was away. And then I set sail, and the people cried '*Ussamkura kussomkara.*' That means 'Come back soon, fat white chief.' Then I steered straight for South Arabia, and what do you think was the first thing I saw when I jumped ashore there? My old faithful schooner, the *Hoptoad* and my faithful old Fridolf, standing by the rail and waving with all his might. 'Fridolf,' I said, 'now I will take command.' 'Aye, aye, Captain,' he said, and so I did. The whole old crew was there, and now the *Hoptoad* is down here in the harbor so you can go and see all your old friends, Pippi."

Pippi was so happy that she stood on her head on the kitchen table, kicking her legs. But Tommy and Annika couldn't help feeling a little sad. It was just as if someone were trying to take Pippi away from them, they thought.

"Now we'll celebrate," cried Pippi as she came down on her feet again. "Now we'll celebrate so that the whole house shakes!" And then she dished up a big supper, and everyone sat down at the kitchen table to eat. Pippi gobbled up three hard-boiled eggs with the shells on. From time to time she bit her Papa's ear, just because she was so happy to see him. Mr. Nilsson, who had been sleeping, came running out and rubbed his eyes in surprise when he saw Captain Longstocking.

"Well, I see you still have Mr. Nilsson," said Captain Longstocking.

"You bet, and I have another pet too," said Pippi. She went out and fetched the horse, who also got a hard-boiled egg to chew on.

Captain Longstocking was very glad that his daughter had settled herself so comfortably in Villa Villekulla, and he was glad that she had had her suitcase full of gold pieces, so that she had not been in need while he was away.

When everyone had eaten, Captain Longstocking took a tom-tom out of his bag. It was one that the natives used to beat time on for their dances and sacrificial feasts. Captain Longstocking sat down on the floor and beat on the drum. It sounded strange and weird, different from anything that Tommy and Annika had ever heard.

"Native-ish!" explained Tommy to Annika.

Pippi took off her big shoes and danced in her stocking feet, a dance that also was weird. Then King Efraim danced a wild war dance that he had learned on Kurrekurredutt Island. He swung his spear and waved his shield wildly, and his naked feet stomped so hard that Pippi cried, "Look out you don't break through the kitchen floor!"

"That doesn't matter," cried Captain Longstocking, and whirled along. "For now you are going to be a cannibal princess, my darling daughter."

Pippi jumped up and danced with her Papa. They danced back and forth facing each other, yelling and shouting, and from time to time leaping high into the air, so that Tommy and Annika were dizzy just from

174

watching them. Mr. Nilsson must have become dizzy too, for he sat and held his hands over his eyes the whole time.

By and by the dance turned into a wrestling match between Pippi and her father. Captain Longstocking threw his daughter so that she landed on the hat shelf, but she didn't stay there long. With a wild cry she leaped across the kitchen and landed right on Papa Efraim, and the next second had tossed him so that he flew like a meteor, head first into the woodbox. His fat legs stuck right up in the air. He couldn't get out by himself, for in the first place he was too fat, and in the second place he was laughing so hard. A rumbling like thunder came from the woodbox.

Pippi took hold of his feet to pull him up, but then he laughed so he almost choked. He was so terribly ticklish!

"Don't ti—ck—l—e me!" he cried, giggling hysterically. "Throw me into the sea or throw me through the window, do anything, but don't ti—ck—l—e the bottoms of my feet!"

He laughed so that Tommy and Annika were afraid that the woodbox would burst. At last he managed to get out, and as soon as he was back on his feet he lunged at Pippi and threw her across the kitchen. She landed on her face on the stove, which was black with soot.

But she was up in an instant and threw herself at her father. She punched him so that the grass in his skirt came loose and flew all over the kitchen. The gold crown fell off and rolled under the table.

At last Pippi succeeded in getting her father down on the floor, and she sat on him and said, "Do you admit that I won?"

"Yes, you won," said Captain Longstocking, and then they both laughed till they cried. Pippi bit her Papa lightly on the nose, and he said, "I haven't had so much fun since you and I got mixed up in that sailors' fight in Singapore."

He crawled under the table and picked up his crown. "The cannibals should see this," he said, "the royal crown lying under the kitchen table in Villa Villekulla."

He put on the crown and combed out his grass skirt, which looked rather scanty.

"You'll have to send that to invisible mending," said Pippi.

"Yes, but it was worth it," answered Captain Longstocking.

He sat down on the floor and wiped the perspiration from his forehead. "Well, Pippi, my child," he said, "do you ever lie nowadays?"

"Yes, when I have time, but it isn't very often," said Pippi modestly. "How about you? You weren't so backward about lying either."

"Well, I usually lie a little for the people on Saturday nights, if they have behaved well during the week. We usually have a little lie-and-song evening, with accompaniment of drums and firelight dances. The more I lie, the harder they beat the drums."

"Is that so?" asked Pippi. "No one here drums for me. Here I go in my loneliness and puff myself so full of lies that it is a pleasure to hear me, but no one even plays on a comb for me. The other night, when I had gone to bed, I lied a long story about a calf who crocheted lace and climbed trees, and just think, I believed every word of it! That I call good lying! But nobody beat a drum for me. Oh, no!"

"Well, then, I'll do it," said Captain Longstocking, and he beat a long riffle on the drum for his daughter, and Pippi sat on his knee and rubbed her sooty face against his cheek so that he became just as black as she was.

Annika was thinking about something. She didn't know if it was quite proper to say it, but she just had to. "It's not nice to lie," she said. "Mommy says that."

"Oh, how silly you are, Annika!" said Tommy. "Pippi doesn't really lie. She just lies for fun. She makes up things, don't you understand, stupid?"

Pippi looked thoughtfully at Tommy. "Sometimes you speak so wisely that I'm afraid you will become great," she said.

✿ ✿ ✿

It was evening. Tommy and Annika had to go home. It had been a full day and it had been such fun to see a real live cannibal king, and of course it was nice for Pippi that her father had come home, but still . . . still . . .

When Tommy and Annika had crept off to bed, they didn't lie there talking, as they usually did. There was absolute silence in the nursery.

Suddenly a sigh was heard. It was Tommy.

After a while another sigh was heard. This time it was Annika.

"What are you sighing about?" asked Tommy crossly.

But he didn't get an answer, for Annika was crying with her head under the quilt.

Pippi Has a
Farewell Party

● ●

When Tommy and Annika came into the kitchen at Villa Villekulla the next morning, the whole house was resounding with the most terrible snores. Captain Longstocking was not yet awake, but Pippi stood in the middle of the kitchen floor, doing her morning exercises. She was just turning her fifteenth somersault when Tommy and Annika interrupted her.

"Well, now I don't have to worry about my future any more," said Pippi. "I'm going to be a cannibal princess. Yes, for half the year I'm going to be a cannibal princess and half the year I'm going to sail around on all the oceans of the world on the *Hoptoad*. Papa thinks that if he rules hard half the year, the people will get along without a king during the other half; for you know an old sea dog like him has to feel a deck under his feet occasionally, and then he has to think about my education too. If I'm going to be a really good pirate, it wouldn't do to spend all my time at court. That's weakening, Papa says."

"Aren't you going to spend any time at all in Villa Villekulla?" asked Tommy sadly.

"Yes, when we've retired and got a pension," answered Pippi, "in about fifty or sixty years. Then we'll play and have lots of fun, won't we?"

This wasn't much comfort to Tommy and Annika.

"Just think, a cannibal princess!" said Pippi dreamily. "Not many children get to be that. Oh, I'll be so fine, I'll have rings in my ears and a little larger ring in my nose."

"What else are you going to wear?" asked Annika.

"Not another thing," answered Pippi. "Never anything else."

She sighed ecstatically. "Princess Pippilotta! What a life! What glamour! And how I shall dance! Princess Pippilotta dances in the firelight to the beating of the drums! Just imagine how my nose ring will jingle!"

"When—when are you going to leave?" asked Tommy. His voice sounded a bit rusty.

"The *Hoptoad* is lifting anchor tomorrow," said Pippi.

All three children were silent a long while; there didn't seem to be anything more to say. At last, however, Pippi turned another somersault and said, "But tonight we'll have a farewell party in Villa Villekulla—a farewell party! I say no more. All who want to come to say good-by to me are welcome."

The news spread like wildfire among all the children in the little town.

"Pippi Longstocking is going to leave town, and she is having a farewell party tonight in Villa Villekulla. Everyone who wants to may go to the party."

There were several who wanted to—in fact there were thirty-four children. Tommy and Annika had persuaded their mother to promise that they could stay up as long as they wanted to that night. She understood that this was absolutely necessary.

Tommy and Annika would never forget the evening of Pippi's farewell party. It was one of those wonderful warm and beautiful summer evenings when you say to yourself, "Ah, this is summer!" All the roses in Pippi's garden glowed in the fragrant dusk. The wind whispered softly in the old trees. Everything would have been wonderful if only—if only—Tommy and Annika couldn't bear to finish the thought.

All the children from town had brought their bird whistles and were playing merrily as they came up the garden walk of Villa Villekulla. Tommy and Annika led them. Just as they reached the porch steps, the door was flung open and Pippi stood on the threshold. Her eyes gleamed in her freckled face.

"Welcome to my humble dwelling!" she said and threw out her arms.

Annika looked at her closely so that she would always remember just how Pippi looked. Never, never would she forget her as she stood there with her red braids and freckles and her happy smile and her big black shoes.

In the distance was heard a soft beating on a drum. Captain Longstocking sat in the kitchen with his native drum between his knees. He was wearing his royal robes today too. Pippi had especially asked him to. She realized that all the children wanted to see a real live cannibal king.

The whole kitchen was soon full of children staring at King Efraim, and Annika thought that it was a good thing no more had come, for there wouldn't have been room for them. Just as she was thinking this, the music of an accordion was heard from the garden, and in came the whole crew from the *Hoptoad*, led by Fridolf. It was he who was playing the accordion. Pippi had been down to the harbor that day to see her friends and had asked them to come to the farewell party.

Now she rushed at Fridolf and hugged him until he was blue in the face. Then she let go of him and cried, "Music! Music!"

Fridolf played on his accordion, King Efraim beat his drum, and all the children blew their bird whistles.

The lid on the woodbox was closed, and on it stood long rows of bottles of soda. On the large kitchen table were fifteen layer cakes covered with whipped cream, and on the stove a huge kettle full of hot dogs.

King Efraim began by grabbing eight hot dogs. All the others followed his example, and soon nothing was heard in the kitchen except the sound of people eating hot dogs. Afterward each child was allowed to help himself to all the soda and layer cake he wanted.

It was a little crowded in the kitchen, so the guests spread out onto the porch and even into the garden. The whipped cream on the cake shone white in the dusk.

When everyone had eaten as much as he could, Tommy suggested that they should shake down the hot dogs and cake by playing a game—Follow the Leader, for instance. Pippi didn't know that game, but Tommy explained to her that one person would be the leader and all the rest had to do everything that the leader did.

"Okay," said Pippi. "That sounds like fun, and it would probably be best for me to be the leader."

She began by climbing up on the laundry roof. To get there she first had to climb up on the garden fence and then crawl up the roof on her stomach. Pippi and Tommy and Annika had done this so often that it was easy for them, but the other children thought it was rather difficult. The sailors from the *Hoptoad* were used to climbing up the masts, so they made the roof without any trouble, but it was quite an ordeal for Captain Longstocking because he was so fat, and besides his grass skirt kept getting caught. He panted and puffed as he heaved himself up on the roof.

"This grass skirt will never be the same again," he said sadly.

From the laundry roof Pippi jumped down to the ground. Some of the smaller children didn't dare do this, but Fridolf was so nice that he lifted

down all those who were afraid to jump. Then Pippi turned six somersaults on the lawn. Everyone did the same, but Captain Longstocking said, "Someone will have to give me a push from behind, or I'll never be able to do it."

Pippi did. She gave him such a big push that once he got started he couldn't stop, but rolled like a ball across the lawn and turned fourteen somersaults instead of six.

Then Pippi rushed up the porch steps and into Villa Villekulla, climbed out through a window, and, by spreading her legs far apart managed to reach a ladder that stood outside. She ran quickly up the ladder, jumped onto the roof of Villa Villekulla, ran along the ridgepole, jumped up onto the chimney, stood on one leg and crowed like a rooster, threw herself down head first into a tree that stood near the corner of the house, slid down to the ground, rushed into the woodshed, took an ax and chopped a board out of the wall, crept through the narrow opening, jumped up on the garden fence, walked along the fence for fifty yards, climbed up into an oak, and sat down to rest at the very top of the tree.

Quite a crowd had gathered in the street outside Villa Villekulla, and when the people went home they told everyone that they had seen a cannibal king standing on one leg on the chimney of Villa Villekulla, crowing "Cock-a-doodle-do!" so that you could hear it far and wide. Of course no one believed them.

When Captain Longstocking tried to squeeze himself through the narrow opening in the woodshed, the inevitable happened—he stuck and couldn't get either out or in. This, of course, broke up the game, and all the children stood around, watching Fridolf cut Captain Longstocking out of the wall.

"That was a mighty good game," said Captain Longstocking, laughing, when he was free at last. "What are we going to play next?"

"In the good old days on the ship," said Fridolf, "Captain Longstocking and Pippi used to have a contest to see which was the strongest. It was a lot of fun to watch them."

"That's a good idea," said Captain Longstocking, "but the trouble is that my daughter is getting to be stronger than I."

Tommy was standing next to Pippi. "Pippi," he whispered, "I was so afraid you would climb down into our hiding place in the hollow oak when you played Follow the Leader, for I don't want anyone to find out about it, even if we never go there again."

"No, that's our own secret," said Pippi.

Her father took hold of an iron rod and bent it in the middle as if it were made of wax. Pippi took another iron rod and did the same.

"Fiddlesticks!" said Pippi. "I used to amuse myself with these simple tricks when I was still in the cradle, just to pass the time away."

Captain Longstocking then lifted off the kitchen door. Fridolf and seven of the other sailors stood on the door, and Captain Longstocking lifted them high into the air and carried them around the lawn ten times.

It was now quite dark, and Pippi lighted torches here and there. They looked very pretty and cast a magic glow over the garden.

"Are you ready?" she said to her father after the tenth trip around the garden. He was.

Then Pippi put the horse on the kitchen door and told Fridolf and three other sailors to get on the horse. Each of the sailors held two children in his arms. Fridolf held Tommy and Annika. Then Pippi lifted the door and carried it around the lawn twenty-five times. It looked splendid in the light of the torches.

"Well, child, you certainly *are* stronger than I," said Captain Longstocking.

Afterward everyone sat down on the lawn. Fridolf played his accordion and all the other sailors sang the prettiest chanties. The children danced to the music. Pippi took two torches in her hands and danced more wildly than anyone else.

The party ended with fireworks. Pippi fired off rockets and pinwheels that lighted up the whole sky. Annika sat on the porch and looked on. It was so beautiful, so lovely! She couldn't see the roses, but she smelled their fragrance in the dark. How wonderful everything would have been if—if— Annika felt as if a cold hand were gripping her heart. Tomorrow—how would it be then, and the whole summer vacation, and forever? There would be no more Pippi in Villa Villekulla, there would be no Mr. Nilsson, and no horse would stand on the porch. No more horseback rides, no more picnics with Pippi, no more cozy evenings in the kitchen at Villa Villekulla, no tree with soda growing in it—well, the tree would of course still be there, but Annika had a strong feeling that no more soda would grow there when Pippi was gone. What would Tommy and she do tomorrow? Play croquet, probably. Annika sighed.

The party was over. All the children thanked Pippi and said goodnight. Captain Longstocking went back to the *Hoptoad* with his sailors. He thought that Pippi might just as well come along with them, but Pippi wanted to sleep one more night in Villa Villekulla.

"Tomorrow at ten we weigh anchor. Don't forget," cried Captain Longstocking as he left.

Pippi, Tommy, and Annika were alone. They sat on the porch steps in the dark, perfectly quiet.

"You can come here and play, anyway," said Pippi at last. "The key will be hanging on a nail beside the door. You can take everything in the chest drawers, and if I put a ladder inside the oak you can climb down there yourselves, but perhaps there won't be so much soda growing there—it's not the season for it now."

"No, Pippi," said Tommy seriously, "we won't come here any more."

"No, never, never," said Annika, and she thought that in the future she would close her eyes every time she passed Villa Villekulla. Villa Villekulla without Pippi—Annika felt that cold hand around her heart again.

Pippi Goes Aboard

Pippi locked the door of Villa Villekulla carefully and hung the key on a nail beside the door; then she lifted the horse down from the porch—for the last time, she lifted him down from the porch. Mr. Nilsson already sat on her shoulder, looking important. He probably understood that something special was going to happen.

"Well, I guess that's all," said Pippi.

Tommy and Annika nodded. "Yes, I guess it is."

"It's still early," said Pippi. "Let's walk; that will take longer."

Tommy and Annika nodded again, but they didn't say anything. Then they started walking toward the town, toward the harbor, toward the *Hoptoad*. The horse jogged slowly along behind them.

Pippi glanced over her shoulder at Villa Villekulla. "Nice little place," she said. "No fleas, clean and comfortable, and that's probably more than you can say about the clay hut where I'll be living in the future."

Tommy and Annika said nothing.

"If there are an awful lot of fleas in my hut," continued Pippi, "I'll train them and keep them in a cigar box and play Run, Sheep, Run with them at night. I'll tie little bows around their legs, and the two most faithful and affectionate fleas I will call Tommy and Annika, and they shall sleep with me at night."

Not even this could make Tommy and Annika more talkative.

"What on earth is wrong with you?" asked Pippi irritably. "I tell you it's dangerous to keep quiet too long. Tongues dry up if you don't use them. In Calcutta I once knew a potter who never said a word. And once when he wanted to say to me, 'Good-by, dear Pippi, happy journey and thanks for your visit,' he opened his mouth and can you guess what he said? First he made some horrible faces, for the hinges to his mouth had rusted and I had to grease them for him with a little sewing-machine oil, and then a sound came out: 'U buy uye muy.' I looked in his mouth, and, imagine! there lay his tongue like a little wilted leaf, and as long as he lived that potter could never say anything but 'U buy uye muy.' It would be awful if the same thing should happen to you. Let me see if you can say this better than the potter did: 'Happy journey, dear Pippi, and thanks for your visit.' Go on, try it."

"Happy journey, dear Pippi, and thanks for your visit," said Tommy and Annika obediently.

"Thank goodness for that," said Pippi. "You certainly gave me a scare. If you had said 'U buy uye muy' I don't know what I would have done."

There was the harbor, there lay the *Hoptoad*. Captain Longstocking stood on deck, shouting out his commands, the sailors ran back and forth to make everything ready for their departure. All the people in the little town had crowded on the dock to wave good-by to Pippi, and here she came with Tommy and Annika and the horse and Mr. Nilsson.

"Here comes Pippi Longstocking! Make way for Pippi Longstocking!" cried the crowd and made a path for Pippi to come through.

Pippi nodded and smiled to the left and the right. Then she took up the horse and carried him up the gangplank. The poor animal looked around suspiciously, for horses don't care very much for boat rides.

"Well, here you are, my beloved child!" called Captain Longstocking and broke off in the middle of a command to embrace Pippi. He folded her in his arms, and they hugged each other until their ribs cracked.

Annika had gone around with a lump in her throat all morning, and when she saw Pippi lift the horse aboard, the lump loosened. She began to cry as she stood there squeezed against a packing case on the dock, first quietly and then more and more desperately.

"Don't bawl!" said Tommy angrily. "You'll shame us in front of all the people here."

The result of this was only to make Annika burst out in a regular torrent of tears. She cried so that she shook. Tommy kicked a stone so that it rolled across the dock and fell into the water. He really would have liked to throw it at the *Hoptoad*—that mean old boat that was going to take Pippi away from them. Really, if no one had been looking, Tommy would have liked to cry also, but a boy just couldn't let people see him cry. He kicked away another stone.

Pippi came running down the gangplank and rushed over to Tommy and Annika. She took their hands in hers. "Ten minutes left," she said.

Then Annika threw herself across the packing case and cried as if her heart would break. There were no more stones for Tommy to kick, so he clenched his teeth and looked murderous.

All the children in the little town gathered around Pippi. They took out their bird whistles and blew a farewell tune for her. It sounded sad beyond words, for it was a very, very mournful tune. Annika was crying so hard that she could hardly catch her breath.

Just then Tommy remembered that he had written a farewell poem for Pippi and he pulled out a paper and began to read. It was terrible that his voice should shake so.

Good-by, dear Pippi, you from us go.
You may look high and you may look low,

190

But never will you find friends so true
As those who now say good-by to you.

"It really rhymed, all of it," said Pippi happily. "I'll learn it by heart and recite it for the people when we sit around the campfires at night."

The children crowded in from all directions to say good-by to Pippi. She raised her hand and asked them to be quiet.

"Children," she said, "hereafter I'll only have little native children to play with. I don't know how we'll amuse ourselves; perhaps we'll play ball with wild rhinoceroses, and charm snakes, and ride on elephants, and have a swing in the coconut palm outside the door. We'll always manage to pass the time some way or another." Pippi paused. Both Tommy and Annika felt that they hated those native children Pippi would play with in the future.

"But," continued Pippi, "perhaps a day will come during the rainy season, a long and dreary day—for even if it is fun to run around without your clothes on a rainy day, you can't do more than get wet, and when we have got good and wet, perhaps we'll crawl into my native clay hut, unless the whole hut has become a mud pile, in which case, of course, we'll make mud pies. But if the clay hut is still a clay hut, perhaps we'll crawl in there, and the native children will say, 'Pippi, please tell us a story.' And then I will tell them about a little town which lies far, far away in another part of the world, and about the children who live there. 'You can't imagine what nice kids live there,' I'll say to the native children. 'They blow bird whistles, and, best of all, they know pluttification.' But then perhaps the little native children will become absolutely desperate because they don't know any pluttification, and then what shall I do with them? Well, if worst comes to worst, I'll take the clay hut to pieces and make a mud pile out of it, and then we'll bake mud pies and dig ourselves down into the mud way up to our necks. Then it would be strange if I couldn't get them to think about something else besides pluttification. Thanks, all of you, and good-by so much!"

The children blew a still sadder tune on their bird whistles.

"Pippi, it's time to come aboard," called Captain Longstocking.

"Aye, aye, Captain," called Pippi. She turned to Tommy and Annika. She looked at them.

How strange her eyes look! thought Tommy. His mother had looked just like that once when Tommy had been very, very ill.

Annika lay in a little heap on the packing case. Pippi lifted her in her arms. "Good-by, Annika, good-by," she whispered. "Don't cry."

Annika threw her arms around Pippi's neck and uttered a mournful little cry. "Good-by, Pippi," she sobbed.

Pippi took Tommy's hand and squeezed it hard. Then she ran up the gangplank. A big tear rolled down Tommy's nose. He clenched his teeth, but that didn't help; another tear came. He took Annika's hand, and they stood there and gazed after Pippi. They could see her up on deck, but it is always a little hazy when you try to look through tears.

"Three cheers for Pippi Longstocking!" cried the people on the dock.

"Pull in the gangplank, Fridolf," cried Captain Longstocking. Fridolf did. The *Hoptoad* was ready for her journey to foreign lands.

Then—"No, Papa Efraim," cried Pippi, "I can't do it; I just can't bear to do it!"

"What is it you can't bear to do?" asked Captain Longstocking.

"I can't bear to see anyone on God's green earth crying and being sorry on account of me—least of all Tommy and Annika. Put out the gangplank again. I'm staying in Villa Villekulla."

Captain Longstocking stood silent for a minute. "Do as you like," he said at last. "You always have done that."

Pippi nodded. "Yes, I've always done that," she said quietly.

They hugged each other again, Pippi and her father, so hard that their ribs cracked, and they decided that Captain Longstocking should come very often to see Pippi in Villa Villekulla.

"You know, Papa Efraim," said Pippi, "I think it's best for a child to have a decent home and not sail around on the sea so much and live in native clay huts—don't you think so too?"

"You're right, as always, my daughter," answered Captain Longstocking. "It is certain that you live a more orderly life in Villa Villekulla, and that is probably best for little children."

"Just so," said Pippi. "It's surely best for little children to live an orderly life, especially if they can order it themselves."

Pippi said good-by to the sailors on the *Hoptoad* and hugged her Papa Efraim once more. Then she lifted her horse in her strong arms and carried him back over the gangplank. The *Hoptoad* weighed anchor, but at the last minute Captain Longstocking remembered something.

"Pippi!" he cried. "You may need some more gold pieces. Here, catch this!"

Then he threw a new suitcase full of gold pieces to Pippi, but unfortunately the *Hoptoad* had got too far away, and the suitcase didn't reach the dock. Plop! Plop! The bag sank. A murmur of dismay went through the crowd, but then there was another plop! It was Pippi diving off the dock. In a few seconds she came up with the suitcase in her teeth. Climbing up on the dock, she brushed away a bit of seaweed that was caught behind her ear.

"Well, now I'm as rich as a troll again," she said.

Things had happened so quickly that Tommy and Annika were bewildered. They stood with wide open mouths and stared at Pippi and the horse and Mr. Nilsson and the suitcase of gold pieces, and the *Hoptoad* in full sail, leaving the harbor.

"Aren't you—aren't you on the boat?" asked Tommy, unable to believe his eyes.

"Make three guesses," said Pippi and wrung the water out of her braids.

She lifted Tommy and Annika, the suitcase, and Mr. Nilsson all up on the horse and swung herself up behind them.

"Back to Villa Villekulla!" she cried in a loud voice.

At last Tommy and Annika understood. Tommy was so happy that he immediately broke out in his favorite song: "Here come the Swedes with a clang and a bang!"

Annika had cried so much that she couldn't stop right away. She still sniffled, but only happy little sniffs that would soon end. Pippi's arms were around her stomach in a strong grip. She felt so safe! Oh, how wonderful everything was!

"What'll we do today, Pippi?" asked Annika when her sniffles had stopped.

"Well, play croquet, perhaps," answered Pippi.

"Goody!" cried Annika, for she knew that even croquet would be quite different when Pippi played.

"Or else—maybe—" said Pippi hesitatingly.

All the children in the little town crowded around the horse to hear what Pippi said.

"Or else," she said, "or else maybe we could run down to the river and practice walking on the water."

"You can't walk on the water. You know that!" said Tommy.

"Oh, it's not impossible," said Pippi. "In Cuba I once met a cabinet maker . . ."

The horse began to gallop, and the little children who crowded around him couldn't hear the rest of the story, but they stood a long, long time, looking after Pippi and her horse galloping toward Villa Villekulla. After a while Pippi and the horse looked like a little speck, far away, and finally they disappeared completely.

PIPPI IN THE
SOUTH SEAS

translated by Gerry Bothmer

CONTENTS

Villa Villekulla

The little Swedish town was very picturesque, with its cobblestone streets, its tiny houses and the gardens that surrounded them. Everyone who visited there must have felt that this would be a calm and restful place to live. But as far as tourist attractions went, there wasn't much to see— almost nothing, in fact. There was a folklore museum, and an old grave mound, and that was all. But wait, there *was* one more thing!

The people of the little town had neatly and carefully put up signs to show visitors the way to the sights. To the Folklore Museum was printed in large letters on one sign with an arrow underneath. To the Grave Mound read another sign.

There was still a third sign, saying, in rather crooked letters:

To Villa Villekulla

That sign had been put up quite recently. It had often happened lately that people would come and ask how to get to Villa Villekulla—as a matter of fact, more often than they would ask the way to the local museum or the grave mound.

One beautiful summer day a man came driving through the little town.

199

He lived in a much bigger town and therefore he considered himself finer and more distinguished than the people who lived in smaller ones. Then, too, he had a very fine car and he was a very grand person, with shoes that were polished till they gleamed, and a thick gold ring on his finger. So it was perhaps not so strange that he thought of himself as fine and distinguished.

When he drove through the streets he honked his horn loudly so that everyone would notice him as he went by.

When the fine gentleman saw the signposts he laughed heartily.

To the Folklore Museum—how do you like that? he said to himself. I can do without that. *To the Grave Mound,* he read on the other sign. This is getting better and better. . . . But what sort of nonsense is this? he thought when he saw the third sign. *To Villa Villekulla*—what a name!

He thought about this for a moment. A villa could hardly be a tourist attraction in the same way that a folklore museum or a grave mound was. He decided that the sign must have been put there for another reason. Finally the answer came to him. The villa was of course for sale. The sign had been put up to show the way to people who might want to buy the house. For a long time he himself had been thinking that he would buy a house in a small town, where there was not so much noise as in the big city. Naturally he would not live there all the time, but he would go there to rest now and then. In a small town people would also be much more likely to notice what an unusually fine and distinguished man he really was. He decided to go and have a look at Villa Villekulla right away.

All he had to do was follow the direction of the arrow. But he had to drive to the edge of the town before he found what he was looking for. And there, printed with red crayon on a very broken-down garden gate, he read:

VILLA VILLEKULLA

Inside the gate was an overgrown garden with old trees covered with moss, and unmowed lawns, and lots of flowers which were allowed to grow exactly as they pleased. At the end of the garden was a house—and what a house! It looked as if it would fall to pieces any minute. The fine gentleman stared at it, and all of a sudden he groaned. A horse was standing on the veranda! The fine gentleman wasn't used to horses standing on verandas. That is why he groaned.

On the veranda steps three small children were sitting in the sunshine. The girl in the middle had lots of freckles on her face and two red pigtails which stuck straight out. A pretty blond curly-haired little girl in a blue checkered dress and a little boy with neatly combed hair sat one on either side of her. On the shoulder of the redheaded girl sat a monkey.

The fine gentleman was puzzled. He must have the wrong house. Surely no one would think there was a possibility of selling such a tumbledown shack?

"Listen, children," he called out to them, "is this miserable hovel really Villa Villekulla?"

The girl in the middle, the redheaded one, got up and came to the gate. The other two trudged slowly behind.

"Lost your tongue?" said the fine gentleman before the redheaded girl had reached him. "Is this shack Villa Villekulla?"

"Let me think," said the redheaded girl and frowned. "It isn't the museum and it isn't the grave mound. *Now* I have it," she cried, "it *is* Villa Villekulla!"

"Don't be so rude," said the fine gentleman and got out of the car. He decided to take a closer look at the place. "I could of course tear this house down and build another one," he mumbled to himself.

"Yes, let's start right away!" cried the redheaded girl. She ran back to the house and briskly started to rip a few boards from the porch.

The fine gentleman paid no attention to her. He wasn't interested in children, and besides he now had something on his mind. The garden in its wild state really looked quite pleasant and attractive in the sunshine. If a new house were built, the lawns cut, the paths raked, and flowers properly planted, then even a very fine gentleman could live there. The fine gentleman decided to buy Villa Villekulla.

He looked around, trying to think of more ways to improve the place. Of course the old moss-covered trees would have to go. He glared sourly at the old gnarled oak with its tremendous trunk and its branches which arched over the roof of Villa Villekulla.

"I'll cut that one down," he said with finality.

The pretty little girl in the blue checkered dress cried out in a frightened voice, "Oh, Pippi, did you hear?"

Unconcerned, the redheaded girl continued to skip around on the garden path.

"Yes, I'll chop down that old rotten oak," the fine gentleman mumbled to himself.

The little girl in the blue checkered dress stretched her hands toward him pleadingly. "Oh, no, don't do that," she said. "It's such a wonderful tree to climb. And it's hollow, so we can play in it."

"Nonsense," said the fine gentleman. "I don't climb trees; you ought to understand that."

The boy with the neatly combed hair came forward. He looked anxious. "But soda grows in that tree," he said imploringly. "And chocolate too. On Thursdays."

"Listen, I think you kids have been sitting in the sun too long," said the fine gentleman. "Everything seems to be going round and round in your heads. But that's none of my business. I'm going to buy this place. Can you tell me where I can find the owner?"

The little blue checkered girl began to cry, and the little boy with the neatly combed hair ran up to the redheaded girl, who was still skipping.

"Pippi," he said, "don't you hear what he is saying? Why don't you *do* something?"

"Why don't I *do* something?" echoed the red-headed girl. "Here I am, skipping for all I'm worth, and then you tell me I'm not doing anything. Skip yourself and see how easy it is!"

She walked over to the fine gentleman. "My name is Pippi Longstocking," she said. "And this is Tommy and Annika." She pointed to her friends. "Is there anything we can do for you—tear down a house or chop down a tree? Or is there anything else that needs to be changed? Just say the word!"

"Your names don't interest me," said the fine gentleman. "The only thing I would like to know is where I can find the owner of this place. I intend to buy it."

The redheaded girl, the one called Pippi Longstocking, had gone back to her skipping. "The owner is quite busy now," she said. She kept on skipping in a very determined way as she talked. "As a matter of fact, terribly busy," she said, skipping around the fine gentleman. "But do sit down and wait a while, and she will probably come along."

"*She,*" said the fine gentleman with a pleased look. "Is it a *she* who owns this miserable house? So much the better. Women don't understand business. In that case there's a hope of getting it cheap."

"We can always hope," said Pippi Longstocking.

As there didn't seem to be any other place to sit down, the fine gentleman sat down on the veranda steps. The monkey anxiously leaped back and forth on the railing. Tommy and Annika were standing at a distance, looking at him in a frightened way.

"Do you live here?" asked the fine gentleman.

"No," said Tommy, "we live in the villa next door."

"But we come here every day to play," said Annika shyly.

"There will be an end to that now," said the fine gentleman. "I don't want any youngsters running around in my garden. Children are the worst thing I know."

"I think so too," said Pippi and stopped skipping for a second. "All children ought to be shot."

"How can you say that?" said Tommy, hurt.

"Yes, I mean it: all children ought to be shot," said Pippi. "But that isn't possible because then no nice little uncles would ever grow up. And we can't do without *them!*"

The fine gentleman looked at Pippi's red hair and decided to have a little fun while he was waiting. "Do you know why you're like a newly lighted match?" he asked.

"No," said Pippi. "But I have always wondered."

The fine gentleman pulled

one of Pippi's pigtails quite hard. "Both of you are fiery on top—ha-ha!

"One has to listen a lot before the ears fall off," said Pippi. "How strange that I haven't happened to think of that before!"

The fine gentleman looked at her and said, "I really think you're the ugliest child I've ever seen."

"Well," said Pippi, "you're not exactly a beauty yourself."

The fine gentleman looked hurt, but he didn't say anything. Pippi stood and looked at him in silence for a while with her head tilted to one side. "Do you know in what way you and I are alike?"

"Just between us," said the fine gentleman, "I hope there is *no* likeness."

"There is," said Pippi. "Both of us have big mouths. Except me."

A faint giggle could be heard from Tommy and Annika.

"So, you're being insolent!" the man shouted. "But I'll soon thrash that out of you."

He reached out his fat arm to grab Pippi, but she quickly jumped to one side and a second later she was sitting perched in the hollow oak. The fine gentleman gaped in astonishment.

"When are we going to start with the thrashing?" asked Pippi, as she made herself comfortable on a branch.

"I have time to wait," said the fine gentleman.

"Good!" said Pippi. "Because I'm thinking of staying up here until the middle of November."

Tommy and Annika laughed and clapped their hands. But that they shouldn't have done, because now the fine gentleman was terribly angry. When he couldn't reach Pippi he grabbed Annika by the nape of the neck and said, "Then I'll give you a hiding instead. It seems as if you need one too."

Annika had never in her life been spanked and she let out a cry of pain and fright. There was a thud as Pippi jumped out of the tree. With one leap she was standing beside the fine gentleman.

"Oh, no," she said. "Better not start a fight now." Then she grabbed the fine gentleman around his fat waist and threw him up in the air several times. And on her outstretched arms she carried him to his car and threw him down in the back seat.

"I think we'll wait to tear down the house until another day," she said. "You see, one day a week I tear down houses. But never on Fridays, because this is housecleaning day. Therefore I usually vacuum the house on Friday and tear it down on Saturday. Everything has its own time."

With great difficulty the fine gentleman scrambled up to the steering wheel and drove off in great haste. He was both frightened and angry and it annoyed him that he hadn't been able to talk to the owner of Villa Villekulla. He was anxious to buy the place and chase away those nasty children.

Then he met one of the town policemen. He stopped his car and said, "Can you help me to find the lady who owns Villa Villekulla?"

"With great pleasure," said the policeman. He hopped into the car and said, "Drive to Villa Villekulla."

"No, she isn't there," said the fine gentleman.

"Yes, I'm sure she's there," said the policeman.

The fine gentleman felt quite safe with the policeman along, and he drove back to Villa Villekulla as the policeman had told him to. He was very eager to talk to the owner.

"There is the lady that owns Villa Villekulla," said the policeman and pointed toward the house.

The fine gentleman looked in the direction in which the policeman was pointing. He put his hand to his forehead and groaned. There on the veranda steps was the redheaded girl, that awful Pippi Longstocking. And on her outstretched arms she was carrying the horse. The monkey was sitting on her left shoulder.

"Hi, Tommy and Annika," shouted Pippi, "let's go for a ride before the next spicalator comes!"

"It's called *speculator*," said Annika.

"Is that—the owner of the villa?" said the fine gentleman in a weak voice. "But she is only a little girl."

"Yes," said the policeman, "only a little girl, the strongest little girl in the world. She lives there all alone."

The horse with the three children on his back came galloping toward the gate.

Pippi looked down at the fine gentleman and said, "It was fun to solve riddles with you a while ago. Come to think of it, I know one more. Can you tell me what the difference is between my horse and my monkey?"

The fine gentleman was really not at all in the mood to solve riddles any more, but he had gained so much respect for Pippi that he didn't dare not to answer.

"The difference between your horse and your monkey—that I really couldn't say."

"It's quite tricky," said Pippi, "but I'll give you a small hint. If you should see them both together under a tree and one of them should start to climb up the tree, then that one isn't the horse."

The fine gentleman pressed his gas pedal all the way down to the floor and took off with a roar. He never, never came back to the little town.

207

Pippi Cheers
Aunt Laura Up

One afternoon Pippi was wandering around in her garden, waiting for Tommy and Annika to come over. But no Tommy came, and no Annika either, so Pippi decided to go and see where they were. She found them in their own garden. But they weren't alone. Their mother, Mrs. Settergren, was also there with a very nice old lady who had come to visit. The two ladies were sitting under a tree, drinking coffee. Annika and Tommy were having fruit juice, but when they saw Pippi they got up and ran to meet her.

"Aunt Laura came," Tommy explained. "That's why we couldn't come over to you."

"She looks so nice," said Pippi, peeking at her through the leaves of the hedge. "I must talk to her. I'm so fond of nice old ladies."

Annika looked a little worried. "It . . . it . . . maybe it's best if you don't talk very much," she said. She remembered that once when Pippi had been to a coffee party she had talked so much that Annika's mother had been very annoyed with her. And Annika was too fond of Pippi to want anyone to be annoyed with her.

Pippi's feelings were hurt. "Why shouldn't I talk to her?" she asked. "When people come to visit, you should be nice and friendly to them. If I sit there and don't say a word, she might think I have something against her."

"But are you sure you know how to talk to old ladies?" objected Annika.

"They need to be cheered up," said Pippi with emphasis. "And that's what I'm going to do now." She walked across the lawn to where the two ladies were sitting. First she curtsied to Mrs. Settergren. Then she looked at the old lady and clapped her hands.

"Just look at Aunt Laura!" she exclaimed. "More beautiful than ever!" She turned to Tommy's and Annika's mother. "Please may I have a little fruit juice so my throat won't be so dry when we start talking?" she asked.

Mrs. Settergren poured a glass of juice and said as she handed it to Pippi, "Children should be seen and not heard."

"Well," said Pippi, looking pleased, "it's nice if people are happy just to look at me! I must see how it feels to be used just for decoration." She sat down on the grass and stared straight in front of her with a fixed smile, as if she were having her picture taken.

Mrs. Settergren paid no further attention to Pippi but went on talking to the old lady. After a while she asked with concern, "How are you feeling these days, Aunt Laura?"

"Awful," replied Aunt Laura, "just awful. I'm so nervous and worried about everything."

Pippi jumped up. "Exactly like my grandmother!" she exclaimed. "She got nervous and excited about the least little thing. If she was walking in the street and a brick happened to fall on her head she'd start to scream and make such a fuss you'd think something terrible had happened.

"And once she was at a ball with my father and they were dancing a *hambo* together. My father is quite strong, and quick as a wink he swung my grandmother around so hard that she flew straight across the ballroom and landed with a crash right in the middle of the bass fiddle. There she was, screaming and carrying on like anything. My father picked her up and held her outside the window—it was four floors up—so that she'd cool off and not be so fidgety. But she didn't like that a bit. She just hollered, 'Let me go this minute!' My father did, of course, and can you imagine, she wasn't pleased about that either! My father said he'd never seen anything like the fuss the dear old lady made over nothing at all. It certainly is too bad when people have trouble with their nerves," Pippi finished sympathetically, and dunked her zwieback into her fruit juice.

Tommy and Annika were fidgeting uneasily in their chairs. Aunt Laura shook her head in a puzzled way, and Mrs. Settergren said hastily, "We all hope you'll be feeling better soon, Aunt Laura."

"Oh yes, I'm sure she will," Pippi said reassuringly. "My grandmother did. She was soon feeling very well."

Aunt Laura wanted to know what cured her.

"Tranquilizers," Pippi said. "That did the trick, I can tell you. She was soon as cool as a cucumber, and she'd sit peacefully for days at a time just not saying a word. If bricks had started falling on her head one after another she'd just have sat there and enjoyed it! If that could happen to my grandmother it could happen to *anybody*. So I'm sure you'll be all well again soon, Aunt Laura."

Tommy crept over to Aunt Laura and whispered in her ear, "Don't mind anything Pippi says, Aunt Laura. She's just making it up. She doesn't even have a grandmother."

Aunt Laura nodded understandingly. But Pippi had sharp ears, and she heard what Tommy whispered.

"Tommy's quite right," she said. "I *don't* have a grandmother. She doesn't exist. Since that's the case, why does she have to be so terribly nervous?"

Aunt Laura looked at Pippi for a moment with a dazed expression, and then began to talk to Mrs. Settergren again. Pippi sat down to listen with the same fixed smile as before.

After a few minutes Aunt Laura said, "Do you know, something very strange happened yesterday—"

"But it couldn't be nearly as strange as what I saw the day *before* yesterday," Pippi said reassuringly. "I was riding in a train, and we were going along full speed when suddenly a cow came flying through the open window with a big suitcase hanging on her tail. She sat down in the seat across from me and began to look through the timetable to see what time we'd get to Falkoping. I was eating a sandwich—I had loads of sandwiches, some sausage and some smoked herring—and I thought she might be hungry, so I offered her one. She took a smoked herring one and swallowed it practically whole!"

Pippi fell silent.

"That was really *very* strange," said Aunt Laura politely.

"Yes, you'd go a long way before you'd find another cow as strange as that one," Pippi agreed. "Just imagine, she took a smoked herring sandwich when there were still lots of sausage ones left!"

Mrs. Settergren interrupted to ask Aunt Laura if she'd like some more coffee. She filled Aunt Laura's cup and her own, and poured more fruit juice for the children. "You were going to tell about the strange thing that happened yesterday," she reminded the old lady.

"Oh, yes," said Aunt Laura, beginning to look worried again.

"Speaking of strange things happening," Pippi broke in hastily, "you'll enjoy hearing about Agaton and Teodor. Once when my father's ship came into Singapore we needed a new able-bodied seaman, and we took on Agaton. He was seven feet tall and so thin that his bones rattled like a rattlesnake's tail when he moved. He had pitch-black hair that came down to his waist, and only one tooth. That tooth was all the bigger, though—it grew all the way down to his chin.

"My father thought Agaton was uglier than anyone should be, and at first he didn't want him on board. Only then he decided that Agaton might be useful to have around to scare any fierce wild horses into stampeding. Well, then we got to Hong Kong, and we needed another able-bodied seaman, so we got Teodor. They were as much alike as a pair of twins."

"That certainly was a strange coincidence!" exclaimed Aunt Laura.

"Strange?" said Pippi. "What was so strange about it?"

"That they looked so much alike," Aunt Laura replied. "That was very strange indeed."

"No," said Pippi, "not really. Because they *were* twins. Both of them. Even from birth." She looked a bit reproachful. "I don't quite understand what you mean, dear Aunt Laura. Is it anything to worry about when twins happen to look alike? They can't help it, you know. Nobody would have *wanted* to look like Agaton—or like Teodor either, for that matter."

"Then why do you speak of strange coincidences?" Aunt Laura asked, looking bewildered.

Mrs. Settergren tried to divert Aunt Laura's attention. "You were going to tell us about the strange thing that happened to you yesterday."

Aunt Laura got up to leave. "That will have to wait till another time," she said. "On second thought, perhaps it wasn't so very strange after all."

She said good-by to Tommy and Annika. Then she patted Pippi's red head. "Good-by, my little friend," she said. "You're quite right, I'm beginning to feel better already. I don't feel nervous at all any more."

"Oh, I'm so glad!" said Pippi, and gave the old lady a big hug. "You know, Aunt Laura, my father was very pleased about getting Teodor in Hong Kong. Because then he said he could stampede twice as many wild horses!"

Pippi Finds a Spink

One morning Tommy and Annika came skipping into Pippi's kitchen as usual, shouting good morning. But there was no answer. Pippi was sitting in the middle of the kitchen table with Mr. Nilsson, the little monkey, in her arms and a happy smile on her face.

"Good morning," said Tommy and Annika again.

"Just think," said Pippi dreamily, "just think that I have discovered it—I and no one else!"

"What have you discovered?" Tommy and Annika wondered. They weren't in the least bit surprised that Pippi had discovered something because she was always doing that, but they did want to know what it was.

"What did you discover, anyway, Pippi?"

"A new word," said Pippi and looked at Tommy and Annika as if she had just this minute noticed them. "A brand-new word."

"What kind of word?" said Tommy.

"A wonderful word," said Pippi. "One of the best I've ever heard."

"Say it then," said Annika.

"Spink," said Pippi triumphantly.

"Spink," repeated Tommy. "What does that mean?"

214

"If I only knew!" said Pippi. "The only thing I know is that it doesn't mean vacuum cleaner."

Tommy and Annika thought for a while. Finally Annika said, "But if you don't know what it means, then it can't be of any use."

"That's what bothers me," said Pippi.

"Who really decided in the beginning what all the words should mean?" Tommy wondered.

"Probably a bunch of old professors," said Pippi. "People certainly are peculiar! Just think of the words they make up—'tub' and 'stopper' and 'string' and words like that. Where they got them from, nobody knows. But a wonderful word like 'spink,' they don't bother to invent. How lucky that I hit on it! And you just bet I'll find out what it means, too."

She fell deep in thought.

"Spink! I wonder if it might be the top part of a blue flagpole," she said doubtfully.

"Flagpoles aren't blue," said Annika.

"You're right. Well, then, I really don't know. . . . Or do you think it might be the sound you hear when you walk in the mud and it gets between your toes? Let's hear how it sounds! 'As Annika walked in the mud you could hear the most wonderful spink.'" She shook her head. "No, that's no good. 'You could hear the most wonderful *tjipp*'—that's what it should be instead."

Pippi scratched her head. "This is getting more and more mysterious. But whatever it is, I'm going to find out. Maybe it can be bought in the stores. Come on, let's go and ask!"

Tommy and Annika had no objection. Pippi went off to hunt for her purse, which was full of gold pieces. "Spink," she said. "It sounds as if it might be expensive. I'd better take a gold piece along." And she did. As usual Mr. Nilsson jumped up on her shoulder.

Then Pippi lifted the horse down from the veranda. "We're in a hurry," she said to Tommy and Annika. "We'll have to ride. Because otherwise there might not be any spink left when we get there. It wouldn't surprise me if the mayor had already bought the last of it."

When the horse came galloping through the streets of the little town with Pippi and Tommy and Annika on his back, the children heard the clatter of his hoofs on the cobblestones and came happily running because they all liked Pippi so much.

"Pippi, where are you going?" they cried.

"I'm going to buy spink," said Pippi and brought the horse to a halt for a moment.

The children looked puzzled.

"Is it something good?" a little boy asked.

"You bet," said Pippi and licked her lips. "It's wonderful. At least it sounds as if it were."

In front of a candy shop she jumped off the horse, lifted Tommy and Annika down, and in they went.

"I would like to buy a bag of spink," said Pippi. "But I want it nice and crunchy."

"Spink," said the pretty lady behind the counter, trying to think. "I don't believe we have that."

"You must have it," said Pippi. "All well-stocked shops carry it."

"Yes, but we've just run out of it," said the lady, who had never even heard of spink but didn't want to admit that her shop wasn't as well-stocked as any other.

"Oh, but then you did have it yesterday!" cried Pippi eagerly. "Please, please tell me how it looked. I've never seen spink in all my life. Was it red striped?"

Then the nice lady blushed prettily and said, "No, I really don't know what it is. In any case, we don't have it here."

Very disappointed, Pippi walked toward the door. "Then I have to keep on looking," she said. "I can't go back home without spink."

The next store was a hardware store. A salesman bowed politely to the children.

"I would like to buy a spink," said Pippi. "But I want it to be of the best kind, the one that is used for killing lions."

The salesman looked sly as a fox. "Let's see," he said and scratched himself behind the ear. "Let's see." He took out a small rake. "Is this all right?" he said as he handed it to Pippi.

Pippi looked indignantly at him. "That's what the professors would call a rake," she said. "But it happens to be a spink I wanted. Don't try to fool an innocent little child."

Then the salesman laughed and said, "Unfortunately we don't have the thing you want. Ask in the store around the corner that carries notions."

"Notions," Pippi muttered to Tommy and Annika when they came out on the street. "I just know they won't have it there." Suddenly she brightened. "Perhaps, after all, it's a sickness," she said. "Let's go and ask the doctor."

Annika knew where the doctor lived because she had gone there to be vaccinated.

Pippi rang the bell. A nurse opened the door.

"I would like to see the doctor," said Pippi. "It's a very serious case. A terribly dangerous disease."

"This way, please," said the nurse.

The doctor was sitting at his desk when the children came in. Pippi went straight to him, closed her eyes, and stuck her tongue out.

"What is the matter with you?" said the doctor.

Pippi opened her clear blue eyes and pulled in her tongue. "I'm afraid I've got spink," she said, "because I itch all over. And when I sleep my eyes

217

close. Sometimes I have the hiccups and on Sunday I didn't feel very well after having eaten a dish of shoe polish and milk. My appetite is quite hearty, but sometimes I get the food down my windpipe and then nothing good comes of it. It must be the spink which bothers me. Tell me, is it contagious?"

The doctor looked at Pippi's rosy face and said, "I think you're healthier than most. I'm sure you're not suffering from spink."

Pippi grabbed him eagerly by the arm. "But there is a disease by that name, isn't there?"

"No," said the doctor, "there isn't. But even if there were, I don't think it would have any effect on you."

Pippi looked sad. She made a deep curtsy to the doctor as she said goodby, and so did Annika. Tommy bowed. And then they went out to the horse, who was waiting at the doctor's fence.

Not far from the doctor's house was a high three-story house with a window open on the upper floor. Pippi pointed toward the open window and said, "It wouldn't surprise me if the spink is in there. I'll dash up and see." Quickly she climbed up the water spout. When she reached the level of the window she threw herself heedlessly into the air and grabbed hold of the window sill. She hoisted herself up by the arms and stuck her head in.

In the room two ladies were sitting chatting. Imagine their astonishment when all of a sudden a red head popped over the window sill and a voice said, "Is there by any chance a spink here?"

The two ladies cried out in terror. "Good heavens, what are you saying, child? Has someone escaped?"

"That is exactly what I would like to know," said Pippi politely.

"Maybe he's under the bed!" screamed one of the ladies. "Does he bite?"

"I think so," said Pippi. "He's supposed to have tremendous fangs."

The two ladies clung to each other. Pippi looked around curiously, but finally she said with a sigh, "No, there isn't as much as a spink's whisker around here. Excuse me for disturbing you. I just thought I would ask, since I happened to be passing by."

She slid down the water spout and said sadly to Tommy and Annika, "There isn't any spink in this town. Let's ride back home."

And that's what they did. When they jumped down from the horse outside the veranda, Tommy came close to stepping on a little beetle which was crawling on the gravel path.

"Be careful not to step on the beetle!" Pippi cried.

All three bent down to look at it. It was such a tiny thing, with green wings that gleamed like metal.

"What a pretty little creature," said Annika. "I wonder what it is."

"It isn't a June bug," said Tommy.

"And no ladybug either," said Annika. "And no stagbeetle. I wish I knew what it was."

All at once a radiant smile lit up Pippi's face. "I know," she said. "It's a spink."

"Are you sure?" Tommy said doubtfully.

"Don't you think I know a spink when I see one?" said Pippi. "Have you ever seen anything so spink-like in your life?"

She carefully moved the beetle to a safer place, where no one could step on it. "My sweet little spink," she said tenderly. "I knew that I would find one at last. But isn't it funny! We've been hunting all over town for a spink, and here was one right outside Villa Villekulla all the time!"

Pippi Arranges a Question-and-Answer Bee

● ●

The long wonderful summer holiday suddenly came to an end, and Tommy and Annika went back to school. Pippi still considered herself sufficiently well educated without going to school and announced very decidedly that she had no intention of setting her foot in school until the day came when she couldn't stand not knowing how the word "seasick" was spelled.

"But since I'm never seasick I don't have to worry about the spelling in the first place," she said. "And if I should happen to be seasick one day, then I'll have other things to think about than knowing how to spell it."

"Besides, you'll probably never get seasick," said Tommy.

And he was right. Pippi had sailed far and wide with her father before he became king of a South Sea island and before Pippi had settled down to live in Villa Villekulla. But in all her life she had never been seasick.

Sometimes Pippi would ride over and pick up Tommy and Annika when school was over. This pleased Tommy and Annika very much. They loved to ride, and there certainly aren't many children who are able to ride home from school on horseback.

"Please, Pippi, come and pick us up this afternoon," said Tommy one day just as he and Annika were going to dash back to school after their lunch hour.

"Yes, please," said Annika. "Because today is the day that Miss Rosenblom is going to give out gifts to children who have been good and worked hard."

Miss Rosenblom was a rich old lady who lived in the little town. She took good care of her money, but once every term she came to school and distributed gifts to the children. But not to all the children—oh, no! Only the very good and hard-working children got presents. To make sure she would know which children were really good and hard-working, Miss Rosenblom held long examinations before she distributed the presents. That was the reason all the children in town lived in constant dread of her. Every day when they were about to do their homework and were trying to think of something more amusing to do before getting started, their mother or father would say, "Remember Miss Rosenblom!"

It was a terrible disgrace to come home to one's parents and brothers and sisters the day Miss Rosenblom had been to school, and not have a small coin or bag of candy or at least some underwear to show for it. Yes, of all things, underwear! Because Miss Rosenblom distributed underwear to the poorest children. But it didn't matter how poor a child was if he didn't know the answer when Miss Rosenblom asked how many inches there were in a mile. It wasn't surprising at all that the children were afraid of Miss Rosenblom!

They lived in terror of her soup too. Believe it or not, Miss Rosenblom had all the children weighed and measured in order to see if there were any among them who were especially thin and pathetic and who looked as if they weren't getting enough to eat at home. All those who were found to be poor and too skinny had to go to Miss

Rosenblom's every lunch hour and eat a big plate of soup. It would have been fine if there hadn't been a whole lot of nasty barley in the soup. It always felt so slippery in the mouth.

Now the big day had arrived when Miss Rosenblom was coming to the school. Classes stopped earlier than usual, and all the children gathered in the school yard. Miss Rosenblom sat at a big table that had been placed in the middle of the yard. To help her, she had two assistants who wrote down everything about the children—how much they weighed, if they were able to answer her questions, if they were poor and needed clothes, if they had good marks in conduct, if they had younger brothers and sisters at home who also needed clothing. There was no end to the things that Miss Rosenblom wanted to know. A box containing coins stood on the table in front of her. There were also a lot of bags of candy, and big piles of under-shirts and socks and woolen pants.

"All children get in line!" shouted Miss Rosenblom. "In the first line I want children who don't have brothers and sisters at home; in the second line children who have one or two brothers and sisters; and in the third, children who have more than two brothers and sisters." This arrangement was made because Miss Rosenblom wanted everything to be orderly. Besides, it was only fair that the children who had many brothers and sisters at home should

get bigger bags of candy than those who didn't have any.

Then the examination began. Oh, how the children trembled! The ones who couldn't answer the minute a question was asked had to go and stand in a corner, and then they were sent home without as much as one piece of candy for their little brothers and sisters.

Both Tommy and Annika were very good at their school work. But in spite of that, the bow in Annika's hair quivered with suspense as she stood in line beside Tommy. And Tommy's face got whiter and whiter the closer he got to Miss Rosenblom. When it was his turn to answer there was a sudden commotion in the line for children without brothers and sisters. Someone was pushing her way forward through the crowd, and who should it be but Pippi! She brushed the children aside and went straight up to Miss Rosenblom.

"Excuse me but I wasn't here when you started," she said. "In which line should I stand, since I don't have fourteen brothers and sisters of which thirteen are naughty little boys?"

Miss Rosenblom looked very disapproving. "You can stay where you are for the present," she said. "But it seems to me that quite soon you will be moved over into the line of children who are going to stand in the corner."

Then the assistants wrote down Pippi's name and she was weighed in order to find out whether she needed any soup. But she weighed five pounds too much for that.

"You don't get any soup," said Miss Rosenblom sharply.

"Sometimes luck is with me," said Pippi. "Now all I have to do is get by without getting stuck with the underwear. Then I'll be able to breathe more freely."

Miss Rosenblom paid no attention to her. She was looking through the dictionary for a difficult word for Pippi to spell.

"Now then," she said finally, "will you tell me how you spell 'seasick'?"

"I'll be glad to," said Pippi. "S-e-e-s-i-k."

Miss Rosenblom smiled—a sour smile. "Is that so?" she said. "The dictionary spells it differently."

"Then it was very lucky that you wanted to know how *I* spell it," said Pippi. "S-e-e-s-i-k is the way I have always spelled it, and it seems to have worked out just fine."

"Make a note of that," said Miss Rosenblom to the assistants and grimly pressed her lips together.

"Yes, do that," said Pippi. "Make a note of this fine spelling and see to it that the change is made in the dictionary as soon as possible."

"I wonder if you can answer this one," said Miss Rosenblom. "When did King Charles the Twelfth die?"

"Oh dear, is he dead too?" cried Pippi. "It's awful how many people die these days! If he had kept his feet dry I'm sure it would never have happened."

"Make a note of that," said Miss Rosenblom to her assistants in an icy voice.

"Yes, by all means do that," said Pippi. "And make a note that it's very good to keep leeches next to the skin. And you should drink a little warm kerosene before going to bed. It's very invigorating!"

Miss Rosenblom looked desperate. "Why does a horse have molars with dark markings running through them?" she asked in a stern voice.

"But are you sure that he has?" said Pippi thoughtfully. "You can ask him yourself. He is standing over there," she said and pointed to her horse, who was tied to a tree. She laughed contentedly. "It's a good thing I brought him along," she said. "Otherwise you would never have known why he has molars with markings in them. Because honestly I have no idea—and, what's more, I don't care much either."

A narrow line was now all that was left of Miss Rosenblom's mouth. "This is unbelievable," she murmured, "absolutely unbelievable."

"Yes, I think so too," said Pippi, pleased. "If I continue being this clever,

I probably won't be able to avoid getting a pair of pink woolen underdrawers."

"Make a note of that," said Miss Rosenblom to the assistants.

"No, don't bother," said Pippi. "I really don't care so much about pink woolen underdrawers. That wasn't what I meant. But you could make a note saying I'm to have a big bag of candy."

"I'm going to ask you one more question," said Miss Rosenblom, and her voice sounded as if she were strangling.

"Yes, keep right on," said Pippi. "I like this kind of question-and-answer game."

"Can you answer this one?" said Miss Rosenblom. "Peter and Paul are going to divide a cake. If Peter gets one fourth, what does Paul get?"

"A stomach-ache," said Pippi. She turned to the assistants. "Make a note of that," she said seriously. "Make a note that Paul gets a stomach-ache."

But Miss Rosenblom was finished with Pippi. "You are the most stupid and disagreeable child I have ever seen," she said. "Go over and stand in the corner right away!"

Pippi obediently trotted off, muttering angrily to herself, "It's unfair, because I answered every question!" When she had walked a few steps she suddenly thought of something and quickly elbowed her way back to Miss Rosenblom.

"Excuse me," she said, "but I forgot to give my chest measurement and my height above sea level. Make a note of that," she said to the assistants. "Not that I want any soup—far from it—but the books should be in order, after all."

"If you don't go over and stand in the corner immediately," said Miss Rosenblom, "I know a little girl who is going to get a sound spanking."

"Poor child," said Pippi. "Where is she? Send her to me and I'll defend her. Make a note of that."

Then Pippi went over and stood in the corner with the children who couldn't answer questions. There the atmosphere was far from gay. Many of the children were sobbing and crying at the thought of what their parents and their brothers and sisters would say when they came home without the least little coin and without any candy.

Pippi looked around at the crying children and swallowed hard several times. Then she said, "We'll have a question-and-answer bee all our own!"

The children looked a bit more cheerful, but they didn't quite understand what Pippi meant.

"Form two lines," said Pippi. "All of you who know that King Charles the Twelfth is dead stand in one line and those who still haven't heard that he is dead stand in the other."

But since all the children knew that Charles the Twelfth was dead there was only one line.

"This is no good," said Pippi. "You have to have at least two lines, otherwise it isn't right. Ask Miss Rosenblom and you'll see." She stopped to think. "I have it!" she said at last. "All very clever and well-trained pranksters will form one line."

"And who is to stand in the other line?" a little girl who didn't want to be thought of as a prankster asked eagerly.

"In the other line we'll put all those who are not quite so clever at playing pranks," said Pippi.

Over at Miss Rosenblom's table the questioning was continuing full force and now and then a child on the verge of tears came shuffling over to Pippi's crowd.

"And now comes the hard part," said Pippi. "Now we're going to see if you have been doing your homework." She turned to a skinny little boy in a blue shirt. "You over there," she said, "give me the name of someone who is dead."

The boy looked a little surprised, but then he said, "Old Mrs. Pettersson in Number Fifty-seven."

"What do you know?" said Pippi. "Do you know anyone else?"

No, the boy didn't. Then Pippi put her hands in front of her mouth in the form of a megaphone and said in a stage whisper, "King Charles the Twelfth, of course!"

Then Pippi asked all the children in turn if they knew anyone who was dead, and they all answered, "Old Mrs. Pettersson in Number Fifty-seven and King Charles the Twelfth."

"This examination is going better than I had expected," said Pippi. "Now I'm going to ask only one thing more. If Peter and Paul are going to divide a cake, and Peter absolutely doesn't want any but sits himself down in a corner and gnaws on a dry little bit of bread, who is then forced to sacrifice himself and down the whole cake?"

"Paul!" shouted all the children.

"I wonder if children as clever as you could be found anywhere else," said Pippi. "But you shall have a reward."

From her pockets she dug out a whole handful of gold pieces and each child got one. Each child also got a huge bag of candy, which Pippi took out of her rucksack.

That is why there was great rejoicing among the children who were supposedly in disgrace. And when Miss Rosenblom's examination was finished and everybody was going home, the children who had been standing in the corner were the quickest to disappear. But first they all crowded around Pippi.

"Thank you, dear Pippi," they said. "Thank you for the gold pieces and the candy."

"It's nothing," said Pippi. "You don't need to thank me. But you must never forget that I rescued you from the pink woolen underdrawers."

Pippi Gets a Letter

The days went by, and all of a sudden it was autumn—first autumn and then winter, a long, cold winter that seemed as if it would never end. Tommy and Annika were very busy at school, and with every day that went by they felt more tired and had a harder time getting up in the morning. Mrs. Settergren began to be really worried about their paleness and their lack of appetite. On top of everything, both of them suddenly caught the measles and had to stay in bed for a couple of weeks.

It would have been two very dreary weeks indeed if Pippi hadn't come and done tricks outside their window every day. The doctor had forbidden her to go into the sickroom, because measles are catching, and Pippi obeyed, although she said she would undertake to crack one or two billion measle microbes between her fingernails during the course of an afternoon.

But no one had forbidden her to do tricks outside the window. The children's room was on the second floor, and Pippi had raised a ladder to their window. It was very exciting for Tommy and Annika to lie in their beds and try to guess how Pippi would look when she appeared on the ladder, because she never looked the same two days in a row. Sometimes she would be dressed as a chimney sweep, sometimes as a ghost in a white sheet, and sometimes she appeared as a witch. Then she would act amusing skits outside the window, playing all the parts herself. Now and then she did acrobatics on the step-ladder—and what acrobatics! She would stand on the topmost rung and let the ladder sway forth and back until Tommy and Annika screamed in terror because it looked as if she would come crashing down any minute. But she didn't. When she was going to climb down again she always went head first just so that it would be more amusing for Tommy and Annika to watch.

Every day she went to town to buy apples and oranges and candy. She put everything into a basket and attached it to a long string. Then Mr. Nilsson climbed up with the string to Tommy, who opened the window and hoisted up the basket. Sometimes Mr. Nilsson would also bring letters from Pippi when she was busy and couldn't come herself. But that didn't happen often, because Pippi was on the ladder practically all the time. Sometimes she pressed her nose against the windowpane and turned her eyelids inside out and made the most terrible faces. She said to Tommy and Annika that she would give each of them a gold piece if they could keep from laughing at her. But of course they couldn't. They laughed so hard that they almost fell out of their beds.

Gradually they became well again and were allowed to get up. But, oh, how pale and thin they were! Pippi was sitting with them in their kitchen the first day they were up, watching them eat their cereal. That is, they were supposed to be eating cereal, but they weren't doing very well. It made their mother terribly nervous to see them just sitting there and picking at it.

"Eat your good cereal," she said.

Annika stirred hers around in the dish with her spoon a bit, but she knew that she just couldn't get any of it down. "Why do I have to eat it, anyway?" she said complainingly.

"How can you ask anything so stupid?" said Pippi. "Of course you have

to eat your good cereal. If you don't eat your good cereal, then you won't grow and get big and strong. And if you don't get big and strong, then you won't have the strength to force *your* children, when you have some, to eat *their* good cereal. No, Annika, that won't do. Nothing but the most terrible disorder in cereal-eating would come of this if everyone talked like you."

Tommy and Annika ate two spoonfuls of cereal each. Pippi watched them with great sympathy.

"You ought to go to sea for a while," she said, rocking back and forth on the chair on which she was sitting. "Then you would soon learn how to eat. I remember once when I was on my father's ship and Fridolf, one of our able-bodied seamen, suddenly one morning couldn't eat more than seven plates of cereal. My father was beside himself with worry over his poor appetite. 'Fridolf, old boy,' he said in a choked voice, 'I'm afraid that you have got a terrible, consuming disease. It's best that you stay in your bunk today, until you feel a little better and can eat normally. I'm coming back to tuck you in and give you some strengthening meducine.'"

"It's called *medicine*," said Annika.

"And Fridolf staggered to bed," Pippi went on, "because he was worried himself and wondered what sort of epidemic he could be having since he was only able to eat seven helpings of cereal. He was just lying there wondering whether he would live until evening when my father came with the meducine. A black, disgusting-looking meducine it was, but you could say what you wanted about it, it was strengthening. Because when Fridolf had swallowed the first spoonful, flames broke out from his mouth. He let out a scream that shook the *Hoptoad* from the stern to the bow and could be heard on ships within a fifty-mile radius.

"The cook still hadn't had a chance to clear away the breakfast dishes when Fridolf came steaming up into the galley, letting out piercing shrieks. He heaved himself down at the table and began eating cereal and he was howling with hunger even after his fifteenth plate. But then there was no more cereal left, and all the cook could do was stand and throw cold potatoes into Fridolf's open mouth. As soon as it looked as if he were going to stop, Fridolf let out an angry growl, and the cook realized that if he didn't want to be eaten up himself, all he could do was keep it up. But unfortunately he only had a miserable hundred and seventeen potatoes, and when he had thrown the last one into Fridolf's gullet he quickly made a dash for the door and turned the lock.

"Then we all stood outside and peeked in at Fridolf through a window. He was whining like a hungry child, and in quick succession he ate up the bread basket and the pitcher and fifteen plates. Then he attacked the table. He broke off all four legs and ate till the sawdust foamed around his mouth, but he only said that for asparagus they had an awfully wooden taste. He seemed to think that the table top tasted better, because he smacked his lips as he ate it and said that it was the best sandwich he had eaten since he was a child. But then my father felt that Fridolf was fully recovered from his consuming disease, and he went in to him and said that now he would have to try to control himself until lunch, which would be served in two hours, and then he would get mashed turnips with salt pork. 'Oh, Captain!' said Fridolf, wiping his mouth. 'Please,' he said with an eager, hungry look in his eyes, 'when is supper going to be served and why can't we have it a little earlier?'"

Pippi put her head to one side and looked at Tommy and Annika and their cereal plates. "As I said, you ought to go to sea for a while and then your poor appetites would be cured in a hurry."

Just then the mailman walked by the Settergren house on his way to Villa Ville-

233

kulla. He happened to see Pippi through the window and called out, "Pippi Longstocking, here is a letter for you!"

Pippi was so astonished that she almost fell off the chair. "A letter! For me? A leal retter—I mean, a real letter? I want to see it before I believe it."

But it *was* a real letter, a letter with many strange stamps.

"You read it, Tommy, you know how," said Pippi.

And Tommy began.

MY DEAR PIPPILOTTA,

When you get this you might as well go down to the harbor and start looking for the Hoptoad. *Because now I'm coming to get you and bring you here to Kurrekurredutt Island for a while. You ought at least to see the country where your father has become such a powerful king. It's really very nice here and I think that you would like it and feel at home. My faithful subjects are also looking forward very much to seeing the Princess Pippilotta of whom they have heard so much. So there is nothing further to be said in the matter. You are coming and this is my kingly and fatherly wish. A real big kiss and many fond regards from your old father,*

KING EFRAIM I LONGSTOCKING
Ruler of Kurrekurredutt Island

When Tommy had finished reading, you could have heard a pin drop in the kitchen.

Pippi Goes on Board

On a beautiful morning the *Hoptoad* sailed into the harbor decorated with flags and pennants from end to end. The town band was on the pier, playing welcome songs with all its might. The whole town had gathered to see Pippi receive her father, King Efraim I Longstocking. A photographer was standing ready to snap a picture of their meeting.

Pippi was jumping up and down with impatience and the gangplank was hardly down before Captain Longstocking and Pippi rushed toward each other with shouts of joy. Captain Longstocking was so happy to see his daughter that he threw her way up in the air several times. Pippi was just as happy, so she threw her father way up in the air still more times. The only one who wasn't happy was the photographer, because he couldn't get a picture when either Pippi or her father was way up in the air all the time.

Tommy and Annika also came forward and greeted Captain Long-stocking—but oh, how pale and miserable they looked! It was the first time after their illness that they had been out.

Pippi of course had to go on board and say hello to Fridolf and all her other friends among the seamen. Tommy and Annika trotted along too.

235

They felt so strange walking around on a ship that had come from so far away, and they kept their eyes wide open so as not to miss anything. They were especially eager to see Agaton and Teodor, but Pippi said that the twins had signed off the ship a long time ago.

Pippi hugged all the sailors so hard that five minutes later they were still gasping for breath. Then she lifted Captain Longstocking up onto her shoulders and carried him through the crowd and all the way home to Villa Villekulla. Hand in hand, Tommy and Annika trudged along behind them.

"Long live King Efraim!" shouted all the people. They felt that this was a big day in the history of the little town.

A few hours later Captain Longstocking was in bed at Villa Villekulla, sleeping, and snoring away so that the whole house shook. Pippi, Tommy, and Annika were sitting around the kitchen table, where the remains of a splendid supper were still in evidence. Tommy and Annika were quiet and thoughtful. What were they thinking about? Annika was just thinking that when you come right down to facts, she would much rather be dead. Tommy was sitting there trying to remember if there was anything in this world that was really fun, but he couldn't think of a thing. Life was an empty waste, he felt.

But Pippi was in a wonderful mood. She stroked Mr. Nilsson, who was carefully making his way back and forth between the plates on the table; she stroked Tommy and Annika; she whistled and sang alternately and took happy little dance steps now and then. She didn't seem to notice that Tommy and Annika were so downcast.

"Going to sea for a bit again is going to be marvelous," she said. "Just think of being on the ocean, where there is so much freedom!"

Tommy and Annika sighed.

"And I'm quite excited about seeing Kurrekurredutt Island too. Imagine what it'll be like to lie stretched out on the beach, dipping my big toes in the South Pacific, and all I'll have to do is to open my mouth and a ripe banana will fall right in it!"

Tommy and Annika sighed.

"It's going to be a lot of fun to play with the children down there," Pippi continued.

Tommy and Annika sighed.

"What are you sighing for?" said Pippi. "Don't you like the idea of my playing with the native children?"

"Of course," said Tommy. "But we're just thinking that it will probably be a long time before you come back to Villa Villekulla."

"Yes, I'm sure of that," said Pippi gaily. "But I'm not at all sorry. I think I can have almost more fun on Kurrekurredutt Island."

Annika turned a pale, unhappy face toward Pippi. "Oh, Pippi," she said, "how long do you think you'll stay away?"

"Oh, that's hard to say. Until around Christmas, I should think."

Annika let out a wail.

"Who knows," said Pippi, "maybe I'll like it so much on Kurrekurredutt Island that I'll feel like staying there forever. . . . Tra-la-la," she sang, and did a few more pirouettes. "To be a princess, that's not a bad job for someone who's had as little schooling as I have."

Tommy's and Annika's eyes, looking out of their pale faces, began to have a peculiar, glassy stare. Suddenly Annika bent down over the table and burst into tears.

"But come to think of it, I don't think that I'd like to stay there forever," said Pippi. "One can have too much of court life and get sick of the whole business. So one fine day you'll probably hear me saying, 'Tommy and Annika, how would you like to go back to Villa Villekulla for a while again?'"

"Oh, how wonderful it will be when you write that to us," said Tommy.

"Write!" said Pippi. "You have ears, I hope. I have no intention of writing. I'll just *say,* 'Tommy and Annika, now it's time to go back to Villa Villekulla.'"

Annika raised her head from the table and Tommy said, "What do you mean by that?"

"What do I mean!" said Pippi. "Don't you understand plain words? Or have I forgotten to tell you that you're coming along to Kurrekurredutt Island? I thought I'd mentioned it."

Tommy and Annika jumped to their feet. Their breath came in gasps. Then Tommy said, "You talk such nonsense! Our mother and father would never allow it."

"Yes, they will," said Pippi. "I've already talked to your mother."

For exactly five seconds there was silence in the kitchen of Villa Villekulla. Then there were two piercing yells from Tommy and Annika, who were wild with joy. Mr. Nilsson, who was sitting on the table and trying to spread butter on his hat, looked up in surprise. He was still more sur-

238

prised when he saw Pippi and Tommy and Annika take one another by the hand and start dancing crazily around. They danced and shouted so that the ceiling lamp loosened and fell down. Then Mr. Nilsson threw the butter knife out the window and started to dance too.

"Is it really, really true?" asked Tommy when they had calmed down and crawled into the woodbin to talk it over. Pippi nodded.

Yes, it was really true. Tommy and Annika were to go along to Kurrekurredutt Island.

To be sure, all the ladies in the little town came to Mrs. Settergren and said, "You don't mean that you're thinking of sending your children off to the South Seas with Pippi Longstocking? You can't be serious!"

Then Mrs. Settergren said, "And why shouldn't I? The children have been sick and the doctor says they need a change of climate. As long as I've known Pippi she has never done anything that has harmed Tommy and Annika in any way. No one can be kinder to them than she."

"Yes, but after all, *Pippi Longstocking*," said the ladies, wrinkling their noses.

"Exactly," said Mrs. Settergren. "Pippi Longstocking's manners may not always be what they ought to. But her heart is in the right place."

On a chilly night in early spring Tommy and Annika left the little town for the first time in their lives to travel out into the great, strange world with Pippi. All three of them were standing at the rail of the *Hoptoad* while the brisk night air filled the sails. (Perhaps it would be more accurate to say all five, because the horse and Mr. Nilsson were there too.)

All the children's classmates were on the pier and almost in tears with regret—mingled with envy—at their leaving. Tomorrow the classmates would be going to school as usual. Their geography homework was to study all the islands in the South Pacific. Tommy and Annika didn't have to do any homework for a while. "Their health comes before school," the doctor had said. "And they'll get to know the South Sea islands first hand," added Pippi.

Tommy's and Annika's mother and father were also on the pier. Tommy and Annika suddenly felt lumps in their throats when they saw their parents wiping their eyes with handkerchiefs. But Tommy and Annika still couldn't keep from being happy, so happy that it almost hurt.

Slowly the *Hoptoad* sailed out of the harbor.

"Tommy and Annika," cried Mrs. Settergren, "when you get out on the North Sea you have to put on two undershirts and—"

The rest of what she was trying to say was drowned in the cries of farewell from the people on the pier, the wild whinnying of the horse, Pippi's happy noisiness, and Captain Longstocking's loud trumpeting when he blew his nose.

The voyage had begun. The *Hoptoad* was sailing out under the stars. Ice blocks were floating around the bow and the wind was singing in the sails.

"Oh, Pippi," said Annika, "I have such a funny feeling. I'm beginning to think that I'll be a pirate too when I grow up."

Pippi Goes Ashore

● ●

"**K**urrekurredutt Island straight ahead!" cried Pippi from the bridge one sunny morning.

They had been sailing for days and nights, for weeks and months, over storm-ridden seas and through calm, friendly waters, in starlight and moonlight, under dark, threatening skies and in scorching sun. They had been sailing for such a long time that Tommy and Annika had almost forgotten what it was like to live at home in the little town.

Their mother would probably have been surprised if she could have seen them now. No more pale cheeks. Brown and healthy, they climbed around in the rigging just as Pippi did. Gradually, as the weather grew warmer, they had peeled off their clothes and the warmly bundled-up children with two undershirts who had crossed the North Sea had become two naked brown children in loincloths.

"What a wonderful time we're having!" Tommy and Annika declared each morning when they woke up in the cabin they shared with Pippi.

Often Pippi was already up and at the helm.

"A better seaman than my daughter has never sailed on the seven seas," Captain Longstocking would often say. And he was right. Pippi guided the

Hoptoad with a sure hand past the most perilous underwater reefs and the worst breakers.

Now the voyage was coming to an end.

"Kurrekurredutt Island straight ahead!" cried Pippi.

There it was, sheltered by green palms and surrounded by the bluest blue water.

Two hours later the *Hoptoad* made for a little inlet on the left side of the island. All the Kurrekurredutts, men, women, and children, were on the beach to receive their king and his redheaded daughter. A mighty roar rose from the crowd when the gangplank was lowered.

"*Ussamkura, kussomkara!*" they shouted, and it meant, "Welcome back, fat white chief!"

King Efraim walked majestically down the gang-plank, dressed in his blue corduroy suit, while on the foredeck, Fridolf played the new national anthem of the Kurrekurredutts on his accordion. "Here comes our chief with a clang and a bang!"

King Efraim raised his hand in greeting and shouted, "*Muoni manana!*" That meant, "Greetings to all of you."

He was followed by Pippi, who was carrying the horse. Then a wave of excitement broke out among the Kurrekurredutts. Of course they had heard about Pippi and her enormous strength, but it was something entirely different to see it before their very eyes. Tommy and Annika and the whole crew trooped ashore, but for the time being the Kurrekurredutts had eyes for no one but Pippi. Captain Longstocking lifted her up on his shoulders so that they would be able to have a good look at her, and again an excited murmur went through the crowd. But then Pippi lifted up Captain Longstocking on one of *her* shoulders and the horse on the other and the murmur swelled into a roar.

The population of the Island of Kurrekurredutt was one hundred and twenty-six people.

"That is approximately the right number of subjects to have," said King Efraim. "More are hard to keep track of."

They all lived in small, cozy huts among the palms. The biggest and finest hut belonged to King Efraim. The crew of the *Hoptoad* also had their huts where they lived while the ship lay anchored in the little inlet. She was anchored there practically all the time these days. Once in a while, though, there would be an expedition to an island about fifty miles to the north where there was a shop where Captain Longstocking bought snuff.

A fine, newly built little hut under a cocoanut tree was ready for Pippi. There was plenty of room for Tommy and Annika too. But before they could go into the hut to wash up, Captain Longstocking wanted to show them something. He took Pippi by the arm and led her back down to the beach.

"Here," he said, pointing with a thick forefinger. "This was the place where I floated ashore the time I was blown into the sea."

The Kurrekurredutts had put up a monument to commemorate the strange event. The stone bore an inscription which read, in Kurrekurredutt words:

Over the great wide sea came our fat white chief. This is the place where he floated ashore at the time when the breadfruit trees were in bloom. May he remain just as fat and magnificent as when he came.

In a voice trembling with emotion Captain Longstocking read the inscription out loud for Pippi and Tommy and Annika. Then he blew his nose with gusto.

When the sun had begun to go down and was ready to disappear in the endless embrace of the South Seas, the drums of the Kurrekurredutts summoned everyone to the royal square, which was situated in the middle of the village. There stood King Efraim's fine throne of bamboo, bedecked with red hibiscus flowers. He sat on it when he ruled. For Pippi the Kurrekurredutts had made a smaller throne which stood next to her father's. In a great hurry they had also put together two little bamboo chairs for Tommy and Annika.

The roar of the drums grew louder and louder as King Efraim mounted his throne with great dignity. He had taken off his corduroy suit and was dressed in royal regalia, with a crown on his head, a straw skirt around his waist, a necklace of shark's teeth around his neck, and heavy bracelets around his ankles. With great majesty, Pippi took her place on her throne. She was still wearing the same loincloth around her middle, but she had stuck some red and white flowers in her hair to be a bit more festive. Annika had done the same. But not Tommy. Nothing could make Tommy stick flowers in his hair.

King Efraim had been away from his ruling duties for quite a while, and now he started to rule with all his might. In the meantime the little Kurrekurredutt children came closer and closer to Pippi's throne. They were filled with awe to think that she was a princess. When they reached the throne they all threw themselves down on their knees before her, touching the ground with their foreheads.

Pippi quickly hopped down from her throne. "What's all this?" she asked. "Do you play 'hunting-for-treasure' down here too? Wait and let me play with you." She got down on her knees and started to nose around on the ground. "There seem to have been other treasure hunters here before us," she said after a while. "There isn't as much as a pin here, that's for sure."

She got back up on her throne. Hardly had she sat down when all the children bowed their heads to the ground again.

"Have you lost something?" said Pippi. "In any case it isn't there, so you might as well get up."

Luckily Captain Longstocking had been on the island long enough for the Kurrekurredutts to learn some of his language. Naturally they didn't know the meaning of such difficult words as "postal money order" and "brigadier general," but they had picked up a lot just the same. Even the children knew the most common expressions, such as "leave that alone" and similar ones. A little boy by the name of Momo could speak the Captain's language quite well, because he used to spend a good deal of time at the huts of the crew, listening to the men talking. A pretty little girl named Moana was also able to understand the language quite well.

Now Momo was trying to explain to Pippi why they were on their knees in front of her.

"You be very fine princess," he said.

"I no be very fine princess," said Pippi in broken Kurrekurredutt. "I be really only Pippi Longstocking, and now I'm through with this throne business."

She hopped down off her throne. And King Efraim hopped down off his, because now he was finished with ruling for the day.

The sun sank like a red ball of fire in the South Seas and soon the sky was bright with stars. The Kurrekurredutts lighted a huge fire in the royal square, and King Efraim and Pippi and Tommy and Annika and the crew from the *Hoptoad* sat down in the grass and watched the Kurrekurredutts dance around the fire. The muffled rumble of the drums, the exciting dance, the strange perfumes from thousands of exotic flowers in the jungle, the glimmering stars above their heads—everything made Tommy and Annika feel very strange. The waves of the sea were ceaselessly pounding in the background.

"I think that this is a very fine island," said Tommy afterward, when he and Pippi and Annika had crawled into their beds in their cozy little hut under the cocoanut tree.

"I think so too," said Annika. "Don't you, Pippi?"

Pippi was lying there quietly with her feet on her pillow as was her habit. "M-m-m," she said dreamily. "Just listen to the roar of the waves. Remember, I said, 'Maybe I'll like it so much on Kurrekurredutt Island that I'll feel like staying there forever'?"

Pippi Talks Sense to a Shark

Very early the next morning Pippi and Tommy and Annika crawled out of their hut. But the Kurrekurredutt children had been up still earlier. They were already sitting under the cocoanut tree, excitedly waiting for their new friends to come out and play. They talked in rapid Kurrekurredutt and laughed, their teeth flashing.

The whole crowd trooped down to the beach, with Pippi at the head. Tommy and Annika jumped up and down with delight when they saw the beautiful white sand where they could dig themselves down, and the blue sea, which looked so inviting. A coral reef a short distance from the island served as a sea wall. Inside, the water lay still and mirror-like. All the children threw off their scanty clothing and, shouting and laughing, dashed out into the water.

Afterward they rolled around in the white sand and Pippi and Tommy and Annika agreed that it would have been much nicer to have really dark skin because white sand on a dark background looked so funny. But when Pippi had dug herself down in the sand up to her neck, so that only a freckled face and two red pigtails stuck out, that looked quite funny too.

All the children settled themselves down in a circle to talk to her.

"Tell us about the children in the northern land you come from," said Momo to the freckled face.

"They love pluttification," said Pippi.

"It's called *multiplication*," said Annika. "And besides," she said, somewhat miffed, "no one can say that we *love* it."

"Northern children love pluttification," Pippi insisted stubbornly. "Northern children become frantic if northern children don't every day get a large dose of pluttification."

She didn't have the strength to continue in broken Kurrekurredutt, but switched over to her own language.

"If you hear a northern child cry, you can be sure that the school has burned down or that a school holiday has been declared or that the teacher has forgotten to give the children homework in pluttification. And let's not even talk about the summer vacation. That brings on such tears and wailing that you wish you were dead when you hear it. No one is dry-eyed when the school gate slams shut for the summer. All the children slowly head for home, singing sad songs, and they can't keep themselves from sobbing when they think that it will be several months before they can get any pluttification to do again. Yes, it's a misery, the like of which you can't imagine," said Pippi and sighed deeply.

"Bah!" said Tommy and Annika.

Momo didn't quite understand what pluttification was and wanted to have a more detailed explanation. Tommy was just about to explain it, but Pippi got in ahead of him.

"Yes, you see, it's like this—seven times seven equals a hundred and two. Fun, eh?"

"It most certainly is *not* one hundred and two," said Annika.

"No, because seven times seven is forty-nine," said Tommy.

"Remember that we're on Kurrekurredutt Island now," said Pippi. "Here we have an entirely different and much more flourishing climate, so seven times seven gets to be much more here."

"Bah!" said Tommy and Annika again.

The arithmetic lesson was interrupted by Captain Longstocking, who came to announce that he and the whole crew and all the Kurrekurredutts were going off to another island for a couple of days to hunt wild boar. Captain Longstocking was in the mood for some fresh boar steak. The Kurrekurredutt women were also to go along, to scare out the boar with wild cries. That meant that the children would be staying behind alone on the island.

"I hope you won't be sad because of this?" said Captain Longstocking.

"I'll give you three guesses," said Pippi. "The day I hear that some children are sad because they have to take care of themselves without grownups, that day I'll learn the whole pluttification table backward, I'll swear to that."

"That's my girl," said Captain Longstocking.

Then he and all his grown-up subjects armed with shields and arrows got into their big canoes and paddled away from Kurrekurredutt Island.

Pippi rounded her hands into a megaphone and shouted after them, "May peace be with you! But if you aren't back by my fiftieth birthday I'll send out an S.O.S. over the radio!"

When they were alone Pippi and Tommy and Annika and Momo and Moana and all the other children looked happily at one another. They were going to have a whole wonderful South Sea island all to themselves for several days.

"What are we going to do?" said Tommy and Annika.

"First we'll get our breakfast down from the trees," said Pippi. Like a flash she was in a cocoanut tree, shaking cocoanuts down. Momo and the

other Kurrekurredutt children gathered breadfruit and bananas. Pippi made a fire on the beach and over it she roasted the wonderful breadfruit. All the children settled around in a circle and had a substantial breakfast consisting of roasted breadfruit, cocoanut milk, and bananas. There were no horses on Kurrekurredutt Island, so all the native children were very much interested in Pippi's horse. Those who dared went for a ride on him. Moana said that one day she would like to go to the northern land where there were such strange animals.

Mr. Nilsson wasn't anywhere in evidence. He had gone off on an excursion to the jungle, where he had met some relatives.

"What are we going to do now?"

asked Tommy and Annika when riding on the horse was no longer any fun.

"Northern children want to see fine caves—yes?—no?" wondered Momo.

"Northern children most certainly want to see fine caves—yes, yes," said Pippi.

Kurrekurredutt Island was a coral island. On the south side the high coral cliffs plunged straight into the sea, and there were the most wonderful caves which had been dug out by the waves. Some were down at the water line and filled with water, but there were others higher up in the cliffs and there the Kurrekurredutt children were accustomed to play. In the largest cave they kept a big supply of cocoanuts and other delicacies. To get there was quite an undertaking. First they had to climb carefully down the steep side of the cliff and hang on to the rocks which jutted out. Otherwise they could easily have plunged down into the sea. Any place else on the island that wouldn't have mattered. But at this particular spot there were plenty of sharks who liked to eat little children. In spite of this danger, the Kurrekurredutt children had fun diving for oysters, but then someone always had to stand guard and shout "Shark! Shark!" as soon as they spotted a fin in the distance.

In the big cave the Kurrekurredutt children also kept a supply of shimmering pearls which they had found in the oysters. They used them to play marbles with and they had no idea that they would be worth any amount of money in Europe or America. Captain Longstocking used to take along a few pearls now and then when he went off to buy snuff. He would trade the pearls for things he thought his subjects needed, but on the whole he felt that the Kurrekurredutts were well off as they were. And the children gaily continued to play marbles with the pearls.

Annika was horror-stricken when Tommy said to her that she would have to climb along the cliff to the big cave. The first part wasn't so bad. There was quite a broad ledge to walk on, but it gradually got narrower and the last few feet to the cave you had to scramble and climb and hang on as best you could.

"Never!" said Annika. "Never."

To climb along a cliff where there was hardly anything to hold on to, and below, a sea filled with sharks waiting for you to fall down! That wasn't Annika's idea of fun.

Tommy was annoyed. "No one should bring sisters along to the South Seas," he said as he scrambled along the cliff wall. "Look at me! You only have to go like this."

There was a loud *plop*, as Tommy fell into the water. Annika screamed. Even the Kurrekurredutt children were terrified. "Shark! Shark!" they cried and pointed out toward the sea. There a fin was clearly visible above the surface, heading rapidly in the direction of Tommy.

There was another *plop*. That was Pippi jumping in. She reached Tommy about the same time as the shark did. Terrified, Tommy was screaming at the top of his lungs. He felt the shark's sharp teeth scrape against his leg. But just at that instant Pippi grabbed the bloodthirsty beast with both hands and lifted him out of the water.

"Don't you have any shame in you?" she asked. The shark looked around, surprised and ill at ease. He wasn't able to breathe above the surface.

"Promise never to do that again and I'll let you go," said Pippi gravely. With all her force she flung him far out into the sea. He lost no time in getting away from there and decided to head for the Atlantic Ocean.

In the meantime Tommy had managed to scramble up on a small plateau, and he sat there trembling all over. His leg was bleeding. Then

Pippi came up. She behaved very strangely. First she lifted Tommy up in the air, and then she hugged him so hard that he lost his breath. Then all of a sudden she let go of him and sat down on the cliff. She put her head in her hands. She cried. Pippi cried! Tommy and Annika and all the Kurrekurredutt children looked at her, surprised and frightened.

"You cry because Tommy almost eaten up?" said Momo.

"No," Pippi answered crossly, and wiped her eyes. "I cry because poor little hungry shark no get breakfast today."

Pippi Talks Sense to Jim and Buck

● ●

The shark's teeth had only scratched Tommy's leg, and when he had calmed down he still wanted to continue the climb to the big cave. Pippi twisted strands of hibiscus fiber into a stout rope and tied it to a stone. Then, lightly as a mountain goat, she hopped over to the cave and secured the other end of the rope there. Now even Annika dared to climb to the cave. When you had a steady rope to hang on to, it was easy.

It was a wonderful cave, and so big that all the children were able to get inside without any trouble.

"This cave is almost better than our hollow oak at Villa Villekulla," said Tommy.

"No, not better, but just as good," said Annika, who felt a lump in her throat at the thought of the oak and didn't want to admit that anything could be better.

Momo showed the visitors how much cocoanut and breadfruit were stored in the cave. One would be able to live there for several weeks without starving to death. Moana showed them a hollow bamboo cane filled with the most beautiful pearls. She gave Pippi and Tommy and Annika each a handful.

"Nice marbles you have to play marbles with in this country," said Pippi.

It was delightful to sit at the opening of the cave and look out over the sea glittering in the sunlight. And it was great fun to lie on one's tummy and spit into the water. Tommy announced a contest in long-distance spitting. Momo was terribly good at it. But he still wasn't able to beat Pippi. She had a way of forcing the spit through her front teeth which no one could imitate.

"If it's drizzling over in New Zealand today," said Pippi, "it's my fault."

Tommy and Annika didn't do so well.

"Northern children no can spit," said Momo with a superior air. He didn't quite consider Pippi as being one of the northern children.

"So northern children can't spit?" said Pippi. "You don't know what you're talking about. That is taught to them in school from the first grade. Long-distance spitting and altitude spitting and sprint spitting. You ought to see Tommy's and Annika's teacher! Man, can she spit! She won first prize in sprint spitting. The whole town cheers when she runs around spitting to beat the band."

"Bah!" said Tommy and Annika.

Pippi raised her hand to shield her eyes from the glare and looked out to sea. "I see a ship out there," she said. "A tiny steamer. I wonder what it's doing in these parts."

And she had reason to wonder!

The steamer was heading toward Kurrekurredutt Island at a good clip. On board there were several South Sea islanders and two white men. Their names were Jim and Buck. They were dirty, coarse-looking men who looked like real bandits. And that is exactly what they were.

Once when Captain Longstocking was in the shop where he bought snuff, Jim and Buck had been there too. They had seen Captain Longstocking put a couple of unusually large and beautiful pearls on the counter and had heard him say that on Kurrekurredutt Island the children used pearls like these to play marbles with. Since that day they had only one goal and that was to go to the island and try to get pearls. They knew that Captain Longstocking was very strong, and they also had a healthy respect for the crew of the *Hoptoad*. They therefore decided to take advantage of an opportunity when all the men were away on a hunt.

Now their chance had come. Hiding behind an island close by, they had seen through their binoculars Captain Longstocking, his crew, and all the Kurrekurredutts paddle away from the island. They were only waiting until the canoes were out of sight.

"Drop the anchor!" shouted Buck when the ship was close to the island. Pippi and all the other children watched them in silence from the cave above. The men dropped anchor, and Jim and Buck jumped into a skiff and rowed ashore. The crew were given orders to stay on board.

"Now we'll sneak up to the village and overtake them," said Jim. "Probably only the women and children are at home."

"Yes," said Buck, "and besides, there were so many women in the canoes I should think that only children are left on the island. I hope they're playing marbles—ha-ha-ha!" His voice carried clearly over the water.

"Why?" shouted Pippi from the cave. "Do you especially like playing marbles? I think it's just as much fun to play leapfrog."

Jim and Buck turned around in astonishment and saw Pippi and all the children sticking their heads out from the cave. A delighted grin spread over their faces.

"There we have the kids," said Jim.

"Perfect," said Buck. "This is in the bag."

But they decided nevertheless to play it safe and be sly. No one could know where the children kept their pearls, and therefore it was best to try to win them over. The men pretended that they hadn't come to

Kurrekurredutt Island to find pearls at all, but were just out for a nice little excursion. They felt hot and sticky, and Buck suggested that, to begin with, they go for a swim.

"I'll row back to the boat and fetch our bathing trunks," he said. This he did. In the meantime Jim stood alone on the shore.

"Is there a good beach around here?" he called to the children in a friendly voice.

"Wonderful," said Pippi. "Absolutely wonderful for sharks. They come here every day."

"Nonsense," said Jim. "I don't see any sharks."

But he was a little worried just the same. When Buck came back with the bathing trunks, Jim told him what Pippi had said.

"Nonsense," said Buck, and he shouted to Pippi, "Are you the one who is saying that it's dangerous to swim here?"

"No," said Pippi, "I never said that."

"That's funny," said Jim. "Didn't you just tell me that there were sharks here?"

"Yes, that's what I said. But dangerous—no, that I wouldn't say exactly. My grandfather swam here last year."

"Well, then," said Buck.

"And Grandfather got back from the hospital already last Friday," Pippi went on, "with the fanciest wooden leg you've ever seen on an old man." She spat thoughtfully into the water. "So I couldn't really say that it's dangerous. Of course a few arms and legs do disappear if one swims here. But as long as wooden legs don't cost more than a dollar a pair I don't think you should deprive yourself of an invigorating swim just because of miserliness." She spat once more.

"My grandfather takes a childish delight in his wooden leg. He says it is absolutely irreplaceable when he goes out to fight."

"You know what I think," said Buck. "I think you're telling whoppers. Your grandfather must be an old man. I'm sure he doesn't want to be in any fights."

"That's what you think!" cried Pippi in a shrill voice. "He's the most ill-tempered old man who ever hit his opponent on the head with a wooden leg. If he can't fight from morning till night he's miserable. Then he gets into such a rage that he bites himself on the nose."

"What nonsense!" said Buck. "No one can bite himself on the nose."

"Yes, they can," Pippi insisted. "He climbs up on a chair."

Buck thought about this for a while, but then he swore. "I don't feel like listening to your silly chatter any longer. Come on, Jim, let's get undressed."

"Besides, I'd like to have you know that my grandfather has the longest nose in the world. He has five parrots and all of them can sit next to each other on his nose."

By now Buck was really angry. "You little redheaded vixen, do you know that you're the worst liar I've ever met? Aren't you ashamed of yourself? Are you really trying to make me believe that five parrots can sit in a row on your grandfather's nose? Confess that it's a lie!"

"Yes," said Pippi sadly. "It's a lie."

"There, you see," said Buck. "Isn't that what I said?"

"It's a terrible, horrible lie," said Pippi, still sadder.

"That's what I thought from the beginning," said Buck.

"Because the fifth parrot," sobbed Pippi and burst out into a flood of tears, "the fifth parrot has to stand on one leg."

"Get lost," said Buck, and he and Jim went behind a bush to get undressed.

"Pippi, you don't even have a grandfather," said Annika reproachfully.

"No," said Pippi gaily, "*must* I have a grandfather?"

Buck was the first one to come out in his bathing trunks. He made an elegant dive from a cliff into the sea and swam out. The children up in the cave watched with great interest. Then they spotted a shark fin, which flashed above the surface of the water for a second.

"Shark, shark!" cried Momo.

Buck, who was treading water and enjoying himself immensely, turned around and saw the terrible creature coming toward him.

There has probably never been anyone who could swim as fast as Buck swam then. In two split seconds he had reached shore and rushed out of the water. He was both frightened and furious, and it seemed as if he thought it was all Pippi's fault that there were sharks in the water.

"Aren't you ashamed of yourself, you nasty brat?" he screamed. "The sea is full of sharks."

"Have I said anything else?" Pippi asked sweetly, and tilted her head to one side. "I don't always lie, you see."

Jim and Buck went behind the bush to get dressed again. They felt that now the time had come to begin thinking about the pearls. No one could tell how long Captain Longstocking and the others were going to be away.

"Listen, children," said Buck. "I heard someone say that there were some good oyster beds in these regions. Do you know if it's true?"

"I'll say," said Pippi. "Oyster shells go crunch-crunch under your feet wherever you walk down there on the bottom of the sea. Go down and see for yourself."

But Buck didn't want to do that.

"There are great big pearls in every oyster," said Pippi. "About like this one." She held up a giant, shimmering pearl.

Jim and Buck got so excited that they could hardly stand still.

"Do you have any more of those?" said Jim. "We would like to buy them from you."

This was a lie. Jim and Buck had no money with which to buy pearls. They only wanted to get them dishonestly.

"Yes, we have at least ten or twelve quarts of pearls here in the cave," said Pippi.

Jim and Buck were unable to hide their delight.

"Wonderful," said Buck. "Bring them here and we'll buy them all."

"Oh no," said Pippi. "What are the poor children going to use to play marbles with afterward? Have you thought of that?"

There was a lot of discussion back and forth before Jim and Buck realized that it would be impossible to get the pearls by clever maneuvering. But what they couldn't get by clever maneuvering, they decided to take by force. Now they at least knew where the pearls were. The only thing they had to do was climb over to the cave and take them.

Climb over to the cave—yes, that was the rub. During the discussion Pippi had carefully removed the hibiscus rope, which was now safely in the cave.

Jim and Buck didn't think that the climb over to the cave looked very inviting. But there didn't seem to be any other way to get the pearls.

"You do it, Jim," said Buck.

"No, you do it, Buck," said Jim.

"*You do it, Jim,*" said Buck. He was stronger than Jim. So Jim started climbing. He frantically grabbed hold of all the jutting rocks

he could reach. Cold sweat was pouring down his back.

"Hold on, for heaven's sake, so you won't fall down," said Pippi in an encouraging way.

Then Jim fell in. Buck was shouting and cursing on the beach. Jim was also screaming because he saw two sharks heading in his direction. When they were no more than three feet from him, Pippi threw down a cocoanut right in front of their snouts. That scared them just long enough for Jim to swim to the shore and crawl up on the little plateau. The water was running in rivulets from his clothes and he looked miserable. Buck was scolding him.

"Do it yourself, and you'll see how easy it is," said Jim.

"Now *I'll* show you how," said Buck and started to climb.

All the children watched him. Annika was almost a bit frightened as she watched him coming closer.

"Oh-oh, don't climb there, you'll fall in," said Pippi.

"Where?" said Buck.

"There," said Pippi, pointing. Buck looked down.

"A lot of cocoanuts get wasted this way," said Pippi a moment later when she had thrown one in the sea to prevent the sharks from eating up Buck, who was desperately floundering in the water. But up he came, mad as a hornet, and he certainly wasn't one to be afraid. He immediately started climbing again, because he had made up his mind once and for all to make his way into the cave and get his hands on the pearls.

This time he managed much better. When he was almost at the opening of the cave he called out triumphantly, "Now, you little demons, this time you're going to get it."

Then Pippi stuck out her index finger and poked him in the stomach.

There was a splash.

"You could at least have taken this with you when you took off!" Pippi shouted after him as she landed a cocoanut bang on the snout of a shark that was coming too close. But more sharks came and she had to throw more cocoanuts. One of them hit Buck on the head.

"Oh dear, was that you?" said Pippi when Buck yelled. "From up here you look like a big, nasty shark."

Jim and Buck now decided to sit it out until the children were forced to come down.

"When they get hungry they'll leave there," said Buck grimly. "And then they'll see something." He shouted to the children, "I feel sorry for you if you're going to have to sit in that cave until you starve to death!"

"You have a kind heart," said Pippi, "but you won't have to worry about us for the next two weeks. Then we might have to start rationing the cocoanuts a little."

She cracked a big cocoanut, drank the milk, and ate the wonderful meat.

Jim and Buck swore. The sun was setting and they began making preparations to spend the night ashore. They didn't dare row out to the steamer to sleep because then the children could get away with all the pearls. They lay down on the hard rocks in their wet clothes. They were very uncomfortable.

Up in the cave all the children were merrily sitting and eating cocoanuts and mashed breadfruit. It was so good. The whole situation was so exciting and pleasant. Once in a while they would stick their heads out to look at Jim and Buck. By now it was so dark that they could see only a fuzzy outline of the men on the plateau below. But they could still hear them swearing down there.

Suddenly there was a shower of the violent tropical kind. The rain came down in torrents. Pippi stuck the tip of her nose out of the cave. "You certainly are the lucky ones!" she shouted to Jim and Buck.

"What do you mean by that?" said Buck hopefully. He thought that the children had perhaps changed their minds and wanted to give them the pearls. "What do you mean by saying we're lucky?"

"I mean, just think how lucky it is that you were already soaked before this rainstorm came. Otherwise you would have got soaking wet in this rain."

More swearing could be heard from down on the plateau, but it was impossible to tell whether it was Jim or Buck.

"Good night, and sleep well," said Pippi. "Because that's what we're going to do now."

The children lay down on the floor of the cave. Tommy and Annika lay one on either side of Pippi, holding her hands. They were quite comfortable. It was so warm and snug in the cave. Outside the rain was pouring down.

Pippi Gets Bored with
Jim and Buck

• •

The children slept soundly all night. But Jim and Buck did not. They kept on grumbling about the rain, and when it stopped they started to argue about whose fault it was that they hadn't been able to get hold of the pearls and which one of them had really had the stupid idea of going to Kurrekurredutt Island in the first place. And when the sun rose and dried their clothes, and Pippi's cheerful face popped out of the cave, saying good morning, they were more determined than ever to get the pearls and leave the island as rich men. But they couldn't figure out how to do it.

While all this was going on, Pippi's horse had begun to wonder where Pippi and Tommy and Annika had disappeared to. Mr. Nilsson had returned from his family reunion in the jungle and he was wondering the same thing. He also wondered what Pippi would say when she found out that he had lost his straw hat.

Mr. Nilsson jumped up on the horse's tail and the horse trotted off to find Pippi. Finally he found his way to the south side of the island. That is where he saw Pippi stick her head out of the cave, and he whinnied happily.

"Look, Pippi, there's your horse!" cried Tommy.

266

"And Mr. Nilsson is sitting on his tail," said Annika.

Jim and Buck heard this. They realized that the horse who was trotting along the beach belonged to Pippi, the redheaded girl up in the cave.

Buck went and grabbed the horse by the mane.

"Now listen, you little monster," he shouted to Pippi, "I'm going to kill your horse!"

"You're going to kill my horse whom I love so dearly?" said Pippi. "My nice, good horse! You can't mean it."

"Yes, I'll probably have to," said Buck. "That is, if you don't want to come here and give us all the pearls. All of them, do you hear! Otherwise I'll kill the horse this instant."

Pippi looked at him gravely. "Please," she said. "I'm begging you—don't kill my horse, and do let the children keep their pearls."

"You heard me," Buck said. "Hand over the pearls this minute! Or else—"

And then in a low voice he said to Jim, "Just wait until she comes with the pearls. Then I'll beat her black and blue to pay her back for this miserable rainy night. As for the horse, we'll take him along on board and sell him on another island."

He shouted to Pippi, "Well, which is it going to be? Are you coming, or aren't you?"

"Yes, I'll come," said Pippi. "But don't forget that you asked for it."

She skipped along the projecting rocks as lightly as if she had been walking down a garden path and jumped down to the plateau. She stopped in front of Buck. There she stood, little and thin, with her two pigtails pointing straight out. There was a dangerous look in her eyes.

"Where are the pearls, you little beast?" shouted Buck.

"There aren't going to be any pearls today. You'll have to play leapfrog instead."

Then Buck let out a roar which made Annika tremble way up in the cave. "I'm going to kill both you and the horse!" he yelled as he lunged toward Pippi.

"Take it easy, my good man," said Pippi. She grabbed him around the waist and threw him ten feet up in the air. He banged himself quite hard on the rocks as he came down. Then Jim came to life. He raised his arm to give Pippi a terrible blow, but she jumped aside with a little chuckle. A second later Jim was also on his way up into the clear morning sky. There they sat, Jim and Buck, on the rock, groaning. Pippi walked up and grabbed them, one in each fist.

"You *can't* be as anxious to play marbles as you seem to be," she said. "There has to be some limit to your playfulness." She carried them down to the skiff and tossed them in.

"Now you go home to your mothers and ask them to give you five cents for marbles," she said. "You'll find them just as easy to play with."

A little while later the steamer was chugging away from Kurrekurredutt Island. Since then it has never been seen in those waters.

Pippi patted her horse. Mr. Nilsson jumped up on her shoulder. Beyond the outermost tip of the island a whole row of canoes came into sight. It was Captain Longstocking and his people returning home after a successful hunt. Pippi shouted and waved at them and they waved back with their paddles.

Then Pippi quickly put up the rope again so that Tommy and Annika and the others could get down from the cave. And when the canoes came gliding in to the little inlet beside the *Hoptoad* a short time later, the whole crowd of children was there to greet them.

Captain Longstocking embraced Pippi. "Has everything been peaceful?" he asked.

"Oh, yes, completely peaceful," said Pippi.

"But Pippi, how can you say that?" said Annika. "We've had terrible things happen."

"Oh, yes, I forgot," said Pippi. "No, it hasn't been completely peaceful, Papa Efraim. As soon as you turn your back, things start to happen."

"But my dear child, what's happened?" said Captain Longstocking anxiously.

"Something really terrible," said Pippi. "Mr. Nilsson lost his straw hat."

Pippi Leaves
Kurrekurredutt Island

● ●

Wonderful days followed—wonderful days in a warm, wonderful world full of sunshine, with the blue sea glittering and fragrant flowers everywhere.

Tommy and Annika were by now so brown that there was hardly any difference between them and the Kurrekurredutt children. And every spot on Pippi's face was covered with freckles.

"This trip will turn out to be a real beauty treatment for me," she said gaily. "I have more freckles and am therefore more beautiful than ever. If this keeps up, I shall be irresistible."

Momo and Moana and all the other Kurrekurredutt children already considered Pippi irresistible. They had never had such a good time before, and they were as fond of Pippi as Tommy and Annika were. Of course they were fond of Tommy and Annika too, and Tommy and Annika were fond of them. So they had a marvelous time together and played and played all day long. Often they would go up to the cave to play.

Pippi had taken blankets there, and when they wanted to they could spend the night and be even more comfortable than they were the first time. She had also made a rope ladder which reached all the way down to the water below the cave, and all the children climbed up and down on it and swam and splashed to their heart's delight. Now it was perfectly safe to swim. Pippi had blocked off a big section with net so that the sharks couldn't get in. It was such fun to swim in and out of those caves filled with water. Even Tommy and Annika had learned to dive for oysters. The first pearl that Annika found was a huge, beautiful pink one. She decided to take it home with her and have it made into a ring, which she would wear as a souvenir of Kurrekurredutt Island.

Sometimes they would play that Pippi was Buck trying to get into the cave to steal pearls. Then Tommy would pull up the rope ladder and Pippi would have to climb up the side of the cliff as best as she could. All the children would shout, "Buck is coming, Buck is coming!" when she stuck her head into the cave, and they would take turns at poking her in the stomach so that she tumbled backward into the sea. Down there she splashed around with her bare feet sticking out of the water, and the children laughed so hard that they almost fell out of the cave.

When they got tired of being in the cave they would play in their bamboo hut. Pippi and the children had built it, though of course Pippi had done most of the work. It was big and square and made of thin bamboo cane, and you could climb around inside it, and on top of it too. Next to the hut was a tall cocoanut tree. Pippi had hacked steps into it so that you could climb all the way to the top. The view was wonderful from up there. Between two other cocoanut palms Pippi had rigged up a swing of hibiscus fiber. It was marvelous, because if you swung as high as the swing would go, you could throw yourself out into the air and land in the water below.

Pippi swung so high and flew so far out into the water that she said, "One fine day I'll probably land in Australia, and then it won't be much fun for the one who gets me on the head."

The children also went on expeditions into the jungle. There was a high mountain and a waterfall that cascaded over a cliff. Pippi had made up her mind that she would like to go down the waterfall in a barrel. She brought along one of the barrels from the *Hoptoad* and crawled into it. Momo and Tommy closed the lid and helped to push the barrel over the waterfall. It bounced down with tremendous speed and then it broke. All the children saw Pippi disappear into the tumbling water, and they didn't think they would ever see her again. But all of a sudden she dived up and climbed ashore, saying, "They certainly go at a fast clip, those water barrels."

The days went by. Soon the rainy season would start and then Captain Longstocking would lock himself into his hut and brood about life, and he was afraid that Pippi wouldn't be happy on Kurrekurredutt Island then. More often lately Tommy and Annika would find themselves wondering how their mother and father were. They were anxious to get home for Christmas. So they weren't as sad as you might expect when Pippi said one morning, "Tommy and Annika, how would you like to go back to Villa Villekulla for a while again?"

Of course, for Momo and Moana and the other Kurrekurredutt children it was a sad day when they saw Pippi and Tommy and Annika go on board the *Hoptoad* for the voyage home. But Pippi promised that they would come back often to Kurrekurredutt Island. The Kurrekurredutt children had made wreaths of white flowers which they hung around the necks of Pippi and Tommy and Annika as a farewell gesture. Their song of farewell sounded sad as it followed the ship out to sea.

Captain Longstocking was also standing on the beach. He had to stay behind in order to rule. Fridolf had taken it upon himself to get the children home. Captain Longstocking slowly and deliberately blew his nose in his big pocket handkerchief as he waved good-

272

by. Pippi and Tommy and Annika cried, and the tears streamed down their faces as they waved to Captain Longstocking and the island children as long as they were in sight.

The *Hoptoad* had a fair wind behind her during the whole voyage home.

"We'd better dig out your undershirts in good time before we reach the North Sea," said Pippi.

"What an awful thought," said Tommy and Annika.

It soon became evident that despite the fair wind, the ship wouldn't reach home by Christmas. Tommy and Annika were bitterly disappointed when they heard it. Just think, no Christmas tree and no Christmas presents!

"Then we could just as well have stayed on Kurrekurredutt Island," said Tommy angrily.

Annika thought of her mother and father and knew that she would be glad to get home, no matter when. But it certainly was sad that they were going to miss Christmas. They both felt the same about that.

One dark night at the beginning of January, Pippi and Tommy and Annika spotted the lights of the little town from afar, twinkling a welcome. They were back home again.

"Well, now we have this trip behind us," said Pippi as she walked down the gangplank with her horse.

No one was at the port to meet them because no one had known when they would get home. Pippi lifted up Tommy and Annika and Mr. Nilsson onto the horse and they rode toward Villa Villekulla. The poor horse had a hard time. He had to plow his way through the snowdrifts piled up in the streets and roads. Tommy and Annika stared straight ahead into the snow flurry. Soon they would be back with their mother and father, and they were suddenly aware how much they had missed them.

In the Settergren house the lights were shining invitingly, and through the window they could see Tommy's and Annika's mother and father sitting at the dinner table.

"There are Mother and Father!" said Tommy and he sounded so happy and excited.

But Villa Villekulla lay in complete darkness and was covered with snow.

Annika was terribly unhappy at the thought of Pippi's going back there alone. "Please, Pippi, won't you stay with us the first night?" she asked.

"Oh, no," said Pippi and jumped down in the snow outside the gate. "I have to get some things in order at Villa Villekulla."

She waded through the deep snowdrifts which reached all the way up to her stomach. The horse plowed along behind her.

"Yes, but think of how cold it will be in there," said Tommy. "It hasn't been heated for such a long time."

"Nonsense," said Pippi. "If the heart is warm and beats the way it should, there is no reason to be cold."

Pippi Longstocking Doesn't Want to Grow Up

Oh, how Tommy's and Annika's mother and father hugged and kissed their children, and what a wonderful supper they prepared for them! Afterward they tucked them in, and sat for a long, long time on the edge of their beds, listening to the children's tales of all the strange things they had experienced on Kurrekurredutt Island. They were so happy, all of them. There was only one sad thing, and that was not having had any Christmas. Tommy and Annika didn't want to tell their mother how miserable they were because they had missed having a tree and presents, but that's the way it was. It seemed so strange to be back. It always does when you've been away, and it would have been much easier if they could have come home on Christmas Eve.

Tommy and Annika were also sad when they thought of Pippi. Now of course she would be home in bed at Villa Villekulla with her feet on her pillow, and there was no one there to tuck her in. They made up their minds to go to see her as soon as they could the next morning.

But the following day their mother didn't want to let them go because she hadn't seen them for such a long time, and besides, their grandmother was coming for dinner to welcome the children home. Tommy and Annika wondered anxiously what Pippi could be doing all day, and when it began to get dark they couldn't stand it any longer.

"Please, Mother, we have to go and see Pippi," said Tommy.

"Yes, run along then," said Mrs. Settergren. "But don't stay too long."

Tommy and Annika ran off.

When they got to the garden gate of Villa Villekulla they stopped and stared in amazement. It looked just like a Christmas card. The whole house was softly blanketed with snow and there were gleaming lights in all the windows. A torch was burning on the veranda and shedding its brightness over the snow-covered lawn. One path to the veranda was neatly shoveled, so Tommy and Annika didn't have to wade through the drifts.

Just as they were stamping the snow off their feet on the veranda, the door opened and there stood Pippi. "Merry Christmas!" she said.

She ushered them into the kitchen. And there was a Christmas tree! The lights were lit and seventeen sparklers were burning, filling the room with a nice smoky smell. The table was set with puddings and hams and sausages and all sorts of Christmas delicacies—yes, even gingerbread men and birds' nests. There was a fire in the stove, and the horse was standing at the woodbin, scraping his hoof in a very refined way. Mr. Nilsson was hopping back and forth among the sparklers in the Christmas tree.

"He is supposed to be an angel," said Pippi grimly, "but I can't get him to sit still."

Tommy and Annika just stood there, speechless.

"Oh, Pippi," said Annika finally, "how wonderful! When did you find time to do all this?"

"Me, I'm the hard-working type," said Pippi.

Tommy and Annika were suddenly overwhelmed with happiness.

"I think it's just grand to be back in Villa Villekulla again," said Tommy.

They sat down around the table and ate piles of ham and pudding and sausage and gingerbread men, and everything tasted even better to them than bananas and breadfruit.

"But Pippi, it isn't Christmas at all," said Tommy.

"Yes, sir," said Pippi. "The Villa Villekulla almanac is slow. I have to take it to an almanac-maker and have it adjusted so that it will run properly again."

"How wonderful," said Annika again. "We celebrated Christmas after all—except without Christmas presents, of course."

"That reminds me," said Pippi. "I have hidden your Christmas presents. You have to find them yourselves."

Tommy's and Annika's faces became flushed with excitement as they sprang up and started hunting. In the woodbin Tommy found a big package which was marked "Tommy." Inside was a fine set of paints. Under the table Annika found a package with her name on it, and inside that was a pretty red parasol.

"I can take this with me to Kurrekurredutt Island the next time we go there," said Annika.

High up on the hood of the stove were two more packages. One contained a small jeep for Tommy, and in the other was a set of doll's dishes for Annika. A small package was also hanging on the horse's tail. In it was a clock for Tommy's and Annika's room.

When they had found all their Christmas presents, they gave Pippi big hugs and thanked her over and over again. She was standing at the kitchen window, looking out at all the snow in the garden.

"Tomorrow we'll build a big snow hut," she said. "And we'll have lights burning in it at night."

"Oh, yes, let's," said Annika, feeling happier than ever to be home.

"I'm wondering if we could make a ski slope running down from the roof to the snowdrifts below. I'm going to teach the horse to ski. But I can't decide whether he needs four skis or only two."

"We're going to have a wonderful time tomorrow," said Tommy. "What luck that we came home in the middle of Christmas vacation."

"We're always going to have fun," said Annika. "At Villa Villekulla, on Kurrekurredutt Island, and everywhere."

Pippi nodded in agreement. They had crawled up on the kitchen table, all three of them. Suddenly a dark shadow passed over Tommy's face.

"I never want to grow up," he said emphatically.

"I don't either," said Annika.

"No, that's nothing to wish for, being grown up," said Pippi. "Grownups never have any fun. They only have a lot of boring work and wear silly-looking clothes and have corns and minicipal taxes."

"It's called *municipal*," said Annika.

"Well, anyway, it's the same nonsense," said Pippi. "And then they're full of superstitions and all sorts of crazy things. They think that something terrible is going to happen if they happen to stick their knives in their mouths while they're eating, and things like that."

"And they can't play, either," said Annika.

"Ugh, how awful to have to grow up."

"Who says you have to grow up?" said Pippi. "If I remember right, I have a few pills somewhere."

"What sort of pills?" said Tommy.

"Some very fine pills for people who don't want to grow up," said Pippi and jumped down from the table. She hunted through closets and drawers and after a while she produced something that looked like three yellow peas.

"Peas!" said Tommy surprised.

"That's what you think," said Pippi. "These are no peas. They are

279

chililug pills and were given to me in Rio by an old Indian chief when I happened to mention that I wasn't wild about the idea of growing up."

"You mean that those tiny little pills can do it?" said Annika skeptically.

"Absolutely," said Pippi. "But they have to be taken in the dark, and then you have to say this:

> *Pretty little chililug,*
> *I don't want to get bug."*

"You mean big," said Tommy.

"If I say 'bug' I mean 'bug,'" said Pippi. "That's the trick, you see. Most children say 'big,' and that's the worst thing that can happen. Because then you start to grow more then ever. Once there was a boy who ate pills like these. He said 'big' instead of 'bug' and he started growing until it was a nightmare—many, many feet every day. It was terrible. He was all right as long as he could go around grazing under the apple trees, the way a giraffe does. But then he got too big and that didn't work any longer. When some ladies came to visit and they wanted to say, 'My, what a nice big boy you've grown up to be,' they had to shout into a megaphone so that he would hear them. All you saw of him was his long, skinny legs disappearing up among the clouds like two flagpoles. He was never heard of after that—oh, yes, once he was. That was when he took a lick at the sun and got a blister on his tongue. Then he let out such a roar that the flowers down on earth wilted. But that was the last sign of life from him—although his legs are probably still wandering around down in Rio, making awful mix-ups in the traffic."

"Oh, I wouldn't dare eat one of those pills," said Annika, terrified, "in case I might say the wrong thing."

"You won't say the wrong thing," said Pippi reassuringly. "If I thought you'd do that, I wouldn't give you one. Because it would be boring to have just your legs to play with. Tommy and me and your legs—that would be fine company!"

"You won't make a mistake, Annika," said Tommy.

They turned the Christmas tree lights out. The kitchen was in complete darkness, except near the stove where the fire glowed behind the stove door.

They sat down in silence in a circle in the middle of the floor, holding one another by the hand. Pippi gave Tommy and Annika each a chililug pill. Chills ran up and down their spines. Just think, in a second the powerful pill would be down in their stomachs, and then they would never have to grow up. How marvelous that would be!

"Now," Pippi whispered.

"Pretty little chililug, I don't want to get bug," they said all together and swallowed their pills. The deed was done.

Pippi turned on the ceiling light. "That's it," she said. "Now we don't have to be grown up and have corns and other miseries. Though the pills have been lying around in my closet for so long that one can't be absolutely sure that all the strength hasn't gone out of them. But we have to hope for the best."

Annika suddenly thought of something. "Oh, Pippi," she said in alarm, "you were going to be a pirate when you grew up."

"Pshaw, I can be one anyway," said Pippi. "I can still become a nasty *little* pirate who spreads death and destruction around me."

She was quiet for a while, thinking. "Just imagine," she said. "If a lady walks by here one day many, many years from now and she sees us running around in the garden, perhaps she will ask Tommy, 'How old are you, my little friend?' And then you'll say, 'Fifty-three, if I'm not mistaken.'"

Tommy laughed merrily. "She'll probably think that I'm small for my age," he said.

281

"Of course," said Pippi. "But then you can explain that you were bigger when you were smaller."

Just then Annika and Tommy remembered that their mother had told them not to stay away too long.

"I think we'll have to go now," said Tommy.

"But we'll be back tomorrow," said Annika.

"Fine," said Pippi. "We'll get started on the snow hut at eight o'clock."

She walked with them to the gate and her red pigtails danced around her as she ran back to Villa Villekulla.

"You know," said Tommy a while later when he was brushing his teeth, "if I hadn't known that those were chililug pills I would have been willing to bet that they were just ordinary peas."

Annika was standing at the window of their room in her pink pajamas, looking over toward Villa Villekulla. "Look, I see Pippi!" she called out, delighted.

Tommy rushed over to the window too. Yes, there she was. Now that the trees didn't have any leaves they could look right into Pippi's kitchen.

Pippi was sitting at the table with her head propped against her arms. She was staring at the little flickering flame of a candle that was standing in front of her. She seemed to be dreaming.

"She—she looks so alone," said Annika, and her voice trembled a little. "Oh, Tommy, if it were only morning so that we could go to her right away!"

They stood there in silence and looked out into the winter night. The stars were shining over Villa Villekulla's roof. Pippi was inside. She would always be there. That was a comforting thought. The years would go by, but Pippi and Tommy and Annika would not grow up. That is, of course, if the strength hadn't gone out of the chililug pills. There would be new springs and summers, new autumns and winters, but their games would go on. Tomorrow they would build a snow hut and make a ski slope from the roof

282

of Villa Villekulla, and when spring came they would climb the hollow oak where soda pop spouted up. They would hunt for treasure and they would ride Pippi's horse. They would sit in the woodbin and tell stories. Perhaps they would also take a trip to Kurrekurredutt Island now and then, to see Momo and Moana and the others. But they would always come back to Villa Villekulla.

And the most wonderful, comforting thought was that Pippi would always be in Villa Villekulla.

"If she would only look in this direction we could wave to her," said Tommy.

But Pippi continued to stare straight ahead with a dreamy look. Then she blew out the light.

AFTERWORD
ABOUT ASTRID LINDGREN
AND PIPPI LONGSTOCKING

Astrid Lindgren is often asked how she came to write about Pippi Longstocking. She replies: "In 1941, my seven-year-old daughter, Karin, was sick in bed with pneumonia. Every evening when I sat by her bedside, she would nag, 'Tell me a story!' And one evening, completely exhausted, I asked her, 'What should I tell?' And she answered, 'Tell about Pippi Longstocking!' She had come up with that name right there on the spot. I didn't ask her who Pippi Longstocking was; I just began the story, and since it was a strange name, it turned out to be a strange girl as well. Karin, and later her playmates, showed a strong love for Pippi, and I had to tell the story again and again.

"One day in March 1944 I fell and sprained my ankle, and to make time pass while I recuperated, I started to put the Pippi stories down in shorthand. It was Karin's tenth birthday in two months, and I decided I would write out the Pippi story and give her the manuscript for a birthday present. . . . And then I decided to send the story to a publisher. . . . I remember concluding in my cover letter, 'In the hope that you won't notify the Child Welfare Committee'—really because I had two children of my own, and what kind of mother had they who wrote such books!"

The publisher rejected the manuscript, but two years later, when another publisher held a contest for girls' books, Lindgren submitted *Pippi Longstocking* and won first prize, along with a book contract.

Although *Pippi Longstocking* (*Pippi Långstrump* in the original Swedish) was immediately popular in Sweden, it also provoked controversy. The heroines of most children's books of the time were quiet, sweet, and gentle, and Pippi, of course, was none of these things. Articles appeared questioning the judges' taste in giving the award to such a book, and some adults even wrote letters to the editor complaining about Pippi's manners.

But Pippi was becoming popular enough to draw the attention of foreign publishers. *Pippi Longstocking* was first published in America in 1950 by The Viking Press, which the author found amusing—her American publisher was named for the early Scandinavians! But Pippi got off to a slow start in the states, and in 1951 her American editor, May Massee, wrote to Lindgren, "It doesn't look as though Pippi will have the enormous success here that she had in Sweden."

Who knew then that Pippi would prove to be one of the most enduringly successful characters in all of children's literature, with (to date) three

Astrid Lindgren and her daughter Karin at the time Pippi Longstocking was created

feature films, translations in more than fifty languages, and more than 6 million copies sold in the United States alone.

What is it about Pippi Longstocking that has made her so consistently popular? Pippi is a children's heroine unlike any other. She lives exact-

Astrid Lindgren and Karin today (still with the same sleigh bed!)

ly as a child might choose in a fantasy world of her own imagining. There are no parents to interfere with anything she might like to do, since her mother is an angel watching Pippi lovingly from heaven, and her father is king of a South Sea Island. She has a suitcase full of gold coins and a chest of drawers that houses a seemingly endless supply of gifts. And she can always beat adults at their own game. When a teacher asks her, "You want to be a really fine lady when you grow up, don't you?" Pippi replies, "You mean the kind with a veil on her nose and three double chins under it?"

As if to underscore the point that Pippi represents a child's fantasy of what life could be, Lindgren has often said, "It is my childhood that I long to return to. . . . And if I dare be so bold as to speak of inspiration, I must say that it is there in my childhood that I get many of the impulses that later appear in my stories."

Astrid Lindgren was born in 1907 in an old red house surrounded by apple trees on a large farm called Nas, near the town of Vimmerby, Sweden. She says, "There was a particular apple tree outside our house—we used to wake early and be the first outside to eat whatever apples had fallen from it

Astrid Lindgren circa 1965

during the night. And then there was the 'owl tree,' where the owls had their nests. But during the day it was our climbing tree. It was hollow, just like Pippi Longstocking's tree, but it was an elm—not an oak, as in the 'Pippi' books. And we loved it. My brother once put a hen's egg in the owl's nest, and the owl hatched a chicken for him! [Lindgren later had one of her characters do the same thing in her book *The Children of Noisy Village*.] That tree is still there, though now it's aged and battered."

A short biography cannot do justice to Ms. Lindgren's rich and varied life. After her rural upbringing, Ms. Lindgren moved to Stockholm to earn a living as a secretary—every one of her books was first written down in shorthand! Married and the mother of two children, Lars and Karin, Lindgren held a classified job for the Swedish government after World War II, and after the publication of her first few books became a reader and translator for her publisher, Ab Raben and Sjogren. Among other titles, she is responsible for bringing Robert McCloskey's *Homer Price* and E. B. White's *Charlotte's Web* to Swedish readers.

But if that is a somewhat predictable path for a children's writer, Ms. Lindgren has also been an instrument of social change in her native

AFTERWORD

Sweden. Her idyllic childhood, the freedom she experienced, and her affinity with the environment, have been a great influence on her political views. In 1976, she wrote an article complaining of the high taxation rate, recounting the story of a man forced to beg because taxes had left him impoverished. When the government was defeated in that year's election, Astrid Lindgren was credited with assisting in its downfall and helping bring lower taxes to Sweden. How much of Lindgren is in Pippi Longstocking? We remember Pippi's words, "Grown-ups never have any fun. They only have a lot of boring work and wear silly-looking clothes and have corns and minicipal taxes."

When she celebrated her eightieth birthday, Astrid Lindgren was visited by the prime minister of Sweden as well as the American and Soviet ambassadors. But much more important to Lindgren than the honors was the news the prime minister brought: the government was going to enact a new Swedish Animal Protection act, which popularly became known as "Lex Lindgren" (that is, Lindgren's Law). The law read, "Chickens are to be let out of cramped cages, cows are to be entitled to grazing space, and sows are no longer to be tethered." The campaign grew out of a newspaper article that Lindgren had written about a cow that had to run more than six miles to find a bull! She had then collaborated on a series of articles about the maltreatment of animals, and the tremendous public response caused the Ministry of Agriculture to capitulate. As Lindgren said, "There is something in life that cannot be accounted for in monetary terms and that is respect for the living."

That respect for the living, for nature,

A postage stamp of Astrid Lindgren issued in Sweden in 1996

AFTERWORD

for childhood, and for its precious freedoms, is the context that informs all of Lindgren's work. She has said, "I don't write books for children. I write books for the child I am myself. I write about the things that are dear to me—trees and houses and nature—just to please myself."

When an interviewer once commented that Pippi Longstocking seems as if she has always been around, Astrid Lindgren replied, "Maybe she was just waiting for someone to pick her up and write about her."